CALCULATED RISK

Timberwolf Press

Tune in to the dramatic series
and visit the online world of *Calculated Risk* at
http://www.TimberWolfPress.com

6875

CALCULATED RISK

DENISE TILLER

TIMBERWOLF PRESS ALLEN, TEXAS
HTTP://WWW.TIMBERWOLFPRESS.COM

Copyright © 2000 Timberwolf Press, Inc.
All Rights Reserved

Timberwolf Press, Inc.
202 N. Allen St., Suite A
Allen, Texas 75013 USA

This title is also available in the following media:

E-Book
Cassette Tape
Audio CD
CD-ROM
MP3 Download
Weekly Episodic Dramatic Audio Series

Visit our Web site at **http:/www.TimberwolfPress.com** for details!

982737509097213974

This book is a work of fiction. All characters, events and dialogues portrayed herein are fictitious. Any resemblance to real persons, living or dead, is purely coincidental. Any use of the names of real persons, places, organizations or products is for literary purposes only, and does not change the entirely fictitious nature of this work.

Trademarks are the property of their owners.

Calculated Risk
is copyright © 2000 by Denise Tiller
All rights reserved. No part of this work may be reproduced in any form, on any media, by any electronic, magnetic, digital, optical, mechanical or by any other means without express written permission from the publisher, Timberwolf Press, Inc.

Printed in the United States of America
10 9 8 7 6 5 4 3 2 1

ISBN: 1-58752-015-X

Dedication and Thanks

To John, Sasha, Tori, BZ, Mary, and Kati

ACKNOWLEDGEMENTS

So many people helped in the creation of *Calculated Risk* it's impossible even for an actuary to count all of them. I want to thank the Lesser North Texas Writers Group for nurturing my initial attempts at fiction, the GUPPIES for their support, Sharon Ervin for getting me an editor appointment at OWFI, and the Kansas City Writers Group for welcoming me after we moved and then encouraging me to find a publisher.

Diana Healy and Kathleen Gregory Klein have my undying gratitude for their insightful comments from the first page of *Calculated Risk* to the last. They kept me focused and challenged me grow as a writer throughout the entire process.

I also want to thank Paige Wheeler for her interest in my career and the staff at Timberwolf Press, particularly Patrick Seaman for his innovative approach to publishing and Carol Woods for her gentle editing style.

Above all, I must thank my family: my parents, Egon and Marguerite Fagerberg who show my Christmas letters to all their friends, my husband John who coauthored my first book and encouraged me although he thought my initial draft sounded like bad Hemingway, and my muses, Kati, Mary, Elizabeth, Vicki, and Sasha who not only love and inspire me, they write better than I do and never complain about TV dinners.

Finally, I must thank Jack, Liz, and the other voices in my head that entertain me as I zoom down the car pool lane. They provide me with a legitimate reason for talking to myself.

98273750909721397495909

1

03809798274981798409197

It was a damned good thing I didn't carry my gun in my car. After two hours of battling that gigantic parking lot also known as the Santa Ana Freeway, I had a bad case of road rage and blared my horn in a breach of California driving etiquette.

I'd spent the afternoon in downtown L.A. drinking Diet Coke and giving a group of investors interested in buying a small life insurance company a crash course in actuarial science. When we broke about six o'clock, a nearly full moon hung over the darkened Los Angeles basin but the city lights obscured the stars. I left with the assignment and clients who appreciated that actuaries did more than count dead bodies and crank numbers out of a mysterious black box.

If I could only use that black box to get home before I lost my mind counting minutes and mile markers. A series of rush hour accidents slowed Orange County's main artery to a drip. My Corvette drop-top wasn't built to inch along at an average speed of ten miles per hour. I was stuck in a herd of red-tailed road hogs and if one more suburban cowboy riding his SUV tried to trample me, I was ready to shoot.

If it hadn't been Valentine's Day and if I weren't late for a romantic candlelight dinner, I might have been more philosophical. I punched redial on my cell phone and got Jack's voice mail for the third time. Didn't the man ever pick-up?

The majestic white-peaked and floodlit summit of Disney's Matterhorn in Anaheim appeared on the horizon, marking the northern boundary of my territory. The sight of the familiar landmark brought some relief. I was on home turf. The congestion on the freeway ended and the stampede began. I carefully calculated velocities and distances between cars, taking advantage of every opportunity to dodge around slower vehicles. My Vette responded to the slightest touch, the space-age instrument panel springing to action. The cavalry of thoroughbreds under the hood raced forward. God, I loved this car. What a rush.

I hit another bottleneck in Santa Ana transitioning to the Newport Freeway but I knew the traffic patterns like an actuarial table. I wove through traffic and hurried through Newport Beach down to Balboa Peninsula and my apartment.

The sixties-style stucco building didn't contain a single element that could be considered architecture. It sat in the less fashionable Upper Peninsula, but it was a block from the beach, it had a garage, and I could see a slice of ocean between buildings from my second floor deck. I dashed up the wooden stairs and opened the door. Puddles, my six-month-old blonde cocker, greeted me, yipping and swirling. I hustled her out before she lived up to her name on the marble entry.

Once we got back, I switched on the lights in my office and pulled a pile of papers off the telephone to check my voice mail. The first message was from a client. I saved it for morning, and listened to the next voice.

"Hi, Lizzie, darlin'." Jack spoke in his lazy, Alabama drawl. Although he'd lived in Southern California for sixteen years, he'd kept his accent. "Sorry you ran into all that traffic, but I'm tied up here. It's going to be another hour or so. Hope that's okay. I'm looking forward to dinner."

"Happy Valentine's Day," I muttered and frowned at my Mickey Mouse watch. That's what I got for dating a workaholic police detective who couldn't take time off to eat and didn't have the nerve to call me on my cellular. At least he'd sent a dozen roses earlier, proving he hadn't forgotten the occasion. Still, his definition of an hour or so left me with roughly seventy-five minutes on my hands and I didn't feel like sitting.

Both my living room and dining room faced the ocean. I turned on lamps and opened the sliding doors to the deck to let in some breeze. While my apartment lacked style on the outside, inside it had the features I cherished the most: windows, open space, a fireplace, and bookcases. Peter, a talented decorator, believed in Feng Shui. He insisted I needed a serene, uncluttered environment to counteract my hyper-kinetic personality and encyclopedic brain. He'd helped me find some simple, classic pieces of furniture, insisting on rounded edges and soft fabrics in muted shades of pink and maroon. His lectures on balancing my yin and yang sounded like a lot of hocus-pocus to my pathologically logical mind, but I couldn't imagine living in anything more pleasant than my spacious, sunny library. I still missed him; he'd been my best friend Scott's lover.

Everything was ready for a romantic evening. A glass vase on the coffee table held Jack's red roses. Candles and a smaller, fresh flower centerpiece graced the oval dining table. This afternoon, Sam, the cleaning man, had worked his normal magic. The place sparkled and the combination of lemon furniture polish and flowers gave it a delightful fruit salad smell. I'd prepared the beef burgundy earlier so it just needed reheating. Jack was the only thing missing. I could put on some music, start the fire, and curl up on my comfy couch with a good book, but the drive had left me keyed.

"I'm going for a run," I told the dog.

Puddles followed me to the bedroom and watched me punt my high heels into a corner and toss my blue pinstriped suit and white silk blouse over the foot of the brass bed. The bed was the most obviously feminine fixture in my apartment with its dust ruffle, quilt, and shams. Sleep ranked high on my list of favorite past-times and I chose not to consider the number of geese who gave their annual crop of feathers to fill the comforter and six pillows with down.

I changed into black running tights and a sweatshirt. Running kept my five-foot-ten frame at a firm one-thirty five and let me eat chocolate. I squeezed my butt under the sleek, stretch fabric. Perfect. The only thing that diet and exercise couldn't help was cleavage, but a fiber-fortified Super Bra took care of that.

Eager for her dinner, Puddles escorted me to the kitchen. I popped the casserole into the oven. Since I grew up without a mother, I started cooking for Dad at an early age, but it was Scott and Peter who showed me how to elevate cooking and dining to an art. I had every gadget and appliance a gourmet chef would want and enough white-tiled counter space to prepare feasts. All it took was the right ingredients and a little effort to make Jack drool.

Once Puddles tucked into her food, I grabbed my blue University of Michigan windbreaker and fanny pack from the hall closet. The pack carried the usual things: a twenty-dollar bill, cell phone, a can of pepper spray, keys.

The tide was out and the moon illuminated the sky with a silver glow. I waded across the beach to the hard sand down by the water and inhaled the sweet ocean air, stretching to get out the kinks. Waves rippled across the dark Pacific and whooshed across the shore near my feet. The beach was nearly deserted except for a few couples either walking hand-in-hand by the surf or huddling under blankets. I loved the solitude of running at night with nothing but the roar of the ocean and my thoughts for company.

As my pulse picked up, my attitude improved. By the time I reached Balboa Pier, my mood was soaring. Nothing beat a good run along the beach at night, except for maybe sex and chocolate, and that would come later. I checked my Mickey Mouse watch as I passed under the lights. Nine o'clock? How did it get so late? Oh, well. Another five minutes wouldn't kill me and I'd still have plenty of time to shower and change before Jack arrived.

A few hundred yards further down the shore I noticed a large mass near the water. As I drew closer, moonlight reflected off human flesh. I stopped dead. A body. Oh, shit. If it had washed ashore, I didn't want to see it. If it hadn't?

My pulse went into overdrive as I whipped around, assessing the situation. Whoever had done this could still be here and I was at the widest, most eroded part of the beach with a wall of sand on one side, the ocean on the other, empty darkness looming ahead, and the pier a hard run behind me. I could phone for help from there. No one would blame me for leaving.

Bleep. My conscience penalized me for the wrong answer. I pulled out my cell phone and pepper spray and dialed 9-1-1 as I slowly crept forward. My voice squeaked. "Hi, my name's Liz Matthews. I'm on the beach about a quarter of a mile south of the Balboa Pier and there's a body by the water."

"Are you certain?"

"Oh, yes." The body moved and I rushed ahead. A woman lay curled up, her pants pulled down below her knees. The surf washed over her but she made no attempt to move.

"God! You're hurt. Hold on."

I grabbed the woman under her arms. She struggled and made gagging noises. An ice-cold Pacific wave splashed over my shoes. I cursed and dragged her above the water line.

"It's okay. I'm trying to help."

She choked and sputtered but stopped fighting. I put her down and dropped to my knees. She had something in her mouth. Sand. I laid my phone and pepper spray where they wouldn't get wet and tried digging it out. She threw up water.

"You're going to be fine. I've already called an ambulance."

The woman whimpered. I wiped my hands on my shirt and pulled up her running tights to restore her dignity. I picked up my phone. "Are you still there? She's really hurt."

"Can you describe her injuries?"

"It's hard to see in the dark, but it looks like someone beat her. I think she was raped, too. And she seems to be in shock." Her entire body shook and she grabbed my sleeve. I glanced around to make certain we were still alone and tucked my phone under my chin. "We need an ambulance and the police. Now!"

I wrapped my windbreaker around her and grabbed my pepper spray. "It's okay. You're safe." I patted her shoulder but it didn't convince either of us and I pleaded with the dispatcher. "Are they on their way?"

"Yes. Please stay on the line."

The dispatcher told me what to do, but I only half-listened as I kept watch. The woman shivered and I held her to keep both of us warm. It was like embracing a soggy sponge and her wet hair smelled of seaweed. "Are you okay?"

She sobbed and shook.

"I'm Liz Matthews. Can you tell me your name?"

"N-N-Nicola."

"Hi, Nicola. The police and the paramedics are on their way. It won't be long."

A lifetime passed before the dispatcher spoke. "They're on the beach, can you see them?"

"Just a minute. We're too low."

I tried to stand. "Nicola, I have to climb up that hill and signal the police. I'll be right back."

Her fingers clawed into my arm. "No! No!"

"You're safe, Nicola. Honest."

I tried to pull free, but she clutched tighter. The only alternative was to take her with me. Somehow, I pulled her to her feet and got one of her arms around my shoulder and put my arm around her. The sand cliff loomed over us. I strained up the steep slope, hampered by loose sand, soggy shoes, and a little over one hundred pounds of all but dead weight at my side. Adrenaline and an overwhelming desire to get to safety kept me going. We crawled the last two feet and Nicola collapsed beside me.

Headlights flashed across the beach. I struggled up onto one knee and waved my arm in a wide arc while I shouted at the dispatcher. The headlights turned in my direction. I stashed the pepper spray. Moments later, an officer jumped out of the vehicle and shined a light in my face. I blinked and shielded my eyes.

"You reported a rape."

"Yeah, I'm still on with the dispatcher." I held out my cellular and pointed it at Nicola. "That's her."

He held the flashlight above her head and I sucked in air when I saw the raw abrasions on her chin, cheeks and nose. The paramedics ran across the sand carrying large cases and nudged me aside. I put my cell phone away and wobbled to my feet. My knees held but my teeth chattered as the wind chilled my wet clothes and my adrenaline rush subsided. The officer tucked the flashlight under his arm to illuminate his notepad. I gave him my name and address and described what I'd found.

His pen stopped. "If you didn't see anyone, how'd you know she'd been raped?"

"Her running tights and panties were down below her knees and she was just lying there with the waves going over her." I motioned down toward the spot but the relentless ocean had partially destroyed the crime scene. "I pulled up her clothes. I hope that was okay."

He peered at me. "What are you doing out here so late?"

"I always run at night."

An EMT interrupted us. "We're about ready to transport, but she wants to talk to you, Miss."

I crouched beside her as she huddled in a blanket. Her voice shook as she whispered. "Come with me, please."

Although I'd never met Nicola before, she needed a friend with her. I couldn't walk away now, even if my beef burgundy turned to charcoal.

2

403809798274981798409197

I squeezed in by the gurney and held on as the ambulance lurched forward. Despite the heavy blankets pulled up to her chin, Nicola trembled and cried. I shivered, too, and the paramedic passed me a warm blanket. It raised my skin temperature, but it didn't help the chill from long buried memories that filled my insides. When my cell phone chirped, I flinched.

"Are you okay? Where the hell are you?" Jack cut off my greeting. His voice was uncharacteristically rapid.

"I'm fine," I lied. "But dinner has to wait, I'm on my way to the hospital—"

"Jesus! What'd he do to you?"

Me? I blinked as my brain processed the information. Of course, Jack knew already. Gossip travels with the speed of light in the cop world and this message must have been garbled in the translation. "Nothing. I'm just here for moral support."

"Oh, God." He exhaled so heavily I almost felt it. "You scared the shit out of me. Got a message that Liz Matthews reported a rape. I didn't know what the hell was going on."

"Well, I'm okay."

"Good. Just stay put. I'm on my way. I got the case."

I put the phone away and plucked a bit of seaweed from Nicola's damp red hair. Simply knowing Jack was on his way made me feel warmer and I babbled. "That was my boyfriend. He's a cop. He's on his way to talk to you."

Nicola closed her eyes and I reassured her. "He's a nice guy, you'll like him. The only problem is he's overly polite. He'll 'Ma'am' you to death. It drives me crazy but it's a Southern thing. He says his mama raised him to be a gentleman to make up for the failings of his gender."

She didn't respond. I stroked her hair and felt ineffectual. As soon as we pulled up to the hospital, ER staff hurried Nicola inside. The admitting clerk ambushed me, but a promise was a promise, and I shook her off and trotted after the gurney. The hospital computer would have to wait until Nicola felt calm enough to tell me her last name and address.

By the time I got to the private treatment room in the depths of the ER, a team of nurses surrounded her. I stood to the side and shivered in the blanket as they assessed her condition. Dad had always joked that I had a standing appointment in the emergency room when I was a girl because I made a habit of falling out of trees, stopping fights, and playing hockey with the boys. While upscale Hoag Hospital with its soothing, lavender-tinted walls offered a nicer decor than the sickly, pea-green paint from my childhood in Detroit ERs, the antiseptic scent made my scars crawl with the memories of past stitches.

"Liz!" Nicola screamed.

"It's okay. I'm here." I pushed through the crowd and put my hand on her arm. "I promise. I won't leave."

She searched my face for assurance and her voice shook. "Why?"

I shrugged. "I just know what it's like to be in these places. It's good to have a friend to hold your hand."

Nicola bobbed her head once. Tears ran down the side of her face and mingled with the salt water in her soggy red curls.

A woman in green scrubs conferred with the paramedics in the doorway. She made notes on a clipboard, then came over and introduced herself in a soothing tone. "Hello, Nicola, I'm Doctor Rosen. May I take a look?"

Nicola sniffed her assent but she watched Doctor Rosen with the concentration of a cornered animal. The doctor pulled down the blanket to expose Nicola's neck. A line of four dark purple bruises ran down her throat, perfect impressions of the fingers of the bastard who'd tried to strangle her. Nicola hissed when she touched the spot.

Doctor Rosen gently pushed back Nicola's thick hair. Her left ear was swollen and bloodied. Her forearms bore large bruises from fighting off her attacker and she had blood around her fingernails. A nurse took notes as the doctor described the bruises and wounds, but I didn't need a pen and paper to record the brutality. The pictures would be in my memory forever.

After she finished the exam, the doctor wheeled up a stool. "Nicola, I know you're very upset, but I have to ask a question. Have you been sexually assaulted?"

Nicola sobbed her answer.

"It's okay. It's not your fault. This is what we can do." Dr. Rosen explained the procedures in detail. "I know it's not very pleasant but if you want to press charges—"

"Yes."

"Fine. I'm afraid you need to sign this form. It details what I just told you." Nicola scribbled with a shaky hand. Dr. Rosen patted Nicola's arm. "I know you've been through a horrible experience. I don't want to make it worse. I'll be gentle, but if you ever feel uncomfortable, tell me and I'll stop. Do you want your friend to stay?"

Nicola nodded and they began with photos of her injuries. She squeezed her eyes shut and clenched her teeth as the flash popped. The bright light made me see spots. Then they stripped off her clothes and saved them in bags. More photos followed while the nurse prepared the rape kit. One glance at the stainless steel instruments and collection containers made me shudder. They scraped under her fingernails for blood and tissue. When they started the pelvic examination, I studied a diagram of the human body on the wall. Tension knotted in my shoulders and neck, scrunching them together.

Nicola nearly squeezed the circulation out of my hand. Her breathing became rapid. "Stop!"

Dr. Rosen stopped. "I'm sorry, Nicola. Do you want to take a break, or do you want me to stop completely."

Nicola shook her head but I urged her. "Come on, we've got to get this bastard behind bars before he does this to someone else. You can do it."

"Finish." Her voice quivered and she clamped her eyes shut while they collected semen and pubic hair.

There was a soft rap at the door and a woman slipped into the room. Her hair was twisted into a silver and black rope that hung to her waist. Her face had the strength and compassion of someone who weathered emotional storms on a regular basis. She pulled up a chair and introduced herself as Maya from the Rape Crisis Center. She expressed her sympathy and offered help. Nicola relaxed her grip on my hand and I flexed my shoulders to loosen the muscles.

In a few minutes, there was a second knock and the door opened. A man drawled, "Excuse me, police."

Doctor Rosen didn't bother to glance up. "We're not through yet."

"That's okay." Jack motioned to me. "I want Liz."

I excused myself, but Nicola clutched my hand despite my promises to return quickly. Maya intervened and assured Nicola she'd be safe. I hesitated, not wanting to abandon Nicola, but my desire to see Jack tugged harder. As soon as Maya pried Nicola's fingers from my hand, I hurried out into the corridor, dropping my blanket on the floor.

Jack belonged to the select group of men who'd look great in a Speedo, if he'd wear one. He looked awfully good in his navy blue suit. The gun, the badge, the neatly groomed short black hair, and other cop accouterments added to his charm in a macho way.

The Freudian implications of dating a man in my father's profession worried me a little. Dad did an outstanding job of raising me alone, even though he still tried to run my life. But, because of Dad, I set high standards for men and Jack was the only guy who'd come close to the mark. Just seeing him made me so damned happy my face hurt from smiling.

The officer from the scene stood beside Jack, and I braked to avoid throwing myself into Jack's arms for a potentially embarrassing public display of affection while he was on duty. But Jack didn't care. He gave me a rib-crushing hug that lifted my soggy running shoes from the floor. I threw my arms around his neck in a stranglehold and absorbed his strength.

"Jesus, Lizzie. You're soaked." He let go and eyed my wet clothes. "You'll catch your death."

"I'm fine." I brushed sand from his suit. "I'm just glad you're here."

He gave me a quick kiss and shrugged an explanation to the officer. "My girl."

The officer nodded and Jack put on his business face. "Okay, Liz, tell me what happened."

Actuaries are trained to observe, record, regurgitate, and analyze data. I described everything in detail. When I finished, Jack asked the officer what he had found.

The officer referred to his notebook. "I tried to question the victim, but she was incoherent. It appears the victim was running toward the Balboa Pier when she was attacked. Judging from the footprints, the actor came down from the top of the dunes and intercepted her. He was probably hiding up there waiting for someone to come by. He ran back up toward the street. I found signs of a struggle and these." He held out a plastic bag with cheap purple, green, and gold necklaces.

I frowned. "Tacky toy jewelry?"

Jack took the bag. "You are such a Yankee. These are Mardi Gras necklaces. Wonder what the hell they're doing here."

The officer left after Jack arranged to meet him later at the crime scene. We stood alone in the corridor. Emergency room business was pretty light on Valentine's Day. Most Newport Beach residents were probably at home celebrating with their lovers instead of dealing with a rape. I wanted to throw myself back into Jack's arms, but he had enough on his mind and I nodded toward the treatment room door. "I probably ought to get back in there."

He shook his head and pulled me to an empty treatment room across the hall for an extended hug. I lingered in the security of Jack's embrace, inhaling his scent.

"You sure you're okay?" His breath was warm on my ear.

"Yeah, but that poor woman. It's just so awful."

"I know. You think she can give me a description?"

I shook my head and pulled away. "She can barely talk. But I've got to get back. I promised."

Before I could leave Jack caught my wrist. "Just a minute. I've got a question first. What the hell were you doing out running on the beach so late at night?"

I shrugged. "I always run at night. You know that."

"But I thought you had sense to run up by the houses."

"I had my cell phone with me."

"Cell phone?" His eyes searched the ceiling. "And what were you going to do if that fellow had attacked *you*? Ask him to wait while you called the police?"

"No, but as soon as I saw some suspicious looking guy—"

"Liz, I'm betting that lady didn't have time to blink."

"But I can take care of myself."

"Okay. Show me." He squared his shoulders and egged me on. "Walk past me. Let me see what you'd do."

I made a face and humored him. He caught me from behind with an arm around my neck. "Okay, Blondie, now how's that phone going to help you?"

If he wanted to play games, fine. We'd wrestled before and my two free arms had to be better than his one. I snaked the phone from my fanny pack, but he stripped it from my hand and put it in his pocket.

"Now let's see what else you have in your bag of tricks."

That was a problem. I stomped on his feet and grabbed his hair, but his damn cop cut was too short. He dug into my pack.

"Well, look here. Pepper spray. Wasn't that thoughtful of you to give me a weapon? Shall we try it?"

He pointed it my face. I squeezed my eyes shut and buried them in his sleeve. "No! Jack! Don't! Please!"

He released me and held the spray in his palm. "This is stupid. He could have used it on you."

"But he didn't." I snatched it and stuffed it in my bag.

Jack's expression darkened. "Only because you got lucky. If you'd been a few minutes earlier, you'd be the one crying in that examination room and I'd be out looking for that mother-fucker so I could kill him."

My cheeks felt hot and I folded my arms. He ducked his head. "Lizzie, I don't want to fight. I'm proud of what you did. But sometimes I've got to whack you upside the head to get your attention. Pepper spray gives women a false sense of security and you've already got more balls than I do."

"Sweet talk." I muttered, but he was probably right.

"It's true. I don't run alone on the beach at night. Why do you put yourself in situations where you'd need pepper spray?"

The tension returned to my neck and I rubbed at it. "I have to get back."

I brushed past him and returned to the treatment room, apologizing to Nicola for the delay. A nurse brought in a tray of syringes and prepared injections of antibiotics, tetanus, painkillers for the stitches, and painkillers for the mind. The sight of needles and the scent of alcohol made me light-headed and I looked away. Nicola clutched my hand and winced.

If someone hadn't heard me scream back in college and pulled the guy off me, I could've gone through something like this. Even with the advantage of a clear head and pepper spray tonight, fighting off a rapist wasn't something I wanted to try again. I glanced back at Jack and caught him standing in the doorway staring gloomily at me. He mouthed, "I'm sorry."

Pride tastes a lot like crow, only drier, but I swallowed it and whispered back, “Me, too.”

His smile made it worthwhile and I passed it on to Nicola. “We’re going to catch this son-of-a-bitch, I promise. All you have to do is describe him.”

She burst into tears. “I can’t.”

3

403809798274981798409197

When Doctor Rosen finished, Maya and I wrapped Nicola in blankets and got her in a chair with a cup of tea and a box of tissues. We sat on either side of her, so close our shoulders nearly brushed hers. Jack pulled up the stool and introduced himself. He jotted down her name and address. Nicola Jackson lived a few blocks from me.

"Ms. Jackson, I'm sorry about what happened. The Department and I will do everything we can to find the man who hurt you, but I need your help. I have to ask some highly personal questions if you wish to prosecute. I don't want to make you feel uncomfortable."

"I understand." Nicola sniffed. "I'm an attorney."

"Good. Would you like these ladies to stay, Ma'am?" She nodded and he continued. "Can you tell me what happened?"

"Man jumped out in front of me. Shouted 'boo'. Laughed. I tried to outrun him. He pulled me down." She twisted a tissue. "He kept hitting me. Calling me names. Terrible names. He kept saying 'tell me you want it'."

She hung her head and trembled. Maya put her arm around her while I held her hand. Nicola struggled to talk between sobs. "I tried. I really tried. He kept hitting me. Holding my face in the water. I thought I was going to die."

She doubled over and wailed. I slipped to my knees and stroked her tangled hair. “You did all you could.”

She shook her head. “I gave up.”

A moan came from deep inside her soul and pierced mine. She cried harder than I thought possible. I shook her. “No, it’s not true. You couldn’t stop him.”

Jack leaned forward. “Ma’am. Listen. You did the right thing. You stayed alive.”

Maya rubbed Nicola’s back. “You had to survive. You have to survive now.”

Slowly, the tears subsided but the humiliation she’d suffered weighed down her shoulders. When she was calm enough to talk, Jack asked, “Did you get a look at his face?”

“No. He had a mask. A horrible mask.”

Between sobs, she described a male Caucasian, early to mid twenties, a little taller and about thirty pounds heavier than me, the generic Southern Californian beach dude. Mercifully, Jack ended the interview. We made an appointment to meet at Nicola’s in the morning. After he left for the crime scene, Maya and I bundled Nicola into Maya’s car and she drove us to Nicola’s apartment on the Peninsula. Simply stepping out of the emergency room and the scent of trauma made me feel better but Nicola cowered until she stood in her living room.

Although the sedatives left Nicola so drowsy she could barely walk, she insisted on taking a shower. I insisted on having the bathroom door open a crack in case she fell asleep. While the shower ran, I glanced around. Her one-bedroom apartment was smaller than my place but it had a better view and she had decorated it in books and work just like I did. Her floor-to-ceiling shelves contained books on law, politics, and hard-core feminist issues, while mine contained actuarial science, business, and mysteries. Her pewter stein and crystal paperweight both said ‘Harvard’. A photograph hanging on the wall showed a triumphant Nicola finishing the Boston Marathon. Her desk in the corner held a computer and printer/fax machine but the odds were good her real workstation was her gold velvet sofa and the coffee table. Her leather briefcase had exploded on the table, burying it in legal documents, gel pens, and sheets of yellow paper.

Going through her bedroom would have been snooping, so I tried the kitchen. Food could provide comfort during a crisis, but Nicola obviously didn’t cook much. Her kitchen would fit in my closet. While she had lovely china and stemware, all she had to eat was frozen low-fat dinners. I zapped a mug of milk in the microwave for Nicola and found a bottle of single malt scotch in the cupboard for myself. I poured a shot. The warmth felt good on my throat and it dulled a little of the edge. I slumped on the couch in her living room, suddenly tired.

Nicola emerged from the bathroom. Her skin, flushed from hot water and thorough scrubbing, matched her pink terry robe. I made her drink the milk and tried to persuade her to go to bed but she wanted to talk.

She sat on the sofa and squeezed my hand. Her voice was soft and her swollen lips barely moved as she spoke. "I don't know how to thank you."

"I'm just returning a favor. Pass it on someday." I gave her Jack's business card. "I wrote my number on the back. Promise to call me if you need anything. You sure you're going to be okay tonight?"

She nodded. "You're coming by in the morning with him, aren't you?"

"I promised."

She studied the card through half-open eyes. "Jack Black. Silly name. It can't be real."

"No, it isn't. He changed it in second grade after he fought the whole class to keep them from teasing him about it."

"So, what's his real name?" Her esses slurred as she fought sleep and the card slipped through her fingers.

"I can't tell you." I picked up the card and placed it on the coffee table. "You'll have to ask him."

"Don't you know?"

"Yes. But it's his name."

Her eyes closed. "You're a good friend. I like that."

She fell asleep. I put a pillow under her head and tucked a forest-green afghan around her, then sat in a chair and closed my eyes. When Jack rapped gently on the door, I shook the darkness from my brain and let myself out. He gathered me into his arms. His strength made me realize how exhausted I was. I didn't want to let go.

"How you doing, darlin'?" he murmured in my ear.

"Tired." I rested my head on his shoulder and let him support some of my weight. "She wouldn't let me call anyone."

"Some folks lick their wounds in private. Let's go home."

That sounded great. The sooner I got another stiff drink, a hot shower, and food the better. Jack wrapped his suit coat around me. It carried the comforting scent of his aftershave and his body heat. He helped me into his vintage Mustang convertible and I collapsed in the seat. "Any luck?"

"No, Ma'am. The crime scene's underwater. Can't get good shoe prints out of sand. Got fellows out knocking on doors, but I wanted to be with you." He yawned and unknotted his tie with one hand. "I need to be back out on the beach at dawn."

A block before my place, Jack made a left and parked in front of his well-kept depression-era beach cottage. He hustled inside and came out carrying a brown-paper grocery sack, a Rottweiler shadow at his heels. "You don't mind if Useless tags along, do you? He's been alone all day."

I shrugged and scooted forward to let Useless in the back. Even before we started dating, I realized Jack and his dog came as a package. The dog had better manners than most people. Useless stretched out on the seat while Jack drove around the corner to my place.

Puddles greeted us at the door of my condo with welcoming yips. Her toenails made staccato clicks on the tile entryway floor as she danced while Useless sniffed her.

The heavy aroma of burned food hung in the air. I rushed to the kitchen and opened the oven. The smoke made me cough. I grabbed potholders, took out the casserole, and plopped it on the range. The mushrooms had evaporated, the pearl onions had shriveled into raisins, and the beef was fossil fuel.

I almost cried. "It's ruined."

Jack switched on the exhaust fan and poked at the blackened mass with a wooden spoon. "Guess we'll have to make do with something else."

My emotions welled in my throat and my voice croaked. "I wanted tonight to be perfect."

"I'm not here for food." He put his arm around me.

"Yeah, right. More sweet talk." I shrugged away and scraped the cremated stew into the wastebasket. Even Useless turned up his nose.

Jack took the pan and filled it with hot water in the sink. "There's no point in getting worked up over burnt meat. I'll fix dinner for you tomorrow at my place. We'll get all dressed up, okay?"

"But what about tonight?"

"Not a problem." He picked up the wall phone and ordered a large pizza with everything but anchovies. "Dinner will be here in thirty minutes. I'll toss a salad, but in the meantime—" He pulled a bottle of champagne from the grocery bag and grinned. "Instant party. We just need a fire and a little music."

He worked the cork off with his thumbs. A fine mist rose over the mouth of the bottle. He poured the champagne into two flutes and toasted me. "Happy Valentine's Day."

Our glasses clinked and I took a long sip. "I really need this. I can't get what happened out of my head."

"Come here. Let me help."

He led me to the dining room and turned a chair around so I could sit backwards while he massaged my neck. At first it hurt, but as his fingers worked the muscles, the tension eased and my head fell forward. My eyes closed and my breathing deepened as I concentrated on the pleasure of Jack's touch. The breeze flowing through the open sliding door mingled the perfume of the fresh flowers on the table with the scent of salt air and I remembered Nicola lying in the surf, paralyzed by fright. He hit a sore spot and I jerked.

"Don't think about it."

He worked the knot and I gritted my teeth. "It just keeps popping in my head. I feel sorry for her. I was almost raped once, but this is so much worse."

"What happened?"

"It was totally stupid. I went to a frat party when I was a freshman. Some guy got me a drink and offered to show me around the house. When we got upstairs, the room started changing colors and I felt like the inside of a lava lamp. The next thing I knew, he was taking off my clothes. I screamed and fought until someone pulled him off me." Jack's fingers gently stroked my shoulders. "The really dumb thing was I blamed myself and didn't report it until he raped another girl."

"It wasn't stupid. It's what these fellows count on." He kissed the top of my head. "Let me take care of you tonight. Why don't you take a shower while I walk the pups? I'll finish this after dinner."

Dad raised me strong and independent. I didn't need anyone to take care of me, but I enjoyed having Jack do it because he did it out of respect. I twisted around for a real kiss. He winked, then grabbing the trash bag from the kitchen, he whistled at the dogs. Useless and Puddles scrambled after him to the door, their stubby tails waggling.

I dragged myself to my bathroom and started the shower. The ocean had left my shoes squishy and I took a whiff. Gross. My running tights had bonded to my skin and I peeled them off. I stepped into the scalding water and scrubbed sand, salt, and sweat from my body. Too bad the memories wouldn't rinse away as easily.

After the shower, I slipped into a black velour robe and checked the mirror. At least it didn't crack, but then it was fogged over. I fastened my hair up with a clip because Jack liked it that way and added some blush and perfume.

We had decided to keep our first Valentine's Day simple. All Jack wanted was two photos of me, one for his desk at the station and the other for his dresser. No man had ever asked for that before and it did more for my yin and yang than all of Peter's decorating advice. The photo session, my first since my senior year in high school, inspired me to get a little, red lace thing from Frederick's and six blue, ocean-mist scented pillar candles in various sizes for the bedroom. The little, red lace thing would have to wait for another night and mood, but I deserved the candles even if Jack didn't get in my bed tonight.

I arranged the candles in two groups of three on either end of my dresser and struck a match. The flames released the fragrance and their light reflected in the mirror, bathing the room in a soft glow. I hung up my work clothes and fluffed the down pillows on my brass bed.

I carried the wrapped, framed photos and card into the living room and placed them next to the roses on the cherry coffee table. Jack and the dogs were still out. I gave it a ninety-nine percent probability that he was on his cell phone checking on the rape investigation, but he'd be back before the pizza. Without Jack and the dogs, uncomfortable quietness echoed off the walls. I turned on all the lights and scanned my eclectic music collection for something to elevate my mood. I chose a swing CD. With the volume cranked up, I went to the kitchen and assembled the salad, breaking up the lettuce and tossing the icky bits into the sink. I barely heard the phone over the whir of the garbage disposal. The caller ID displayed a local number.

A woman asked, "May I speak to Elizabeth Matthews?"

Her voice sounded tense and I stiffened. "Speaking."

The caller paused. "Elizabeth, this is your mother."

My cheeks burned as if she'd slapped my face. "I don't have a mother!"

I slammed the receiver down and pressed my hands against my ears to block the echoes of playground taunts. "We know what happened...Your mother left because she didn't love you."

I squeezed harder. "It's not true. She's not my mother."

"Lizzie! Who was that?"

I jumped and dropped my hands when I saw Jack peering into my face. "Wrong number. I didn't hear you come back." I pulled a long knife from the block and dismembered a defenseless cucumber with savage chops.

Jack sucked in air. "Who's not whose mother?" He leaned against the refrigerator with his arms folded, waiting for an answer. Meanwhile I attacked a ripe tomato. Red juice and seeds sprayed across the counter.

"Thought you said your mama was dead."

"She is as far as I'm concerned," I muttered as I hacked. "She abandoned Dad and me when I was a baby. I haven't heard from her in almost thirty years." I waved the knife, dripping with juice, in his face. "And if that woman thinks..."

The phone rang and I slammed the blade into the cutting board. It stuck straight upright and he raised his eyebrows.

He answered with a calm, cop-voice. "Liz Matthew's residence...I know, Ma'am, but she doesn't want to talk to you...Yes, I'm sure you'd like to explain, but I don't think anything you can say will help." He sighed. "Yes, Ma'am, I'll give her a message. Just a minute."

My jaw ached from clenching my teeth. Jack tucked the phone under his chin and shrugged helplessly, then pulled a small leather notebook from his hip pocket. "Okay, Ma'am." His pen flowed across the paper. "What were the charges?" He lifted the pen and listened. "Sounds right."

I shook my head. She'd been arrested, too. Probably wanted bail money. As if.

He scribbled some more. "Yes, Ma'am, I'll tell her, but I can't make her call you. She'll get in touch if she wants to."

He returned the receiver to the cradle, and I jutted out my chin. Each shoulder carried a chip the size of a brick while I waited for him to deliver the message, but he stuffed it in his pocket and picked up the champagne. "I'm going to start a fire."

I took my glass and followed him to the living room, plopping on the soft, dusty pink sofa as he twisted the gas starter and threw on a match. Flames exploded, sending a wall of heat across the room. He halved the stereo volume, then fetched his paper bag and sat beside me. The dogs curled up in front of the hearth.

"Got a present for you. Afraid it's not much." He pulled a gift wrapped in pink tissue from the sack.

After roses and champagne, I hadn't expected anything else. I tore off the wrapping and found a gold makeup case with a toothbrush, toothpaste, my favorite perfume, and a house key on a red ribbon. I examined it, trying to decipher the guy-code.

"I thought you could keep it at my place and I brought one to keep here for me." He took a masculine shaving kit from the grocery bag and grinned. "I even brought a dish and dog food for Useless. That way if we wanted to spend the night, we could. And key's to my house, you can use it anytime."

I'd never traded keys before. My cool, sophisticated veneer cracked, as did my voice. "Is this like going steady?"

He nodded and entwined his fingers in mine. "Darlin', I love you. I know you're skittish about relationships, but I want to wake up and see you next to me."

My cheeks burned hotter than the fire. If it hadn't been my place and if my legs would've worked, I might've run because actuaries knew far more relationships fail than work. The odds between a divorced cop and a woman with a runaway mother would be even worse. On the other hand, he made me feel too comfortable to move my butt off the couch. "I'm pretty scary in the morning. I don't talk."

"That's okay. I'll bring you coffee in bed." He grinned. I surrendered. We sealed the deal with a lingering kiss and he whispered, "May I stay tonight?"

I snuggled in the safety of his arms and nodded. "I want you to make love to me and get all the ugliness out of my head."

He slipped a warm, smooth hand into my robe and caressed my breasts, sending lovely, lusty thoughts to my brain, but dinner was due any minute and I wiggled away. "After the pizza. You need to open your present."

I put the makeup case next to his red roses and handed him the photos. Even though he'd asked for them, I held my breath as he opened the wrapping. "Oh, Lizzie." His face lit up as he admired the pictures. "These are beautiful. I'm a lucky man. I'm going to take this to the station first thing."

I let out the air, but my chest remained inflated. He thanked me with a deeper kiss. As we cuddled on the couch, curiosity overpowered my anger. "Is she in trouble?"

"No, Ma'am, your little sister is."

Sister? I used to ask Santa for a sister, but the nerve of that woman throwing me away then having another. "I'm an only child."

"Well, your mama's got a fourteen-year-old on probation for possession of drugs, thought maybe you could help her."

"Not my problem." Jack sat silent as the Sphinx. If I wanted to know more, I'd have to ask. "What else did she want?"

"She wants to see you, apologize."

"It's too late." I stiffened and stared at the flames.

"What happened? Why'd she leave?"

"Don't know. I thought it was my fault. Dad wouldn't talk about her. He threw out everything that reminded him of her, even my baby pictures. I used to worry he'd leave, too."

I'd never said those words aloud before and I swallowed hard. Jack stroked my hair. "Oh, darlin', your Daddy would be sitting between us right now if he could."

"I figured that out. That's why I'm in California." I brushed my cheeks with my fingertips. "Some girls teased me about her abandoning me, so I told them she was dead. It shut them up and it made me feel better, so I had an imaginary funeral and buried her." I squinted at the fire. "Is that sick?"

"Oh, Lizzie, no." He held me tightly. "I'm glad you told me. Let me call her, tell her not to bother you again."

I shook my head. "The least she owes me is an explanation." I walked to the phone and punched star-six-nine. How had she found me? And why did she think I could help with her daughter, her other daughter? When she answered, I made it quick. "Meet me Saturday morning at Balboa Pier."

4

403809798274981798409197

The ringing filtered through layers of goose down and sleep until it penetrated my subconscious mind. I pulled the pillow from my head and took off the eye mask. The sun had barely yawned through my window. Saturday already. I mumbled something resembling ‘hello’ into the telephone.

“He raped another woman last night. When is it going to stop?” Nicola sounded frightened.

“Soon.” I rubbed my eyes and glanced at the empty place on my bed where Jack should’ve been. The rapist had struck two more times since I’d found Nicola on the beach Tuesday night. Nicola had become a prisoner in her apartment, too terrified to leave. “Make coffee. I’m coming.”

Jack and I had spent a quiet Friday night at my place. He’d gotten called out about the rape just after we’d fallen asleep, the aura of lovemaking still enveloping us. Although I knew he wouldn’t come back, I couldn’t fall asleep again for hours, worrying about him and about Nicola. I punched his speed dial number just to hear his voice and he answered on the second ring, already wide-awake. He didn’t have any good news to share about the investigation but he did promise to be at Peninsula Park at nine o’clock when I met with my mother.

After the abbreviated evening, I needed an IV drip of caffeine to get human. It took all my fortitude to crawl out of my warm, soft bed and drag myself to the kitchen to start the coffee maker. While it hissed and gurgled, I went back to the bedroom and slipped into black bike shorts, a sweatshirt, and running shoes.

Over the last three days, Nicola and I had spent hours talking but I couldn't persuade her to leave her apartment. It was time to bring in the pros, my good friends Ben and Jerry. After I walked Puddles, I grabbed three pints of assorted flavors from my personal collection, put them in a paper bag, and stuffed them in my backpack. I filled an insulated travel mug with an energy boosting mixture of coffee, cream, and chocolate syrup and headed to Nicola's apartment. By the time I reached her place, the mug was empty and the exercise had almost woken me up. I stifled a yawn and knocked softly. "Nicola, it's me."

Chains rattled and bolts clunked as she opened the door. As soon as I stepped in, she went through the locking ritual. It took a moment for my eyes to adjust to the darkness. Despite the gorgeous Southern California sunshine and a spectacular view of the ocean from her living room, Nicola had closed the drapes. The swelling on her face had gone down and the abrasions had scabbed over, but the bruises remained dark blue-green. She wore baggy Harvard sweats. Her red hair hung in damp curls from yet another shower. Ben, Jerry, and I had arrived just in time.

Nicola wrapped her arms around herself. "I'm sorry I bothered you, but every time he rapes another woman..."

"I know, but the sketch of the mask is in the morning newspaper and it'll be all over the beach by noon. See, I've got some of the flyers." I pulled a handful of sheets from my backpack and waved them. "We can tack them up around town."

She shook her head so I thrust my backpack at her. "I brought breakfast."

She pulled out the bag. Her face screwed in confusion. "Ice cream?"

"Of course. What did they teach you at Harvard?" I mimicked her Boston accent, dropping the R's. "It has dairy, fruit, nuts, and chocolate. That's four major food groups."

She examined the cartons as if they were evidence in a trial. "I guess it would be okay."

"Of course it's okay. That's the joy of living alone. No one can tell you what to eat. Now, I can put it in bowls, but I find eating it from the container makes me feel empowered."

A small smile fought its way out of her lips. "Oh, Liz. Are you always so cheerful?"

"God, no. It's caffeine and sugar and I could use another dose. I've got to deal with my mother this morning."

"I'd almost forgotten. Perhaps you'd like brandy with that. It helps when I talk to my mother."

"I'll take you up on that afterwards."

Internet printouts dealing with rape blanketed the coffee table. Nicola gathered all the sheets and forced them into a pile to make room for the ice cream. We squeezed into her pretend kitchen, bumping elbows as Nicola poured fragrant coffee into glass pedestal mugs and I got out the spoons and napkins. She led the way to the living room, and we settled on the couch with the cartons lined up on the table. She chose my favorite, New York Super Fudge Chunk. She took a bite and furrowed her brows. She had a second taste and moaned, "God. I could eat this every morning."

"Me, too. The only problem is, you have to burn off the calories. I thought maybe you'd like to run later."

She stared at the ice cream, her face frozen. "Not today."

"Nicola, you can't live like this."

"I appreciate everything you've done, but leave me alone."

Her voice sounded colder than the ice cream. I laid my spoon on the napkin. "Okay. I'd better go. See ya."

She put her hand on my arm. "Wait. Don't leave. I'm sorry." Her voice faltered. "I'm scared."

"I know. That's what he wants. You can't let him win."

She blinked. Her serious manner made me appear to be a ditzy blonde slacker, but the difference between us sprang from hair color experiences. Blondes don't have to prove women are superior; they're born knowing where men keep their brains. Nicola was a fighter and the threat of losing made her think.

She studied her locked door as if the rapist were on the other side. "Okay."

I saluted her with my mug. "Then get ready."

I cleaned up while she changed. The Chamber of Commerce had ordered the February weather just to make the rest of the country envious. Sunlight glittered off the sand and the temperature was expected to climb to near seventy. During the summer, Balboa Peninsula was crowded and noisy, a hideous place to live. But in the late winter, it was heaven and we only had to dodge a few skaters and cyclists.

After our run, I barely had time to go home, shower, and change into jean shorts and a sports shirt for the meeting with my mother. I waited at a picnic table under a palm tree in Peninsula Park at the foot of Balboa Pier, drumming my artificially elongated nails on the green enamel wood tabletop. The small grass-covered oasis between the parking lot and beach seemed like the perfect, neutral site, a place where I wouldn't feel confined and I could leave at any time. I watched the parking lot as the first group of tourists arrived for a day at the beach. The children ran ahead, giggling and shouting while their parents struggled behind bearing coolers, umbrellas, boom boxes and towels.

A few minutes later, Jack approached, whistling and balancing two paper cups on top of a small white box, a newspaper tucked under his arm. His white dress shirt, navy slacks, and cop accessories made a bold fashion statement.

"Morning, darlin'," he drawled as he slipped onto the bench beside me.

"Morning. How'd it go last night? Is the woman okay?"

He frowned. "She's still in the hospital. The son of a bitch is escalating. I'm afraid I've got to cancel lunch."

"Oh, Jack! You've got to eat sometime."

"Look, I promised to be here when you met your mama and I am. I even brought breakfast." He opened the box of cinnamon rolls and waved a cup under my nose. My favorite aromas, freshly brewed mocha coffee, cinnamon, and recently showered and shaved man blended. "Made reservations for dinner tonight. Fanciest place in town. Got to wear a coat and tie."

"You'd better." I took a cup. "And her name's Ann."

"Okay," he said, arranging napkins and rolls. "Did you see the paper?"

I shook my head as he handed me the *Orange County Register* folded to display a sketch of a bird of prey. "It looks Aztec or Mayan."

Jack shook his head. "Think Mardi Gras."

"Why do you think it's connected to Mardi Gras?"

"The colors and the timing. Mardi Gras ends a week from Tuesday and I got a hunch it belongs to a Krewe."

"Crew? What do boats have to do with this?"

He chuckled and took the paper. "I keep forgetting you damn' Yankees don't know about these things. I'm talking Krewes with a 'K'. They're social organizations. Each Krewe has a parade every year with a different theme."

"At least you've narrowed it down."

"Not really," he snorted. "There's over a hundred Krewes in New Orleans alone and they're damn' busy this week."

"But this is California."

"Krewes are a vital part of the Mardi Gras celebration. Even out here." He smoothed the newspaper out. "We're passing this picture out everywhere."

I touched his knee. "Can I help?"

He shrugged. "Just promise you won't go wandering around the beach alone at night anymore."

"If you promise to wear your vest." He whimpered as I ran my hand up his thigh. "I think body armor's sexy."

The whine deepened into a primitive moan. "Oh, God. That vest is mighty hot. Don't know that I can make love in it."

"Then I'll be on top."

His testosterone surged and his hand slipped into my knit shirt. "We can stop by my place when we're done here."

"Nope, it only happens if you wear it to work first."

I wiggled away and broke the cinnamon roll into bits, unable to eat. Jack whistled as he scanned the area. He stopped abruptly and I followed his line of sight. My throat closed. I felt like Dorian Gray staring at his portrait twenty years later.

Everyone said I resembled my father, but I couldn't deny Ann's genetic contribution. I had her to blame for my curl-resistant blonde hair and sun-sensitive porcelain skin. At least her fine bones had tempered Dad's hulking frame. Her pale blue sweater and skirt made her appear delicate.

I marched toward her, but the smell of tobacco contaminated the salt air. My nose crinkled. She smoked. I took off my sunglasses and tossed my hair. The chips on my shoulders grew to the size of the palm trees towering over us and I swaggered as I balanced them.

She stopped, too. Her mouth formed a small 'O'. Her voice sounded like a breeze. "Elizabeth. You're beautiful."

"Yeah, right." At least she didn't sound surprised. "What do you want?"

She flinched as if I'd slapped her. "I just wanted to apologize for what I've done."

Apologize? What about her kid, her other kid? I folded my arms. "So? What did you do?" Was I being a brat, or just defensive? I didn't care. If I didn't let her in my life, she couldn't leave me again.

She twisted her fingers and ducked her head. "Your father didn't tell you?"

"Dad can't even say your name."

"I don't blame him." She nodded. "It was all my fault. He's a good man."

"Yeah, he is." Which meant she left because of me. I sucked up all my emotions. "So why did you leave me?"

"I didn't want to." She looked into my face. "I was young. Too young to have a baby."

"You were nineteen. I've got the birth certificate. I can do the math."

She struggled. "Your father was the first man I really knew. It happened so fast. I got pregnant. I didn't know babies were so much work. I wanted to have fun, but your father liked the late shift." Tears formed. "I was lonely. One night, he caught me coming out of a bar with a man. I thought he'd kill us. He told me to leave and not come back."

My hands trembled as I rubbed my temples and assimilated all she had and hadn't said. My voice shook. "And where was I all this time, Mommy Dearest."

She shrank. "In your crib. I know it was wrong but—"

I jumped in her face and shouted. "You left me alone!"

"I'm sorry." She raised her hands in self-defense and Jack gripped my upper arm, anchoring me to the sidewalk.

"Sorry isn't enough. You risked my life to get laid. How many other children have you abandoned?"

She shook her head. "None. I just have your sister."

"And where is she?"

"I don't know. We had a fight last night, she ran away."

"At least she had the choice."

Ann buried her face in her hands and wailed. Jack took charge. "Ladies, we need a time out. Ma'am, could you sit at that bench over there? I'll be with you in a minute."

He pulled me to the picnic table, but I couldn't sit. A group of teen-aged boys with boogie boards and wet suits stared but took the long way around us. "The girls in school were right." The words tangled in my throat and I choked them out. "She didn't love me."

"Oh, darlin'." He folded me into his arms, holding me so tightly I could barely breathe. "That's not true. It took that woman every ounce of courage she had to come here today. If she didn't love you, she couldn't have done it." He patted my back and clucked sympathetically. "I know you're hurting. Let me calm your mama down so you can talk it out."

I scrunched up the pain and let him go. Deep inside, I'd always known Ann had cheated on Dad, but it didn't explain the years of silence.

Part of me hoped she'd been so horribly disfigured in an accident that she'd hidden herself away in a convent, or that she'd left with my identical twin sister, so I wouldn't have to admit that she didn't want me.

Jack strolled across the lawn to Ann, handing her a handkerchief. She wiped her tears, then rummaged through her large white purse, pulling out a wallet and handing him a piece of paper. He put it in his notebook and wrote as she talked.

Jack returned. "Your mama's been up all night worrying about your sister. She thinks the girl spent the night on the beach." He stroked my hair. "She gave me a photo. I promised to ask around. Maybe you ought to wait on more talking till your sister turns up."

"I can't." I marched across the grass with Jack at my heels. Ann cringed, her eyes red and puffy. Jack was right. Raging would only give me a sore throat. I tucked my hands under my arms.

"I'm sorry I yelled. Dad raised me better than that. I hope you find your daughter. If she wants to talk to me, *she* can call. I'll phone *you* when I'm ready." She nodded and my nose went up in the air. "You smell like an ashtray. Don't smoke next time and don't expect too much."

I stumbled to the table, fighting to breathe. Jack sat beside me. "You did the right thing. Don't fret about it."

"But I don't have little compartments like you do."

"Hell, if I carried all my work around with me, I'd probably be a drunk." He squeezed my hand. "How about a walk?"

"But this isn't about work. It's about…" I didn't want to say the word. Family. I steadied myself. "I want to see my sister's picture first."

"You don't need it. Just saw you off at the ankles and you'll have her." He passed me the photo. "Your mama says she sprayed her hair orange and got a tree tattooed on her arm."

The picture confirmed that we'd been painted from the same palette by the same hand and I wondered if we shared anything else. "I always wanted a sister. What's her name?"

"Willow. Willow Forrester."

"Oh, shit." I grimaced and gave him the picture. "No wonder she ran away. Poor kid. Are you going to turn this in?"

"Now that's a problem. If I do, we'll have to tell the judge. She's already on probation and she cut class yesterday."

"Then I'll find her myself. The beach isn't that big."

I popped to my feet, but Jack pulled me back. "Whoa there, Mizz Sayers. Before you go traipsing all over creation, make a few calls first. Your mama gave me her friends' phone numbers."

I pulled out my cell. No one answered at the boyfriend's house and the first girl friend got snotty. But the second girl wavered and I poured on the dire consequences to Willow if I had to involve the police. She gave me a name and an address, almost.

"She said the boyfriend's Uncle Jimmy lives near the Newport Pier in that house that looks like a boat. She said they spend a lot of time there."

I knew the place since I ran past it every day. It sat at the end of row of million dollar houses right on the beach. With its gray stucco walls, round windows, tubular metal railings, and deck chairs on the front porch it appeared ready for a cruise. I shook my head. My little sister obviously ran in wealthier circles than I did. The thumping of a bass line greeted us as we stepped to the door. Jack rang the bell.

No one answered. I peered in the front windows. The white-on-white living room and dining room belonged in a decorator show home, but there was no sign of life. I went through the gate at the side of the house. There was barely room for my shoulders between the stucco wall and the wooden privacy fence.

"Liz!" Jack called as I squeezed down the path. "You can't go snooping."

The music grew louder as I approached a set of French doors. I scanned the family room. A folded newspaper and a coffee cup sat on the end table. Two running shoes attached to inert hairy legs stuck out from behind the dark-red leather sofa. I yelled for Jack.

He scuttled down the walk, cursed, and whipped out his cell phone, calling for backup and an ambulance, then pulled out his gun and told me to stay put. One kick burst the door open and I followed him in. He squatted beside the body of a man with curly, graying hair and a full beard lying on the terra cotta tile floor. The man was dressed for exercise, except for the bullet hole in his chest. The body smelled of sweat and blood.

Coffee tastes better the first time. I swallowed before I threw up. I didn't stop to clean up, but ran through the house searching for Willow. Upstairs, a semi-nude girl sprawled on rumpled black sheets on the king-sized waterbed in the master suite. The face, the orange streaked hair, and the willow tree tattoo couldn't be denied. I touched her throat. Her skin felt warm and her pulse faint. Her respiration was shallow. An open bottle of pills lay on one side of her and a gun on the other.

The music stopped. An eerie silence washed over the room. I slapped her. The water sloshed. "Willow! Wake up!" No response. I tried again, then pulled her torn T-shirt to cover the parts Jack didn't need to see and shouted for him.

Footsteps thudded up the stairs. Jack yanked me from the bed. "Oh, fuck!" The veins in his neck bulged. "What the hell are you doing here? Did you touch anything?" I jumped back and shook my head. "Then put your hands under your arms and don't move!"

I did what he said and tried to pull my head into my shoulders just to be safe. He checked her pulse and pupils, and then yelled for an officer. When one appeared, Jack left him in charge, and grabbing the back of my shirt, hauled me to the family room. My feet barely touched the ground. Another officer came through the French doors. He stopped when he saw us and stared at me while he reported no sign of forced entry.

Jack kept his hand twisted in the neck of my shirt, his expression cold, his fury barely controlled, and instructed the officer. "Secure the crime scene. I'll be right back."

The officer nodded in my direction. "What about her, Sir?"

"She's my girl friend." Jack muttered through clenched teeth and pushed me outside. He didn't stop until we hit the beach and his anger thawed. "Don't you have enough sense not to walk into a crime scene? Jesus!" He threw his arms in the air and searched the heavens. "You could've gotten hurt and if you touched that weapon, I might as well turn in my badge."

I held up my hands. "I'm sorry. I didn't touch anything. Honest. I don't want to get you in trouble. Is she going to be okay?"

He blew out his emotions in one puff and his expression softened. "I don't know. It's hard to tell with overdoses. I'm sorry I yelled."

"You think she killed him?"

"I don't know yet." He ran his fingers through his hair and his voice dropped. "I'm only preserving the evidence until I can hand this off, but you have to stay here. If you go back in, I'll lock you in a squad car."

Been there, done that. Two squad cars had already parked on the dead-end street next to the house. The officer in charge of the scene strung yellow police tape across the porch, blocking the entrance. He eyed me and jotted down my name and address before he took his position by the gate. The yellow tape and police vehicles attracted a crowd of neighbors and people off the beach and the Newport Pier. In-line skaters and cyclists slowed as they passed by on the sidewalk in front of the house to gawk and avoid hitting pedestrians.

I paced up and down in the sun, checking my watch at the end of every circuit to time the EMTs' arrival. They rushed inside a few minutes later and I phoned Jack to make certain my sister was still alive. When the paramedics brought Willow out on a gurney, Jack put his hand on my shoulder and shook his head. "I think you ought to go with her."

He helped me into the ambulance. As we pulled away, I glanced down at the tubes and wires connected to Willow.

"Stupid little brat." I took her hand. "I've waited this long for a sister. You're not going to die on me now."

5

403809798274981798409197

"You don't know your sister's address or phone number?" The hospital clerk stared at me over the frames of her pastel pink eyeglasses, her fingers poised over the computer keyboard.

I squirmed on the edge of the chair beside the admitting desk. As soon as I'd walked in the door, someone had pulled me into the cubicle to add to the red tape the hospital generated. I wanted to get to the treatment area and check on Willow. "She's my half-sister. We just met and she's unconscious. Can't we do this later? I want to get back there and see how she's doing."

"But we need to contact her mother."

"Fine. Just give me the phone book."

She opened a desk drawer and handed me the *Orange County White Pages*. The thin sheets rattled as I whipped through it. Thank God, Ann was listed. The clerk tapped in the information as I dictated. When she finished, she motioned to the phone.

"Do you want to call her, or should I?"

It seemed like something family should do but as soon as Ann answered, I didn't know what to say. She hung up as soon as she heard about Willow.

With the clerk satisfied that a responsible party was on the way, I hurried down the hall to the treatment area. It wasn't hard finding Willow's room. ER and EMT personnel swarmed around her, talking in low voices while the heart monitor beeped. A woman was siphoning blood out of Willow's arm and I stopped and looked away. Another woman with a stethoscope hanging around her neck took my elbow and guided me out of the room.

"Are you the sister?" she asked.

"Yeah, is she okay?" I tried to pull back but she pushed me into the hallway.

"She's doing as well as can be expected. Do you know why she took the pills?"

I didn't know why she did anything and I shook my head. "Can't I be with her? She's just a kid!"

"We need room to work. Why don't you sit in the waiting room? We'll call you if there's any change in her condition."

That didn't sound good, but arguing wasn't working. The waiting area offered semi-comfortable upholstered chairs and up-scale home and fashion magazines only a few months old, far more pleasant than the Emergency Rooms of my childhood with their hard plastic seats and ages-old automotive literature. It even smelled less of disinfectant than the hospitals back home. Still, sitting is the last thing I can do during a crisis, especially in a place filled with sick people. In one corner, a young woman held a wailing baby while her husband looked on helplessly. Another woman held a bloody cloth to her son's broken nose. Several weekend athletes nursed injuries, but the rest of the occupants appeared feverish, coughing, sneezing, or some combination of those symptoms. I stood by the Emergency Room entrance and tried to chew my fingernails. The acrylic coating made them too crunchy to be comforting so I tapped my foot instead.

The poor kid. At fourteen, I'd wallowed in a cesspool of self-pity. Everything about my body irritated me and I wished myself dead on several occasions, but even in the depths of my despair, I'd never sunk low enough for suicide. I wondered what pushed Willow into the abyss.

I sneaked back to the treatment room, but the nurse chased me out again and I said a little prayer while pacing near the ER entrance. I had so many questions for Willow, starting with why did she swallow those pills and moving on to what on earth was she doing alone in a house with a man old enough to be my father? Judging from the murder scene, Willow was up to her triple pierced earlobes in excrement. She'd better have good answers or we'd get acquainted with a wall of glass between us.

Ann blew in through the automatic doors, her face full of worry. The unresolved anger fermenting in my veins bubbled up again. I pressed my temples to force it back and showed her to the treatment room.

A baby-faced doctor who probably graduated from medical school that morning met us in the hallway holding a clipboard. He shook our hands and spoke in a low voice. "I'm afraid Willow's swallowed a drug cocktail. She's breathing on her own but her heart beat is a little irregular and she's not getting enough oxygen. The next few hours will be critical."

"But she will be okay?" Ann almost pleaded.

"We're waiting to see if she regains consciousness."

Ann looked at me for help and I stumbled through the question. "But her brain, I mean, it's working, right?"

The doctor nodded and said we could see her for a few minutes. Ann and I approached Willow's bed cautiously. Willow had less color than the white sheets. Tubes and electrodes connected her to monitors, IVs, and oxygen. I strained to decipher the displays but Ann went even paler than Willow and gasped. "Oh, my God. It's all my fault."

I caught her before she hit the floor. She didn't weigh that much. A nurse helped me get her to a chair and gave her a glass of water. She leaned forward with her head down and I knelt in front of her. "Are you okay?"

She looked at me through red-framed eyes and whispered. "Yes. I don't mean to be a bother. I'm sorry."

"Don't worry about it." I stood and rubbed my arms, feeling totally helpless. When Ann recovered, I helped steer her to the waiting room. The admitting clerk joined us and showed Ann to a chair in her cubicle near the computer, offering her tissues and encouragement. Ann composed herself and hunted through her purse for her insurance card. Once the hospital computer had its fill of information, I took Ann to a corner of the waiting area as far as possible from sick people. We sat side by side as if we were a pair of china bookends that had been fractured and glued back together.

Ann sniffed into the tissue. "Thank you for finding Willow."

Fresh tears tracked down her cheeks and I shifted. "It's okay. Would you like some coffee or something?"

She shook her head.

"What did you mean, this was all your fault?"

Ann dabbed her eyes. "She's making the mistakes I did."

"You swallowed a handful of pills, too?"

Her voice was barely audible. "I didn't have anything after I lost you."

She cradled her face in her hands. I reached out to touch her but my fingers stopped just short of her shoulders. She wasn't the only one who'd gotten hurt. I went outside to get some air and stood at the edge of the parking lot overlooking the Pacific, the breeze whipping my hair. After a lifetime of keeping my feelings in check, I felt caught in an emotional blender. Seeing Ann made me feel disloyal to Dad. Why had I done it? I walked around the hospital twice, searching for an answer and wishing Ann to be a card-carrying bitch so I could scream at her. Why did she have to be this mousy little woman who aroused my sympathy?

The second time I passed the emergency room, Ann stood outside blowing cigarette smoke into the sky. As soon as she saw me, she tossed the cigarette on the ground and smashed it with her toe.

"Sorry." She stared at the crushed butt. "I gave up smoking years ago but I was so upset this morning I bought a pack." She darted for the door but I blocked her.

"Why did you abandon me?"

"I told you, your father—"

I shook my head. "That's bull. You could have gotten a lawyer and fought him."

"I didn't have any money."

"You could have found some. What about your parents?"

"They never forgave me for getting pregnant and marrying a Catholic. They never saw you."

My shoulders sagged. Although I'd buried my mother in my head, I'd clung to the hope that my grandparents loved me, just like Grammie and Grampa, and that someday they'd find me—that they wanted to find me. I folded my arms to keep the hurt inside. "You could have called. You could have written. You could have sent me a goddamned birthday card."

"I wrote you, but your father sent everything back."

I felt cold. "Dad wouldn't do that."

She foraged through her purse. "I saved them. I brought one."

"How convenient. Do you always carry stuff like that with you?" The *nerve* of this woman!

"No. I knew I'd see you today and…" She gave me a sealed envelope, postmarked just days prior to my thirteenth birthday. A bold, black 'X' covered my name and address, and Dad had scrawled 'Return to Sender' across it.

My fingers could barely grasp the card. I pressed it to my chest and turned away. The old glue on the envelope opened easily. The frilly pink card was silly and sentimental; nothing like Dad would buy. It contained a photo and she'd added a note in a spidery hand that she loved me and missed me. "Please write, please call, please forgive me," she'd written.

The words did the sidestroke and I closed the card and my eyes. I hadn't expected this from either of my parents. But did a birthday greeting, nineteen years belated, change anything? Was she sincere, or was she only attempting to manipulate her way back into my life? Dad obviously believed I needed to be protected from her or he wouldn't have returned it. I certainly didn't want to get hurt again.

I stuffed the card into my backpack. Ann twisted the handle of her white purse while she waited for my reaction. But if she expected me to jump into her arms, she'd underestimated Dad's influence. Cops questioned everything and so did I. "Why are you doing this to me now? What do you want? Money?"

She held her purse like a shield. "No, I just wanted to see you."

"And that's it?" This was unreal. What about Willow?

She shook her head and opened her mouth but nothing came out. My eyes narrowed. "What is it?"

"I-I want to hold you. Just one more time. I had to leave so fast; I never got to do it. Please?"

Something the size of my heart caught in my throat. Money wouldn't cost me as dearly, but I braced myself and nodded. In a swift motion, she threw her arms around my neck and sobbed. Her tears streamed down my neck. I felt dizzy, nervous. My hands fluttered until they landed on her back. "Ann. Mom. Please, don't cry."

Her shoulders quivered and I patted them until her sobs subsided. She pulled away and wiped her face with her hands. I clawed through my backpack searching for anything that remotely resembled a tissue. All I found was a shabby fast food napkin and I handed it to her.

"Can I do anything for you?"

"Just help Willow. Talk to her, please. You're the only family she has and she won't listen to me."

I was thinking in terms of getting her coffee. "Look, I don't want to get in the middle of any mother-daughter fight."

She nodded and blew her nose. "But I don't want her to die or go to jail. Is that wrong?"

"No, of course not. Maybe you should start at the beginning. Why do you think she tried to kill herself?"

"It's that boy. Ever since she started dating him, she's been nothing but trouble."

"Time out." I made a 'T' with my hands. "You let a fourteen-year-old date? How old is this boy?"

"Eighteen. I told her she couldn't see him anymore and this is what happened." She motioned toward the ER.

Eighteen? I shook my head. Suicide seemed extreme in response to a parental edict, but what was Ann thinking, letting her date in the first place? "Maybe you should try therapy."

"We have. She just rolls her eyes."

I rolled mine, too. Did I have 'sucker' written across my forehead? "So, what's your problem with this boy now?"

"The way he treats her. He puts her down. He won't let her see her friends. He got her on drugs."

Those were damned good reasons. I told her I needed to think. She went back inside; I did laps around the parking lot to clear my brain. Any woman who let a fourteen-year-old date was asking for trouble, and she'd found it. Dad taught me family ranked above everything else. My sister needed help. I didn't know what to do, but I couldn't make things worse.

They moved Willow to ICU shortly before noon. As soon as the nurses had her settled, they ushered Ann and me into her room. Willow seemed so thin and so young, all bony arms and legs, like me at fourteen. She lay in the bed, still, limp and devoid of color. Only the beeping of the monitors indicated she was alive and I didn't know if she had either the physical strength or the strength of character to survive.

Ann clasped her hands as if she were praying and glanced at the baby-faced doctor. "She'll wake up soon, won't she?"

The young man chose his words carefully. "We really don't know. It may be hours. It may be days. But you can talk to her. Sometimes that helps."

Ann stepped closer to the bed and ran her fingers across Willow's forehead, barely touching her skin. "Sweetheart, it's Mommy. I love you."

The pain slashed through my heart and a low moan tried to break out of my throat. I bolted from the room, past the nurse's station, and through the waiting area. The lack of an open elevator stopped me and I stabbed the button. Damn her! Damn her! Damn her! I stabbed the button again and again. Why didn't she love me?

"Elizabeth?"

I flinched at the sound of Ann's voice. She touched my arm. "Are you okay?"

"No." I sniffed the hurt back inside and moved away. "Why did you have to call me? I had everything under control."

"I'm sorry." She bowed her head. "My mother died a few months ago. We hadn't spoken since before you were born. I couldn't go to my grave without apologizing to you." She peered up at me. " I love you and it means so much to have you here."

A ding announced the elevator and the door slid open. A priest slipped out and headed toward ICU. Watching him took my thoughts home to Detroit and Dad, my grandparents, aunts, uncles, cousins, and extended family at Catholic School. That was enough love for anyone. I shouldn't mourn things I never had. Maybe Ann loved me a little. She had left Willow's side to come after me. I pulled on my adult skin and caught the elevator door. "Look, I need a drink. You want anything?"

Ann shook her head. The strongest beverage the vending machine offered was Diet Coke and I used it to wash down a candy bar. Since they only let us see Willow once an hour and I couldn't take any more revelations from my mother, I spent most of the afternoon camped in a sheltered spot under the canopy of the main entrance sorting out emotions. Just when I thought the post office was going to change my address to Hoag Hospital, Jack showed up with Detective Hal Peters. I hustled out to meet them.

Jack wrapped me in his arms. "You okay, darlin'?"

"Yeah, I'm glad you're here. Willow's still unconscious." I described her condition as we walked arm-in-arm toward the entrance. When we reached the canopy, Jack stopped.

"Hal's handling the murder case. He has some questions for you."

Hal resembled a blonde grizzly bear in a business suit and was one of the few people next to Dad who made me feel petite. I looked up at him "Why? I don't know anything about what happened."

"You barged into a crime scene."

The next time I run across a dead body, I might keep running. Hal asked questions in triplicate and lectured me about jeopardizing the investigation. By the time he finished, I regretted not taking the gun.

"What have you told your mother?" Hal asked.

"Nothing, why?"

Jack put his hand on my back. "Hal needs to talk to your mama. I'll drive you home so you can get your car."

Damn. For the first time in my life, I'd kept my mouth shut when I should have talked. "That's okay, Honey. This is family business. I think I should stay."

I stuck out my chin, daring them to send me home. They shrugged. We pulled Ann out of the ICU waiting room and wound our way through the labyrinth of corridors to the cafeteria. After a day with nothing more to eat than a Snickers bar, even hospital food smelled appetizing and appeared edible. We pushed our trays through the line past the fruit and salad bar to the real stuff. Ann took a piece of apple pie. I choose the heart-healthy turkey with dressing and a big slab of chocolate cake. Jack added a second slab of cake and paid for all of us.

The hospital cafeteria was nearly deserted in the late afternoon except for a few visitors scattered around the room. Jack carried our tray to a table in the corner near a potted palm. He and Hal snagged one side of the table leaving me to sit by Ann. The aroma of turkey and sage brought to mind fond memories of holidays past and the many birds Dad and I destroyed before we got the knack of cooking, but at least we'd never turned one into rubber. I couldn't manage a bite.

Hal handled the questions. "Tell me about Willow. What does she like to do? Any hobbies?"

Was this Hal talking? Hobbies? This wasn't cop talk.

"Willow's an artist. Painting, sculpture. Her teachers think she could get a scholarship." Maternal pride filled Ann's face. It made her pretty but the smile evaporated and she studied her untouched pie. "I guess that won't happen now."

"When did you first suspect she was on drugs?"

"I didn't. Not until she was arrested. I don't even know where she found the money to buy them. I blamed her change of behavior on that awful boy."

"What's this boy's name?"

"Ryan Lefebvre. He's a rich kid. Lives up in the foothills, drives a little red Mercedes convertible."

"Was she in the habit of staying out all night?"

Okay, Hal was acting like a cop after all.

"No. She broke her curfew a lot, but last night was the first time she didn't come home." Ann touched the napkin to her eyes. "This last week has been so terrible. I grounded her after she got arrested, but she sneaked out on Valentine's Day to see him, then he got her to cut school yesterday. When she got home, I told her she'd never see him again. She got hysterical and ran out."

Dad would never have tolerated behavior like that from me.

Ann sobbed and Hal waited a discreet interval before he questioned her again. "Do you know a James O'Reilly?"

She shook her head. "I think he's Ryan's uncle."

"It appears your daughter spent the night at Mr. O'Reilly's house. We found Mr. O'Reilly shot to death. We found the gun beside your daughter."

Her freckles stood out like dots of ink on white paper. I put my arm around her. Her voice dropped. "Oh, no. Oh, no."

"Do you know why Willow would want to harm him?"

"No." She looked at me. "Willow wouldn't hurt anyone."

I nodded. "I think we need to call a lawyer."

103809798274981798409197

Stupid hospitals. I had to walk clear out to the parking lot to use my cell phone to call Nicola. Hoag Hospital perched on a bluff overlooking the Pacific and the cool, late afternoon wind blowing off the ocean went straight through my knit shirt and chilled my bare legs. I paced to keep warm and counted the rings. Nicola's answering machine screened the call.

"Nicola, pick up, it's Liz. I need you."

She answered and I launched into a rapid report about my mother, Willow, and the dead man. She interrupted. "Liz, breathe." As I gulped in air, Nicola made the switch from rape victim to lawyer and continued. "You know I don't practice criminal law, but there's no need to panic. It will be days before the police can complete the investigation. This is what you need to do."

She spoke in bullet points as she took control of our conversation, instructing me as if she were lecturing a class at Harvard Law. I took notes on the back of a receipt while I shivered.

"But even if they can't charge her until they finish the investigation, what if they decide to hold Willow in jail when she wakes up? She's on probation for possession."

"Suicide is a serious matter. Your sister needs professional help."

Nicola explained the commitment procedure. "Now, I hate to be crass, but does your mother have insurance?"

I thought back to the admitting information. "Yes."

"Then I'm certain your sister will get at least a week in a secure, psychiatric facility. She won't be going anywhere or seeing anybody while she's getting the help she needs. The police will be satisfied with that." She gave me the names of three attorneys. "Come over later, I want to hear everything."

A rock concert on wheels zoomed past and I had to repeat my promise to stop by. The red Mercedes convertible parked in the fire lane near the ER. After nine years in Southern California, few things surprised me. The driver had pulled into the parking lot as if he were on his way to a fire; it was possible Newport Beach gave their Fire Chief a red Mercedes.

The driver styled his hair in the rearview mirror, then mercifully killed the engine and the music. He sauntered into the Emergency Room. My jerk detector went off and I trotted after him. His vanity plates read 'SSSSSST'. Oh, shit.

Ryan 'Hot Stuff' Lefebvre pushed to the head of the line at the admitting clerk's desk. His face belonged on a box of nutritious cereal guaranteed to make the consumer healthy, wealthy, and popular and his body wasn't bad for a kid. He dressed in designer-label clothing and a phone hung on his belt, but he wore his Y-chromosomes like epaulettes. If he'd come to my house when I was fourteen, Dad would've had all his guns on the coffee table.

"I need to see Willow Forrester."

The clerk peered over those same pink eyeglass frames. "If you'll wait a minute, sir, I'm helping someone."

He put his hand on the desk. "I need to see Willow now."

The clerk took off her glasses. "She's in ICU."

"Then she's still alive."

"Yes, but she's critical. She can't have visitors."

"Well, they'll let me see her. I'm her boyfriend."

Mr. I-own-the-hospital hurried down the hall. The admitting clerk glared after him and so did I. As a rule, I don't toy with the baby male ego; it's just too easy. But my jerk meter had redlined and this creep was dating my little sister. He deserved the full treatment.

I leaned across the clerk's desk and whispered. "He's been buying Willow drugs and he's parked in the fire lane out there. Red Mercedes. You can't miss it."

The clerk nodded and picked up her phone. It was one, but big sister wasn't through yet and I caught up with Ryan in the ICU waiting room. Ann sat alone in a corner, thumbing blindly through a magazine, and Ryan rushed to her. "Mrs. Forrester, where's Willow? I have to see her."

Ann glanced up. If looks could kill, that young man would have sprawled on the floor dead. "No, not as long as I have breath in my body."

I stopped a few feet behind Ryan. Ann didn't appear to need any help, so I waited my turn. The boy raised his hands. "But I love her."

"You call that love? You knew she was on probation. You knew she wasn't supposed to see you. But you got her to cut class and you hid her from me last night." She waved at the ICU. "This is what happened."

He shrugged. "It's not my fault. She was stoned when she called me. Uncle Jimmy said she could sleep it off there if we promised to talk to you in the morning."

Ann stood. "I don't believe you. And I think you're the one buying her those drugs. She can't afford them."

Ryan drew himself up. He had an inch on me. Two, if I counted his stylishly coifed hair. "Mrs. Forrester. I'm an athlete. I don't use drugs."

My turn. "Yeah, right. Half the pro athletes in the country belong at Betty Ford." I rolled my eyes. "Don't they teach debate in high school anymore?"

Ryan spun around. I gave him my best Valkyrie Warrior-Goddess pose with my hands on my hips and my chin high. All the hot air inside him blew out and his jaw flapped in the breeze. Fourteen-year-old girls with no self-esteem never gave boys much lip, especially golden boys with phones who drove Mercedes convertibles. But I had enough ego to give transfusions.

"I'm Willow's sister. What the hell are you doing here?"

He stammered. "I wanted to find out about Willow. I dropped by Uncle Jimmy's to get her and I saw the police tape. One of the neighbors told me about Uncle Jimmy and said they'd taken a girl away in an ambulance."

I stepped closer. "Why'd you leave her there last night?"

He held his hands in front of him. "She was high and I couldn't make her leave. I figured she'd be safe enough."

I stood in his face. "Well, apparently she wasn't. Just what kind of man was your Uncle Jimmy?"

He inched back. "He's really my godfather, one of Dad's friends, but he's real cool."

"Did he pass out drugs?"

"I don't think so. But they're everywhere, you know."

I jabbed him in the chest with a scientifically reinforced fingernail. "No. I don't know. I manage to avoid them and if you really loved Willow, you'd help her avoid them, too."

His eyes narrowed and his breathing deepened. "It's not like she's addicted or anything. It's just something she does to relax. You probably drink."

"As a matter of fact, I do, but I'm old enough to know my limits and I'm not going to end up in jail or the hospital because of it. Is that what you want for her?"

He puffed up like a cobra. "No, of course not. Dad paid for her lawyer and I'm sure he'll pay for her doctors, too."

I almost levitated. Nobody rubbed his money in my face, particularly a high school kid. I had to side with Ann; like the Stone Age, Ryan was history.

"Ryan, I have two words for you. Statutory. Rape."

His mouth gaped and he turned a violent shade of fuchsia as he choked on his anger. I was about to suggest performing the Heimlich Maneuver when a nurse inserted herself in the center of our argument. Although she only came up to my chin, she glared down her nose at us. "You people will have to take this outside. We have critically ill patients here."

Ryan protested. "But I need to see Willow."

"Are you immediate family?"

"Well, no, but—"

"Then you'd better leave before I call Security."

From the way the nurse looked at me, I decided to accompany Ryan. Once out in the corridor his color returned to basic California Tan and he balked.

"I don't know what I did to make you mad, but I'm sorry." A casual stroke of his hand smoothed his expression and hair. "We haven't even been introduced. I'm Ryan Lefebvre."

I gave him my name and he grinned as if we were best buds. "I hope you're not still angry. I've been totally crazy since I found out about Willow. Is she okay?"

"I don't know, she's in a coma."

"Oh, God." He rubbed off the smile and shuddered. "She has to wake up. Please, I need to see her. Can you help?" He thrust a blue velvet jewel case in my hand. "I want to slip this on her finger so she sees it when she opens her eyes."

He had an idea there. The engagement ring with a diamond the size of a marble opened *my* eyes, and to think Sleeping Beauty had settled for a kiss. I blinked, snapped the case shut, and shoved it at him. "No way. You're both too young."

Jack and Hal found us playing hot potato with the case. I made the introductions. Ryan insisted on showing them the ring explaining the size, color, and clarity, as well as the price. He all but got on his knees and pleaded with me to put it on Willow's finger. I declined and Hal took him away for a chat.

"Little creep." I muttered after they left.

"He surely is, but you can handle him. I need to get back to work. Want a lift home to get your car?"

I glanced at my jean shorts and sport shirt. A shower and fresh clothes wouldn't hurt and I hated being a pedestrian. I found Ann and briefed her about the commitment process and the ring. She nodded and I stuffed the list of lawyers in her hand.

As we strolled down the hall, Jack put his arm around me. "Still want to go out for dinner tonight?"

"You'd better believe it. I need a break from all this."

"I understand. I checked with Willow's probation officer. The kid's a mess. Her daddy was an alcoholic, drank himself to death, and beat your mama pretty regularly."

My stomach twisted. "God. How could she put up with that?"

"I don't know. But besides the drugs, Willow's been burning herself with cigarettes and shoplifting. She needs professional help. There's not much you can do."

My shoulders sagged under the weight of Willow's problems. As we stepped outside into the liquid gold of a Southern California afternoon, I put on my mirrored sunglasses and noticed Ryan's little red Mercedes tethered to a tow truck. Estrogen rushed through my veins. Jack was wrong. I *could* help Willow and this was the beginning.

7

"See, darlin'. You eat the tails, then you suck the heads till the eyes pop out."

Jack demonstrated. A small, reddish crustacean face poked out of his mouth, and I shuddered. "Oh, Jack, that's awful. How can you do that?"

He threw the remains of the crayfish into a bowl with its decapitated brethren while I swished a raw oyster in a combination of cocktail sauce, horseradish, and Tabasco. I tossed the spicy mixture down and gasped. My sinuses would be clear for weeks.

"Just showing you how it's done. At least mine are cooked." He grinned and sucked another. The antennae twitched.

I laughed. It usually took six months and a credit history to get Saturday night reservations at the Crescent City Café where New Orleans met the Pacific. I marveled at how Jack had secured a prized table overlooking the harbor with just a few hours notice. But we were giggling like a couple of kids at the trendiest restaurant in Newport Beach.

What we lacked in deportment we made up in style. I wore my best breast-boosting bra under a low cut, sapphire-blue velvet dress that rode high on my thighs. Jack looked like the cover boy of a men's fashion magazine in a charcoal gray pinstripe suit.

We stopped giggling long enough for the waiter to replenish our wine. I swirled the Chardonnay and sighed over the oak aroma. Jack raised his glass. "I'm gonna toast myself this time. I'm one lucky son-of-a-gun."

"So am I." We clinked glasses. Maybe I was simply in love, but the candle-lit restaurant with its plush green carpet and dazzling white linen tablecloths seemed the perfect place for a tryst. The well-cushioned chairs invited lingering and the waiters didn't rush us. It was so quiet we could whisper and if we tired of gazing at each other or the harbor, we could look at the gilt-framed paintings of New Orleans and displays of Mardi Gras memorabilia.

I'd earned the pampering. Except for getting Ryan's car towed and getting Nicola out of her apartment, the rest of my day had been as much fun as swimming in sewage. At least Nicola had shown enthusiasm for planning Willow's defense and a twisted imagination in plotting revenge on Ryan. I'd gone home feeling pretty good.

Then I'd called Dad in Detroit.

Instinctively, I'd always known better than to question him about my mother and I hadn't until I started kindergarten. I'd watched the other kids and their moms for weeks and after the Thanksgiving pageant, once we got home, I asked him about mine. His face contorted like a creature from out of my nightmares. He took me by the shoulders and told me never to mention her again, then he walked out the front door. I thought he'd left forever, so I crawled under my bed and cried and prayed, promising God I'd be the perfect daughter if he brought Daddy back.

He did and I lived up to my end of the bargain, at least until I hit puberty.

Late in the phone conversation, I casually brought up the subject of Ann in my most adult, non-threatening manner. When we hung up, I again felt like crawling under my bed and crying. Damn Dad. He acted as if my even thinking about her was an act of disloyalty. I couldn't tell him I'd seen her and I'd felt my desire to help Willow cool. I wanted to escape for few hours to clear my head, so when Jack picked me up, I'd left my cell phone home.

"You, sir, must be an imposter."

Startled out of my memories, I looked over my shoulder. From the heavy New Orleans accent, I expected to see a Southern gentleman in a Confederate uniform carrying dueling pistols. Instead, there stood a slender man in white chef's uniform. His brown hair was pulled back in a ponytail and a heavy mustache obscured his mouth. A diamond stud glistened in his left ear lobe. Everyone sitting around us stared.

"I haven't heard from my good friend Jack Black in almost three years. I figure he's either dead or in jail or he would have called before this. How dare you appropriate his good name to get a table in my restaurant?"

The man twisted his heavy mustache. Although I couldn't see his lips, the corners of his eyes crinkled. Jack stood and they did the guy hug, slapping each other's backs. "Travis, you're right, but since you opened this place it's easier to get an audience with the Pope." He motioned to me. "I want you to meet somebody special. Liz, this is my good friend, Travis Tourville. Trav, this is my girl, Liz Matthews."

I unfolded and tugged at the hem of my dress before I shook hands with the premier chef of Orange County. His grip was strong and he smelled of green pepper, celery, and onion with a dash of paprika and cayenne. He scanned me from head to toe. My high heels gave me an inch on him and he whistled. "You son-of-a-bitch. How'd you get a good-looking woman like this?"

"I got lucky. And she cooks better than you, too." Jack winked and my already bolstered chest took on yet another dimension.

Travis's back went straight. "Is that a fact? We'll just see about that." He pointed a finger at me. "I'll make you something special. None of that blackened shit Yankees want."

Jack put his hand on Travis's shoulder. "That'd be mighty nice, but what I really need is five minutes of your time."

Travis nodded. "Let me finish in the kitchen. I'll join you for dessert."

Jack held my chair. "You're not upset about me talking business here, are you? I should have told you."

I grabbed his tie and pulled until his lips reached mine. "You'll owe me, but I think we can work something out." We kissed. "Do you really think I'm a better cook?"

He held up his right hand. "As God is my witness."

Jack might have been a little biased. Zeus didn't feast better on Olympus. The crayfish bisque was creamy and flavorful and the sand dabs stuffed with crab melted in my mouth. I nearly licked the sauce from the gold-trimmed plate and I only paused long enough to let the food settle before I asked a question.

"How do you know this guy?"

"He was my first friend when we moved to New Orleans back in high school. I practically lived at his house. His mama's a hell of a cook."

When Travis returned, he'd changed into black slacks and a collarless white silk shirt. He wore my favorite scent, *eau de chocolate*. His mustache almost brushed his ears as I praised his creations. He gave my hand a whiskery kiss then pulled up a chair. "So you old scoundrel, how's life been treating you?"

Men can be so competitive. The guys compared who was the most overworked and under-appreciated. Although Travis had appeared in several magazines and on TV talk shows, he pointed out Jack had time for a girl friend and Jack conceded. He bragged on me so, my underwires nearly burst.

Travis twirled the end of his mustache. "Sounds serious. Have you told her your real name yet?"

"I surely did."

"Hell, it took me two years and a case of beer to get that out of you. She must be damn' special."

I smiled. Only his closest friends knew his mama had christened him Eustace. Jack's ex-wife and I were the only women in the group.

Travis signaled the waiter who placed chocolate crème brûlée, sweet potato pecan pie, and bourbon bread pudding in front of me. "You left room for dessert, didn't you?"

What's three thousand calories? Just a marathon. I attacked the crème brûlée. The warm chocolate went straight to my hips. I gave Travis two thumbs and a spoon up.

A second waiter served coffee. After he left, Travis nodded at Jack. "So, what do you want to talk about?"

"Do you recognize this?"

Jack handed him a drawing and Travis's mustache screwed into a frown as he studied the vulture mask. "Saw it in the paper this morning. That's all. Sorry." He tapped it with a well-groomed forefinger. "But why ask me about it?"

" I've been to every costume shop in Orange County. No one recognizes it. I was hoping it might belong to a Krewe. Heard you had a lot of parade photos."

There was that word again. Jack had explained some of the traditions.

"We can look." Travis stood and offered me his arm. We began the tour at the restaurant entrance with the family portrait behind the maitre d's podium. "Now, this is my daddy's Krewe. The photo's from when he was king. That's me, I was twelve, and these are my sisters Tara and Theresa."

He explained the origin of the celebration, which dated back to the presidencies of Andrew Jackson and Martin Van Buren, as we walked around the restaurant checking the various displays of Mardi Gras mementos, studying every photograph. By the time we completed the circuit, I could have passed a test on New Orleans history, but we hadn't found a match for the mask.

"I'm sorry I couldn't help." Travis held my chair. "Every town in Louisiana has Krewes but there's Tourvilles in almost every parish. I'll scan this and email the folks back home."

Jack settled back with his coffee. "I appreciate that."

Travis tucked the sketch into his pocket. "I don't understand what makes a man do such a thing."

"This fellow's what the textbooks call the anger-retaliatory rapist. It's a fancy way to say he's just plain pissed and he beats the shit out of women to get back at them."

I swallowed some pie. "I thought they were all that way."

"No, he's one of the most violent types. He's not acting out a fantasy. He's not even planning. He picks his victims at random and attacks them in a blitz. And just plain beating them isn't enough. He calls them names and makes them beg."

The camera in my mind replayed the image of Nicola lying on the beach. I pushed the desserts away and Jack put his hand on mine. "Oh, darlin', I'm sorry, I shouldn't talk that way in front of you."

"It's okay." I tried to shrug off the creepy sensation running along my spine. "I want to know what kind of man he is. If he's this violent, he must have a record."

He shook his head. "I don't think so. He's not worried about getting caught. If he'd ever been in, he would be."

Travis waved and a waiter brought a bottle of port and three small crystal glasses. He poured and passed us the drinks. "So why the Mardi Gras mask?"

"He's showing off. Most rapists wear ski masks or stockings so they can't be identified, this fellow's daring me to do something about it."

Daring him? Jack had never let a case bug him like this before and I rested my hand on his thigh. "You think the mask means something?"

"I sure do, and I'm going find out what it is."

"To your success." Travis raised a tiny glass of port and I joined him in the salute.

We laughed and talked. The guys shaved a few miles off my

morning run, finishing the desserts for me. The waiters were clearing the tables and we were enjoying our second round of port when Jack frowned at his pager and excused himself. I threw my napkin on the table as the rich food shifted in my stomach. This couldn't be good.

Jack's face was grim when he came back. "Sorry. I've got to go. There's been another rape. We'd better settle up."

Travis stood. "It's settled."

Jack reached for his wallet; his voice was sharp. "No, sir. I'm not sponging off my friends."

"You're not sponging." Travis put his hand on Jack's arm. "You're inviting me for dinner. I haven't had a real home-cooked meal in years and I'd truly like one. Let me test Liz's cooking." He winked. "Or was that just some of your B.S.?"

" That's a deal. As soon as I catch the fucker." Jack's expression relaxed as he shook on it but I tensed. He might as well invite Martha Stewart and Emeril Lagesse, too. At least we'd have something to celebrate.

Travis escorted us to the entrance and draped strands of purple and gold beads around my neck. By now I knew that the purple stood for justice and the gold said power. Jack held my coat. "He really beat the crap out of this woman. I'm going to swing by the hospital first, see if I can talk to her. I'll call you a cab."

I shook my head. "I might as well ride with you and check on Willow. I can get a cab from there."

The valet had Jack's cherry red Mustang parked under the green awning. I waited until we were on the Pacific Coast Highway before I asked what happened.

"Woman out walking her dog. He must have followed her home. He forced his way into her apartment. She's pretty bad."

I huddled in the coolness of Jack's convertible and stared out the window. First a runner, now this. "Damn. A woman can't even walk a dog in this town anymore. That's pathetic."

"I'm doing the best I can." He glanced at me. "You know, I enjoy walking with you."

"I know, but I don't need an armed escort. I just don't like looking over my shoulder every time I go out at night."

He nodded and held my hand until we pulled into the hospital. An ambulance was parked at the Emergency Room entrance, its lights flashing. We paused beside it. Jack slipped his arms around me. "Do you mind me coming in late?"

I shook my head. Useless and his clothes were already there. He kissed me. "Come find me before you leave."

By now I could get to ICU blindfolded, but Ann wasn't in the waiting area. My paranoia meter inched up and I found a nurse who told me Willow had regained consciousness and had been transferred to the psychiatric unit. She called ahead so I could get through the locked door and I hurried over, cursing myself for not having my cellular with me.

A young, petite nurse let me in. It made me a little nervous hearing the door lock behind me but I was pretty certain I'd pass the test to get out. If not, at least the waiting area appeared comfortable and cheerful enough, its sofas and paintings making it look more like a hotel than a hospital. The nurse effervesced as she led me to Ann. "We're so glad you're here. Your mother's been worried about finding you. Willow's going to be just fine. You can see her as soon as her guests leave, but we need to be quiet because it's after lights-out."

She babbled without taking a breath, her face animated. And I thought *I'd* had a lot of sugar tonight. Ann met me by the nurse's station. After her full day at the hospital, she had the pallor of a patient. Even her pastel blue skirt and sweater seemed worn and faded. The effusive nurse went back to work and Ann whispered. "Thank goodness you're here. I've been leaving messages."

"I left my cell phone at home. Is Willow okay?"

She nodded and smiled. "She's a little weak, but her mind's clear. The doctor says she should recover."

I pulled her further from the nurse's station. "What about committing her?"

"It's all arranged. She'll rest here tonight. They'll transfer her to a place that specializes in teenagers tomorrow."

"Good. Does Detective Peters know she's conscious?"

"He's here with her probation officer." Ann wrung her hands. "They just went in to talk to her, but they're going to wait a few days to see how she responds to therapy before they make any decisions."

"Is your attorney here?"

"No. It's so late."

I shook my head. I should have been here. "Where's her room?"

Ann gave me the number, but to get there, I had to get past the nurse's station and I didn't have a pass to visit Willow. I waited for my opportunity. When the phone rang and the bubbly young nurse glanced down at a chart, chattering with the caller, I took a deep breath of antiseptic-laden air and walked past. The rooms were dark except for Willow's and her door was half-open. I leaned against the wall where

I couldn't be seen by the room's occupants and casually examined my artificially elongated nails, hoping no one would notice a six-foot-something blonde in a short, blue velvet dress and high heels hanging out in the psych ward.

"I just took a couple of pills. I don't know why I'm stuck here." Willow's tone had that whiny quality teenagers used to irritate adults. I remembered it well.

"You took a lot more than a couple of pills." Hal's voice echoed in the stillness. "We've got the lab reports if you want to refresh your memory. Now, let's try this one more time. Tell me where you got that crap?"

"I told you, I found them."

"In your boyfriend's pocket, maybe?"

"No. Ryan doesn't have anything to do with it." Willow went on the attack. "It's Mom's fault. She doesn't understand what it's like to be a teenager. She told me I couldn't see Ryan anymore so I left and you can't make me go back."

"Oh, you don't have to worry about that. If you don't start giving me better answers, your next stop's going to be Juvenile Hall. They'll be worse than your mother. You can kiss your boyfriend good-bye."

I peered into the room. Willow folded her arms and slumped against the pillow. Her color had improved from deathly pale to sickly white. She wore an unfashionable blue print hospital gown and still had an IV taped to her hand but she was off oxygen and the monitors. Her face screwed into a frown.

"You don't know anything. Ryan loves me." She almost stuck out her tongue.

I shook my head. God, she was stupid.

"We'll see about that. Why don't we go over what happened when you woke up this morning? Did you talk to Mr. O'Reilly?"

"No, he wasn't there."

"Where was he?"

"Like, duh?" She sighed heavily. "How should I know? He didn't leave a note."

I admired Hal for not slapping the attitude out of her, but he remained patient. "Then how do you know he was gone?"

She paused, squinting as if she was straining to remember. "I went downstairs and no one was there. I was afraid he'd already called Mom, so I went back up and took the pills."

"You didn't get any phone calls? You didn't make any?"

"No. I fell asleep. Why do you keep asking me all these questions?"

"Because a man's dead and I have to find out why."

Her eyes widened and she sat upright. "Who's dead?"

"Jimmy O'Reilly."

Willow sank back and chewed a thumbnail.

A woman cleared her throat and I glanced over my shoulder. A nurse with short, wavy hair the color of iron and a drill sergeant's bearing stood behind me. She extended her arm and pointed down the corridor. Although I wanted to hear Willow's response, I know when I'm busted and I hurried back to the waiting area with the nurse two steps behind me.

As soon as I reached the safety of Ann's side, I smiled and offered my hand. "Hi, I'm Willow Forrester's sister. I was just waiting to see her."

She gave me a look that improved my posture and made me feel like saluting. Even her voice sounded starched. "We have rules on this floor and I expect visitors and patients to obey them. We don't normally allow visitors after lights-out, but we've made an exception for you this once, and you are to wait here quietly until her guests leave." She pivoted on her heel and marched to the nurse's station and her chronically cheerful co-worker. After she left, Ann leaned her head near mine and whispered, "Is everything okay?"

I nodded. Willow may not have given Hal good answers earlier, but she'd seemed truly surprised to learn Jimmy O'Reilly was dead. We'd have to deal with the probation violations, but this murder nonsense would stop.

We waited together on the couch another fifteen minutes until Hal came out followed by Willow's probation officer, a thin woman with deep lines in her face and almost no lips. Ann started to rise but Hal motioned her to remain seated. He filled up the armchair beside her while the probation office took a seat across from us.

Ann clenched her fists together in her lap. "Is everything okay? Did Willow explain what happened?"

Hal kept his voice low and his face expressionless. "Your daughter told me a story but we'll need to talk some more later. When we do, I suggest you get a lawyer."

Ann clutched my hand and I tried to clarify his statement. "You mean for the probation violations, right? We all agree she needs help with this drug problem but you don't think she murdered any one, do you?"

I leaned forward, expecting Hal to smile and reassure me, but his 'all cop' manner didn't change. "We're too early into the investigation to draw any conclusions and your sister hasn't been exactly cooperative. I'm willing to give her some time to get her head straightened out while I'm waiting for the lab results before I question her. That's all I can say." He stood. "I'm sorry, Liz. We'll keep you informed."

The probation officer spoke briefly to Ann and then followed Hal out. I rubbed my forehead. The stupid kid had mouthed off to Hal, but she didn't know Jimmy O'Reilly was dead. The problem was, I couldn't say anything about it without admitting I'd been snooping. The iron-haired head nurse reminded us she was bending the rules to let us see Willow since Willow wouldn't be allowed any visitors once the doctors began their evaluation in the morning. She tapped the crystal of her watch. "You can have five minutes."

Ann took my hand and led me into the room as if I were a treasure. Willow sat on the bed slouched over a tray stabbing a quivering mound of red gelatin with a plastic fork. Her face needed a good scrubbing and hopefully the orange dye would wash out of her hair. When she saw us, she stopped torturing her dinner and fell limply against the pillows.

Ann chirped. "Sweetheart, there's someone I want you to meet. Your sister."

Willow folded her arms just like I used to do with Dad before a lecture. My mind automatically did the math; I was eighteen years older than Willow, practically Ann's age when I was born, old enough to be Willow's mother. The thought made me shiver, but I stepped forward.

"I'm glad you're feeling better, you scared the hell out of us." Us? Maybe there really was something to this family business, after all. " I've always wanted a sister."

She rolled her eyes and flashed an 'L' made with her thumb and forefinger at me. The tips of the best nails money could buy tingled. If she hadn't been in a hospital bed, I'd've diced her. Loser.

Willow turned her baby blues on Ann. "Mommy, I want to go home. The food sucks and there's no telephone. They won't let me call Ryan. I have to let him know I'm okay."

"Now, Sweetheart, you know the rules, no phones calls."

"But that's so unfair. It's like I'm being punished. There's not even a T.V. in here."

"It's not punishment. You just tried to kill yourself."

Willow's chin shot up. "Well, it's your fault. You told me I couldn't see Ryan anymore. I'd rather die than like live without him."

I almost bit my tongue in half in the effort to keep from channeling

Dad, but it didn't work. "Only a real loser," I returned her 'L', "would kill herself to punish her mother. Do you have any idea how much trouble you're in?" Willow glared. "Stay out of this. It's none of your business."

"Now, Sweetheart, be nice." Ann smoothed Willow's hair. "If it weren't for Elizabeth finding you, you'd be dead."

The plate of gelatin hit me in the chest as Willow shrieked. "You fucking bitch!"

8

4038097982749817984091 97

I hadn't expected any gratitude for saving Willow's life, but I certainly didn't expect her to heave a plate of strawberry gelatin at me, either. At least she threw like a girl. The plastic plate bounced off my padded chest and clattered to the floor. While I picked red slime out of my cleavage, the head nurse charged in.

From Willow's hysterical screaming, I concluded that Ryan was supposed to rescue her, not me. The juvenile drama queen no doubt expected Ryan to be impressed by the depth of her love, but I had ruined her attempt to play Sleeping Beauty.

Since Ann and I couldn't talk to Willow until the doctors finished probing her adolescent mind, I'd spent Sunday morning with Nicola tacking up posters of the rapist's mask around town and Sunday afternoon in bed with Jack catching up on lost love and sleep. This morning I was doing what I do best: actuarial work. Numbers were my friends. Although any competent mathematician could make two plus two add up to almost anything, numbers were more dependable than people, particularly little sisters, and I enjoyed solving problems.

I sat at my computer drinking coffee and massaging numbers, wearing a black velour robe and a telephone headset. Puddles curled up on her chair beside me and slept. While I tried to keep the rest of my apartment clutter free, my office resembled the inside of my brain. Papers covered every available surface; file drawers bulged with information, most of it useful; actuarial, legal, and accounting books crammed the shelves; and diplomas on the vanity wall documented my test-taking ability. The centerpiece was a high-powered computer that performed complex calculations. To the untrained eye, my office resembled Mount McKinley before an avalanche but I knew what was in every layer, I simply didn't believe in stifling creative genius with boring tasks like filing. Poor Peter used to sigh and shake his head whenever he saw the mess.

My current project involved researching and analyzing mortality, persistency, and expense data on direct-mail life insurance and developing a product. I had a meeting with the client in half an hour and the results needed a final polish. As the last page of the report came off the printer, the phone rang. Ann's number showed on the caller ID. The five cups of coffee I'd consumed swirled in my stomach and I clicked on the headset.

"Elizabeth, I'm sorry to bother you." Ann spoke in a low, flat tone.

"Is something wrong with Willow?"

"The doctors say she's hostile and they think, well, that she resents you." Ann stumbled over the words, and the coffee spun faster in my stomach. "They'd like you to come down and talk to them, and, maybe, if it's okay, they're recommending some family therapy."

The words 'family therapy' activated my panic button. My senses went on red alert and my pulse quickened. "No." I shook my head. "It's not my fault. Resentment's not even Willow's primary problem. That started long before I got involved."

"But, Elizabeth—"

A vision of psychiatrists surrounding me, clucking 'Poor Willow' and expecting me to help her when no one was helping me popped into my brain. I squeezed my eyes shut. "No, no, no. We're not a family. I didn't cause any of this to happen. I told you I'd help with the legal things, but not this. I can't. Not now."

"I'm sorry. You're right. I shouldn't have expected you to do this. I'll tell them."

Her voice broke and tears threatened to flood the phone line. I took a deep breath. "Look, Ann, don't cry. I'll think about, but I'm late for an appointment."

I tore off the headset and hurried into my bedroom to change. My panty hose decided to make it a wrestling match and I snagged them on my nails. Damn. I'd built my life around things I could count on, numbers, Dad, and now Jack. A sister would be nice, but my mother and Willow simply didn't figure into my life's equation. I certainly didn't want strangers analyzing my feelings, especially not when I couldn't.

I found a new pair of more cooperative pantyhose and slipped into a little gray power suit. Thank goodness I'd done my makeup and hair earlier. After I hobbled into my heels, I grabbed my briefcase and headed down to the garage and my car.

President's Day traffic was light and I raced away from my problems to the Church of The Risen Son on Jamboree Road without getting a speeding ticket. I parked and showed a little of my old cross-country form as I sprinted down the long sidewalk between towering palm trees and sweet-smelling pink and white spring flowers to the entrance.

When I reached the bronze sanctuary doors, my chest was heaving and I stopped to run my fingers through my hair and brush the stray blonde strands from my suit. With my composure restored, I squared my shoulders and entered the building. Although the exterior of the church resembled the Silverdome in size and shape, complete with satellite dishes and antennas, the interior was quiet, calm, and comforting. My pulse dropped back to normal as I crossed the lush mauve carpet and mentally prepped for my meeting.

The Reverend F. Wesley Anderson, known as the 'Video Apostle' by millions of people across the country who watched his weekly worship service and daily inspirational talk show, had decided to branch out from saving souls to providing their survivors with financial security. I inherited the assignment since Peter had decorated Reverend Anderson's office and subsequently introduced us.

The Reverend's secretary, a blue-haired woman the size of Tinkerbell, zealously guarded his stained glass doors and nodded me into the inner sanctum. Peter's understated, elegant style was obvious throughout the spacious office with its rich, warm woods and soft, muted fabrics. Bookcases lined one long wall while the opposite wall of glass looked out over a meditation garden built around a labyrinth. A helicopter could land on Reverend Anderson's neatly organized leather-topped desk but it fit the scale of the room.

Reverend Anderson sat in a high-backed, wine-colored armchair at his eighteenth century cherry conference table reading the Bible. His gold-rimmed glasses rode low on his long, narrow nose. He resembled a clean-shaven Abe Lincoln with white hair and no skin pigment. In honor of President's Day, he'd chosen a tie covered in tiny American Flags to coordinate with his television-blue shirt. When he saw me, he pushed up his glasses and telescoped to his feet. He made solid eye contact and shook my hand firmly.

"Good morning, Elizabeth. How are you?"

I gave him my most businesslike smile. "Fine, thank you. I have the revised projections ready and I think you'll be happy with the excess of income over outgo."

While Reverend Anderson watched the bottom line as much as any executive, the only prophets he discussed came from the Old Testament and I'd learned to modify my language to suit him. He sat easily erect, ready for my presentation. I laid my leather briefcase on the table and popped open the locks but the report wasn't on top. I rifled through it. It had to be here. I'd printed it out just this morning.

"Oh, shit." I inhaled sharply and tried to suck the word back into my mouth, but it didn't work. Thirteen years of Catholic School had left an indelible mark and cursing in front of a pastor still seemed like a sin. "I'm so sorry. I didn't mean to swear, but I left the report at home."

Reverend Anderson rested his chin on his palm and gazed at me. "I think God will overlook it. What's wrong?"

"Nothing, really. I got a phone call just before I left, and, well, I got distracted. I can be back in half an hour."

Part of Reverend Anderson's success came from his genuine interest in people. He'd watched me nurse Peter through his final illness, so when the Reverend decided to go into the insurance business, he'd called me. He always asked how I was doing and seemed very pleased when I'd fallen in love. He shrugged. "Don't worry. I've got a funeral tomorrow but we can do it Wednesday morning after I tape. Is everything okay with Jack?"

"He's fine, but he's awfully busy." I closed my briefcase and inched back in preparation to escape.

"I can imagine with all the rapes and then poor Jimmy." He shook his head.

I stopped. "You knew Jimmy O'Reilly?"

"Oh, yes. Jimmy was going to publicly witness his faith in our Lord on Sunday and become a full member of the flock."

My mouth gaped wide enough for both of my size ten feet to slip in, high heels and all. "Why?"

His eyebrows rose. "Well, some people actually find comfort in God and my Church."

My scalp almost burst into flames. Why didn't I rip out my tongue before I said anything else stupid? "Reverend Anderson. I'm sorry. I didn't mean it that way. You know how much I respect you after all you did for Scott and Peter. And for me."

"Yes, I do. Now sit down." He pulled out a tall, upholstered chair and motioned to me. "You should know that I respect you, too. Something's troubling you today. If there's anything I can help with, please tell me."

I sank into the chair. My mother's existence had been my most closely guarded secret. Only Scott and Peter knew before Jack found out. I wasn't ready to tell the world, but if the worst happened, everyone would know. Reverend Anderson sat with his hands folded, waiting for me to speak. Although we were alone, I whispered. "The police think my little sister may have killed Jimmy O'Reilly."

"Oh, my." He reached out and patted my arm. "No wonder you're upset. I didn't even know you had a sister."

"I didn't myself until last week. My mother left when I was a baby." I scrunched myself together and gave him a condensed version of the story. When I finished, he took off his gold-rimmed glasses and rubbed his pale eyes.

" It must have been devastating to learn the truth. I'd like to help any way I can."

"Could you tell me about Jimmy O'Reilly. What was he like? Why would anyone want to kill him?"

He settled back in his chair and shook his head, his expression sad. "I don't understand how anyone can take a life, but I'll tell you what I know about Jimmy. He worked as my technical engineer when we built this church. He helped design the audio and video system." A faint smile brushed his lips. "Jimmy loved music and he was a genius with all that equipment. He spent a lot of time here after hours, experimenting."

"The newspaper said he was a semi-retired recording company executive."

"Yes, about twenty years ago he got the opportunity to work in the music industry. It was what he thought he wanted."

"And it wasn't?"

Reverend Anderson smiled. "Sometimes, when we're young, we don't always make the right choices. Jimmy turned his back on God to pursue money and the pleasures of the flesh."

If Reverend Anderson had chosen Jimmy O'Reilly to be the Spotlight Sinner, he must have had some juicy things to confess, perhaps something worthy of murder. I leaned forward. "Like what?"

"Only God and Jimmy know." Reverend Anderson rebuked me gently and I shrank a little. "But the Almighty gave him a wake-up call in the form of a heart attack and triple bypass shortly before his fiftieth birthday. He started watching our services in the hospital and found his way back to the fold."

"So, you think he really was sincere."

"I know he was. None of us have a perfect relationship with our Lord, but Jimmy was trying." He paused. "You know, Elizabeth, God truly works in mysterious ways. I'd like to help you try to re-establish your relationship with your mother."

The panic I'd felt when Ann had suggested family therapy returned and I held up my hands. "I'm flattered you'd even consider helping with your schedule, but there's no relationship to re-establish."

Reverend Anderson pressed his palms together in an attitude of prayer. "I understand your reluctance to get involved with someone who hurt you so badly, but I think perhaps God has given you this opportunity to experience your mother's love. Don't let it slip away. You're a fine woman with many gifts, but there are some things a girl misses growing up without a mother."

Missed? No way. My spine stiffened and I stood. "Thank you, but Dad did a good job raising me. Nothing's missing. I'll see you Wednesday."

I grabbed my briefcase and raced out to my car. The tires squealed as I peeled out of the parking lot onto Jamboree. My Corvette went from zero to sixty in about four seconds as I ran through the gears. I didn't need a mother to be a woman. I'd read all the girl magazines and Scott had helped. Even he knew what boys wanted and providing it wasn't much of a challenge. Some makeup, the right clothes, and a little you-can't-resist-me-attitude and they lined up. If they gave me any trouble, I beat the crap out of them.

I floored it through a yellow traffic light and dodged around a bread truck. The meddlesome old man. I wasn't a drag queen or a fag hag. I was a woman and I didn't need a happy ending with my mother. All I wanted was some answers. A Toyota pulled out in front of me. The brakes screamed. My bumper missed him by six inches and my heart nearly popped through my ribs. The hair on my arms stood straight up. I turned into a strip mall parking lot to catch my breath. There wasn't any reason to kill myself over Ann, and I drove sedately the rest of the way home and went back to work.

About four o'clock that afternoon, I stretched and glanced out my office window. The sun sat low in the sky. With the rapist still loose, paranoia on the Peninsula ran high. By early evening, the beach was dead. Even the guys from my Sunday night roller-hockey game had insisted on escorting me home yesterday, although I assured them any man crazy enough to attack a woman wielding a hockey stick deserved every cut and broken tooth I'd give him.

I phoned Nicola to make arrangements for our run and changed into running tights and a Michigan sweatshirt. As I tied my shoes, Puddles raced to the door yapping about ten seconds before the knock. I peered through the peephole and saw Jack. He was dressed for work in a gray suit but he was carrying an overnight bag. I opened the door and collected a kiss.

"This is a pleasant surprise. What's up?"

His face gave it away. "They found Willow's prints on O'Reilly's gun. I'm sorry. I wanted you to hear it from me."

My stomach sank. "What possible motive do they have?"

"He was going to call her mother and send her home."

"But that's stupid."

"Not to her. Kids kill over shoes." He shrugged. "Look, Lizzie, I don't want you to stew, she hasn't been charged yet. Even if she is, in the worst case, she misses the prom but she's out in a few years."

I backed away, rubbing my arms. "That's pretty cold."

" I just want to prepare you." He dropped the bag and raised his hands. "She's already in a whole mess of trouble over probation violations. She needs help."

"Sending her to jail isn't going to help."

"Who said anything about jail? She's a juvie with a drug problem. With her, they'll probably make a deal, send her someplace where she'll get her head straight."

"Great." I stared at the ceiling. "Like they don't think she's worth a trial. That's not justice."

"I know how you feel." He tugged me into his arms. "But don't be mad at me. I'm only the messenger." He caressed the silky fabric of the running tights covering my backside. His voice dripped testosterone. "I've got to get back to work. I've got a meeting about seven, but I could drop by later. Brought some clothes. Thought I could leave them here so I wouldn't have to go home every time I wanted to change."

I leaned against him. Although his job automatically put him on the wrong side when it came to Willow, he was trying to be supportive. He was also gradually moving in. I poked his ribs. "Okay, but wear your vest."

He squeezed my butt and gave me a kiss. As soon as he left, I grabbed my fanny pack and headed toward Nicola's. The sun, a brilliant gold disk, hung just above the ocean. It shimmered off the water and tinted the sky orange-pink, but few people were out to enjoy it. I ran past the almost deserted Newport Pier to Nicola's apartment. She came out wearing shapeless sweats. Sunglasses and a Red Sox cap helped obscure her face. As we ran, she lectured me about criminal defense strategies and the value of plea bargains. It didn't help. When we got back to her place, she paused at the door.

"Please don't misinterpret this. Your sister deserves the best defense, but are you certain she's innocent?"

"Of course, she's my sister."

While Nicola had the grace not to turn my logic into a sieve, her question chased me home. I took the steps two at a time and locked the door behind me but the question followed me through my apartment and gnawed at me as I stood on my deck watching the ocean swallow the sun. The orange-pink sky faded into dark-blue mist and I went inside. I wouldn't sign my name to an actuarial statement based on so little data. Even Jack was ready to write Willow off. I had to find out more about my sister and do what was best for her.

Jimmy O'Reilly's newspaper obituary had invited all friends of the deceased recording-company executive to celebrate his life at his home tonight. I'd never crashed a wake before, but it appeared Willow spent as much time at Jimmy O'Reilly's as she did at her own house. Jack had rushed me out of the crime scene on Saturday morning before I'd had a chance to really see the place. I needed to learn more about my sister and the murder victim, and the victim's house seemed like a good starting point, so I showered, changed, and drove down for a little research.

Darkness shrouded the beach but the battle-ship gray house with its large porthole windows was lit up for Jimmy O'Reilly's bon voyage party. Given the lack of parking around the Newport Pier area, half of Orange County must have come to pay their respects. I slipped into the line of mourners streaming into the house.

The Widow O'Reilly made the perfect, gold-plated trophy wife. She held court in a white satin chair in the white-on-white living room surrounded by a sea of white lilies. She wore a tiny black Lycra dress that showed off her perfectly toned body and heavy gold jewelry. Hours on a tanning bed had given her skin a deep, golden-brown color and her blond hair glittered with mousse, but someone needed to tell her about sunscreen and moisturizer before she hit thirty.

The widow exchanged air kisses with a woman in a leopard mini-dress whose face was so tight, she probably had to sleep with her eyes open. Two young men wearing heavy black eyeliner, black leather pants, and peek-a-boo black shirts and a young woman who had styled her hair by sticking her finger in a light socket waited to express their condolences. My little black dress and stilettos made me one of the more sedately dressed women.

The place hummed as Jimmy O'Reilly's friends and business associates ate, drank, and schmoozed. I scanned the room. Most of the cocktail parties I went to were attended by men in suits discussing insurance and statistics. Probably ninety percent of these mourners thought an actuary was a place to bury actors and didn't know GAAP from The Gap. I needed a plausible reason for attending the wake before I introduced myself to anyone, so I drifted through the crowd to reconnoiter and eavesdrop.

The formal living room and dining room covered the front of the narrow house and provided a spectacular view of the ocean but the rooms seemed designed to look at, not live in. The furnishings, while elegant and pricey, said more about the thickness of Jimmy O'Reilly's wallet than his personality.

The family room stretched behind the living room. This was where Jimmy O'Reilly must have spent his time with the walk-behind bar, big screen T.V., and walls covered with rock-and-roll memorabilia. I gravitated to the spot behind the deep-red leather sofa where we'd found the body. The terra cotta tile floor had been scrubbed but the blood had left dark stains in the grout.

"They say that's the spot the old man got shot."

The speaker, in his late twenties, wore black silk pajamas and an aura of bourbon obviously expecting this was either a slumber party or formal ninja gathering. His buzz cut accentuated his gaunt frame. I tried not to act like a voyeur or a girl fresh out of convent school. "Oh, really? How awful. Who would do a thing like that?"

"Some little bitch. I find it strangely erotic. Don't you?" A silver stud on his tongue darted in and out of his mouth as he talked.

I gave him an unequivocal "No," and escaped to the dining room. Even with her orange hair and tattoo, Willow didn't belong in this group. She might have envied the expensive, flamboyant clothes and pierced body parts of many of the guests, but these people had power and money. They could care less about a high school freshman.

As I wormed through the crowd in the dining room, I realized why so many people had gathered in it. Travis Tourville, dressed in his chef's whites, stood by the table arranging a display of orange-red crayfish. The rich aroma of food and a familiar face attracted me like a magnet. I wedged in beside him. "Hey, Travis, what are you doing?"

He wiped his hands on a towel and bent over. His heavy mustache tickled my ear. "Catering a goddamn wake. Didn't expect to see you here. That ol' scoundrel around?"

"Hell, no. He's working. Did you know Jimmy O'Reilly?"

Travis snapped his fingers at a waiter. "He's one of my backers. It's the only reason I'm doing this before Mardi Gras." He gave the waiter instructions, and then checked his watch. "That lawyer better get here. I need to get to the restaurant."

"What lawyer?"

"Jimmy's. She called yesterday. Said Jimmy left special instructions for his wake, ordered all this, and told me I had to be here because Jimmy left a letter for me. So, how do you know Jimmy?"

"Ah," I searched for an excuse. "It's kind of a family thing."

Travis glanced around and made a face as if someone had just poured ketchup on his crab crepes. I tried to follow his eyes but the only person I recognized in the crowd was the back of Reverend Anderson's white-blonde head over by the gold-plated widow. I frowned. Damn. He'd know why I was here and I didn't want my reason broadcast around or I'd be out on my butt. Maybe I could avoid him. I glimpsed a perfect male hairdo. I'd try to evade Ryan, too.

When I turned to Travis, he'd pushed into the kitchen. The delicious, spicy scents wafting up from the table pulled my nose to more important business, and I decided to fortify myself before mingling. I went straight for the Oysters Rockefeller, Coconut Shrimp with apricot-horseradish sauce, and rare Cajun Beef Tenderloin. Once armed with food and a glass of white wine, I slowly cruised the dining room in search of small talk about Jimmy O'Reilly and the murder.

The man in an Italian suit smiled at me from the doorway. Michelangelo must have carved his face with the masculine jaw and full, sensuous lips. For a man near fifty, he had a great body and a full head of hair with just enough gray to be sexy. Something about his lips and eyes seemed almost familiar, but I didn't know any men who owned clothes that expensive. I gave him a don't-you-wish-look and edged past him to hear what the widow was saying now that Reverend Anderson had moved into the family room.

The man approached with a smile as smooth and transparent as glass. "Sorry, I've been staring. I knew you'd be incredibly attractive, but you're even more beautiful than I expected."

His rich, melodious voice carried a trace of Southern honey. His ring finger was unmarked. "Corny, but an intriguing line. I'll give you an eight. Who are you?"

"Andre Lefebvre, Ryan's father." He held out his hand but mine were full and I struggled to balance everything and untie my tongue. "I didn't expect to see you tonight."

"I was just curious. I understand Willow spent a lot of time here and I wanted to figure out how she fits in all this." I gestured at the glitterazzi.

"Oh, that's simple." He shrugged. "She doesn't fit in this crowd. Most of these people are in the industry. They're barracudas. I watch my back when I'm around them."

"So, what did she do here?"

Andre took my arm and nudged me to an empty corner of the living room near an alabaster nude. "Let me put this delicately. Ryan and Willow are teenagers. There's a beach outside, free food, and no parents."

My backbone stiffened. "And I'll tell you what I told Ryan, statutory rape."

He raised his hands. "I understand your concern, but you're misinterpreting the situation. Ryan loves Willow because she's not like girls his age. She's innocent."

"Yeah, and easy to manipulate."

He appraised me. "Well, I'm certain once she spends some time with you, that won't be a problem."

"Do you think she killed Jimmy O'Reilly?"

"No. And if you really want to help her, you should convince your mother to let me retain a real lawyer for her."

"We don't want to feel obligated to you."

The ninja swayed toward us. "Hey, Uncle Andre. Just like you to corner the prettiest woman." He leaned into Andre's face. "Where's Aunt Renee?"

Andre's nose crinkled at the ninja's eighty-proof breath. "In Nice, I think. She sends her condolences."

Wife? Condolences? Uncle Andre? The ninja leaned toward me, barely defying the law of gravity and nearly spilling his bourbon. "Aren't you going to introduce us?" He ran his tongue around his teeth to play with the silver stud.

Andre gestured, casually pushing the ninja back. "Liz Matthews, this is Jimmy's son and my godson. I still call him James Junior, but his friends call him Viper. Just take my advice and don't let him show you the snake tattoo."

Viper laughed and swayed his pelvis. "Women love to watch it dance." He leered at me. "Want to see?"

I gave his crotch the briefest glance and snorted. "I'm not interested in little squiggly things."

Viper's face twisted. He grabbed my elbow but before I could throw my wine in his eyes, Andre yanked him outside, spilling bourbon on the arctic-white carpet. The crowd in the living room hushed for a few seconds, then collectively shrugged and went back to their conversations. I peered out one of the large, round windows. The men had stopped on the beach, standing just inside the light from the street lamps. They stood too far away to be heard, but their posturing and gesturing conveyed a heated argument.

Any man who makes lewd comments deserves an emasculating comeback. I couldn't be the first woman to diss Viper, not when he made himself a target. Still, Andre's behavior puzzled me as much as Viper's. A man of his age and stature shouldn't confuse a testosterone display with masculinity.

A male shoulder brushed against mine and my nose picked up the scent of a designer cologne guaranteed to make girls swoon. Ryan stood beside me, dressed in preppy dark Dockers and white shirt. I fought the urge to ask about his car getting towed. He watched the argument on the beach and then flashed the toothy smile at me that had made his dentist wealthy. "What did Viper do now?"

"He grabbed me." I moved away and set my wine glass beside the alabaster nude so I could eat without juggling.

Ryan smirked and eyed my dress, or rather, the parts it didn't cover. "You look really hot tonight. I hope Willow is as attractive as you are when she's twenty-five."

"Yeah, right." Like father, like son. I gave Ryan a five-point penalty for flagrant flattery and popped an oyster in my mouth.

Ryan sidled into my personal space, trapping me in the corner. His voice got husky, "I know you think Willow and I are too young to get married, but I really need to see her. Can you help?"

He touched my arm. Illegal use of hands. I picked up my wine and accidentally spilled it down his shirt. He jumped back and I offered him a napkin with a cheerful grin. "I'm so sorry. It shouldn't stain."

He mopped off his shirt. I stepped away but he followed, keeping a respectful distance between us. "Isn't there any way I can convince you that I love Willow."

"Wait four years."

He pleaded, "Please, just let me see her once."

"I can't. None of us can see her right now. Doctor's orders until they figure out why she tried to kill herself. Do you have any idea why she took all those pills?"

"Sure." His eyes narrowed as he smiled. "She can't live without me."

I felt a chill and stared out the window. Viper took a wild swing at Andre, but the older man caught Viper's arm and twisted it around, almost bringing him to his knees, then he shoved him. Viper wiped his face with the sleeve of his black silk pajamas and stumbled away.

Andre came back in, straightening his tie and smiled at me, but if he expected gratitude, he was mistaken. I tossed my hair. "That wasn't necessary. I can take care of myself."

"You don't know Viper. He has a bad temper, especially around women, and it's best not to let him get started." Andre placed his hand on Ryan's shoulder. "I see you've found the lovely Liz. Wasn't it nice of her to come?"

"Oh, yes. She's going to get me in to see Willow."

"Wait a minute. I didn't say that. No one can see her until after the psychiatric evaluations."

Andre touched my arm. "Well, keep us posted. We're worried about her." He dismissed Ryan with a flick of his hand. "Get back to your friends. I want to show Liz the house."

He led me upstairs. Since I go to every open house on the Peninsula just to dream, I appreciated seeing the custom amenities as well as the opportunity to quiz Andre. Gold and platinum records lined the wood-paneled study.

"Have you known Jimmy O'Reilly long?"

"Forever. We grew up together back in Louisiana. We were blood brothers, formed a band in high school. We came out here after college to make our fortunes."

Andre opened door. "This is Viper's room."

The male smell almost overpowered me. Clothes carpeted the floor. "He still lives with his father?"

"Occasionally. He can't seem to remember to pay his rent."

"What does his stepmother think of that?"

"Krystal doesn't live here. The divorce is almost final."

He skipped the guest room and ushered me to the master bedroom and flicked on the lights. I paused just inside and stared at the neatly-made king-size waterbed. No one would ever guess I'd found Willow sprawled on its rumpled black sheets a few days earlier. The shrink said Willow had tried to kill herself on Jimmy O'Reilly's bed to make a statement, but I couldn't see her choice of location as some sort of twisted teenaged revenge against an adult who stood between her and Ryan. To me, it seemed like a place where she'd be found before it was too late.

"Liz!" Andre called to get my attention and motioned. "Watch this." He pressed a button on a console by the waterbed and the draperies slowly opened, revealing the beach and ocean. My eyes felt as big as my fiber-enhanced chest.

He dimmed the lights. "You can see better now."

I nodded and allowed myself a bit of envy. He pressed another button and the big screen TV came to life. He switched it off and turned on the music. New Age sound surrounded us. "Can you see why the kids come here?"

"Yeah. I could almost move in myself, but I wouldn't let anyone else use it."

"Neither would I. But you haven't seen the best part. Lay on the bed."

Dim lights, soft music. How blonde did he think I was? "No way. You're married and I've got a boyfriend."

He held up his hands. "I'm flattered, and as much as I'd love to seduce you, it's not that. You should see this."

Just to keep him quiet, I crawled on the bed, pulling at the hem of my little black dress to keep the rating PG. It felt a little creepy knowing a dead man had once slept here and even worse considering that my little sister had had sex on it, but I settled in and tried not to think. The water sloshed and he pointed up. The mirror in the ceiling reflected my image back at me and I caught my breath. Andre slipped in on the other side and we rocked in his wake. "You like it?"

"I don't know." I fanned my hair out on the burgundy and gold velvet bedspread and posed. Not bad. He was close enough I could smell his cologne and I watched his reflection carefully. "I've never had a desire to see myself do it. Anyway, this is earthquake country. I don't want to turn into a pin cushion when the big one hits."

"What the hell's going on here!"

It hit. Jack stood in the door, smoke practically coming from his ears.

The bed rocked violently as I scrambled out. "It's not what you think."

He glared at me, then at Andre. "We'll talk outside."

No one takes that tone with me, or jumps to such gigantic

conclusions. I stomped down the stairs after Jack. Hal Peters tried to stop him in the living room, but Jack waved him off and walked out the door. When my high heels sank in the sand of the beach, I struck first. "How dare you embarrass me like that?"

His jaw dropped. "What? You were in bed with a man."

"But he was just showing me the mirror in the ceiling. Jesus, give me some credit."

"Credit? You want credit for that?" He slapped his forehead. "Why the hell do you think he was showing it to you?"

A woman screamed and a sharp crack of a gun sounded over the noise of the surf. Jack drew his weapon and ran. A woman lay bleeding in the alley beside the house. A man was running away. He stopped at the corner, spun, and fired. Jack took the shot in the chest. He went down and rolled against the house.

My heart went through my ribs. "Jack!" I screamed and ran toward him.

403809798274981798409197

For a dead man, Jack wrestled damn hard. “Liz! Stop it!”

I did. He jammed me into the corner where the sidewalk met the rough stucco wall of the beach house and rolled on top of me, covering my face with his chest. The concrete was cold and the stucco scratched through my dress. I couldn’t see or breathe, but I could feel his ribs rise and fall. I could hear his heart beating. Or was it mine? He lifted his head, and then rolled onto his back with a groan.

“God.” He struggled to breathe. “Don’t you have sense—” He paused to suck air into his lungs. “To take cover when you hear gunfire?”

I was still wedged between him and the house and I struggled to sit as I snaked my hand over his shirt. No blood.

“But you got hit. I saw it. I thought you were dead.”

He thumped his chest and grinned. He forced out the words between breaths. “Wore my vest. You promised you’d be on top.”

“Oh, God.” I laughed and cried at once, caressing that wonderful vest. “I’ll be on top all night. But I’m bronzing this baby and putting it on the mantel.”

Travis knelt beside us. "Jack! You okay? I saw it from the kitchen."

Hal ran around from the front of the house, his weapon drawn. "Jesus. What happened?"

"Jack got hit," I said, scuffling to my feet.

Hal pushed me aside and I landed on my butt with my back against the stucco wall. He yanked open Jack's suit coat and searched. "You son of a bitch! What the hell do you think you're doing?"

Jack held up his hands. "I'm okay, Hal. Honest. Wore my vest. He ran that way. Dark pants and jacket."

Hal scowled down the street. "Fuck! I'm not going to catch him on foot." He pulled out his cell phone and called the dispatcher. "Officer down." He gave the address and description of the assailant.

I wormed across the concrete past Hal to Jack. While I couldn't remember the velocity of a bullet, I recalled enough from physics to know for every action there is an equal and opposite reaction. It took an enormous amount of energy to stop anything traveling that fast. Jack's chest had absorbed the shock and he wasn't getting up. I found his hand and squeezed it. "Honey, are you okay. Does it hurt?"

He nodded. "That sucker packs a wallop."

Lights flashed in my eyes. A police cruiser screeched to a halt and a cop jumped out. Hal briefed him. The officer slammed the car door and gunned the engine as he backed out to the main street. I stroked Jack's forehead. The Balboa Peninsula was a long, narrow finger of land. Only three roads and a tiny ferry connected it to the rest of California. In such a finite area, cops were bound to find the man. I wanted to be first in line to kill him.

Hal stooped beside Jack. "How you doing, buddy?"

"Okay. Help me up."

He pulled Jack to a sitting position. Jack moaned and clutched his left arm close to his body. He almost doubled over. I winced, too, and put my arm around him. "Honey, maybe you ought to lay down and wait for the paramedics."

"No. I need to talk to that lady." He pushed me away. "Come on, Hal. Give me a boost."

"Over my dead body." I crawled between them and stuck my arms out. "You're hurt. Hal can talk to her."

"Lizzie, please."

Hal studied Jack. "It's okay, Liz. I'm not going to let anything happen to this guy. He owes me too much."

He took Jack's forearm and hoisted him to his feet. Jack and I groaned at the effort. Hal put his hand on Jack's back to steady him. "See, he's fine."

Just watching Jack hurt tore me up. I pressed my hands to my mouth to push back my fear, and my shoulders trembled.

It took an effort to untangle my legs to get to my feet, even with Travis's help. The hem of my black dress was practically around my waist. I pulled it to a more ladylike length and brushed off the sand and dirt while I waited for my knees to stop wobbling. Once I felt capable of motion, I followed Jack and Hal to the woman lying on the pavement under the street lamp.

She wore a skirted suit. Reverend Anderson knelt by her side. He'd tucked his coat under her head and was attempting to stem the bleeding from the wound in her abdomen with a handkerchief, but it was already hopelessly dark and wet. Travis ordered a waiter to bring clean towels. Hal squatted and studied the wound.

If I couldn't get Jack to sit down, I could hold him up. I slipped under his right arm and clutched his hand. He let his weight rest on my shoulders and pressed his left arm against his body as if he were holding his ribs together. We both shivered in the cool ocean breeze. A crowd gathered around the woman. Most had come from the wake.

"Ma'am, I'm Detective Black. You called this morning. Can you tell me what happened?"

Her voice was soft and shaky. She gasped between words. "Man—jumped—shouted 'boo'—grabbed my brief case—shot me."

Sirens wailed in the distance. "Can you describe him?"

She moaned. "Ski mask."

A waiter ran up with a stack of white dishtowels to help stop the blood. The sirens grew closer and another cruiser squealed into the street.

"What was in the case?"

"Video tape." She swallowed. "Some letters—a will."

The paramedics swarmed over her. Hal ordered the officers to herd everyone back into the house. Jack pulled his arm from my shoulders, then hunched over and hugged his ribs. "Liz, you go in, too."

"No!" I slipped my arm in his and clung to him. "I'm not leaving. You need to sit and let the paramedics look at you."

"Lizzie, I got work to do and you're standing in the middle of a crime scene."

"Do I look like I care? You could be bleeding to death."

Travis took my side. "Come on, Jack. Humor the woman. At least sit down."

Jack grumbled and hissed as he let Travis ease him into the front seat of the patrol car. He leaned his head back and wheezed from the exertion. "Thanks, Trav. You said you saw this from the window. What happened?"

"I was washing up when I heard a scream. I saw a man and a woman wrestling over a briefcase. He shot her and ran. Then I saw you go down."

Jack hugged his ribs tighter. "Can you describe him?"

Travis stroked his mustache and squinted as if he were seeing the man again. "Medium build. Dark clothes. Ski mask."

"Did you hear him say anything?"

"Not really. Before I looked up, I thought I heard someone shout 'boo' and laugh. A real crazy laugh."

"Take Liz inside."

I threw a fit, but moving the Pacific to Detroit would have been easier. I pointed a manicured dagger in his face. "You've got five minutes, then I'm driving you to the hospital."

Travis pulled me into the house. Most of the mourners, led by the grieving widow and Andre, had gathered in the living room of the beach house, all demanding information at once from the officers. We left the poor men with the unenviable task of controlling high-powered people accustomed to having things their way and searched for a quiet spot in the family room.

"Hey, Liz. Sit down. I'll get you something to drink."

I sank into an over-sized chair and thousands of tiny fingers raced up my thighs as my black panty hose disintegrated. I wiped at the filth on my dress. Damn Jack and his damn job. Didn't he realize he belonged in a hospital?

Andre slipped onto the ottoman in front of me and eyed my torn stockings. "Are you okay?"

I tucked the hem of my dress around my legs and sat primly. "Yeah, I'm fine. Trying the punk look."

"I prefer the other. What happened out there?"

I hugged myself. "We heard gunfire. Saw a man running away. He shot Jack. Thank God, Jack was wearing his vest."

Andre furrowed his perfectly shaped eyebrows. "Shooting a cop. That's bad business."

"Yeah, I wouldn't want to be in his shoes when they catch him. I just wish they'd let me have him first."

"Did you get a good look at him?"

I shook my head.

"How about that poor woman. Did she see who did it?"

Andre's questions were getting on my nerves and I didn't have many left. "I can't say. You'll have to ask the police. They'll find him soon. The Peninsula's not that big."

"I hope so. And I hope your boyfriend will be okay. If you like, I'll explain what happened upstairs."

"Nothing happened."

"That's true. But I would like to buy you dinner sometime to discuss Willow and Ryan, if your boyfriend doesn't object. Here's my card. That's my private line."

Andre left to find a more congenial audience. Travis handed me a cup of coffee topped with whipped cream. Bourbon vapors drifted up in the steam. I took a sip and gasped.

Travis sat on the ottoman and sipped his own coffee. The whipped cream collected on his heavy mustache. "Old Number Seven's one of the best cure-alls."

"I almost lost him." I squeezed my eyes shut.

"Aw, Jack's too contrary to die. They'd kick him out of Heaven *and* Hell." He touched my hand. "Honest, he's okay."

"Then why wouldn't he let me stay with him?"

"Jack's always been one to lick his wounds alone."

"Elizabeth?" I glanced up and saw Reverend Anderson standing over me, rolling up the bloodstained sleeves of his white dress shirt. Travis rose and shrugged his way through the crowd to the kitchen. Reverend Anderson watched Travis's retreat with a puzzled expression, and then gazed at me through his gold-rimmed glasses. "I'm going to the hospital with that poor woman but I wanted to make certain you were all right."

"I'm fine. How's Jack?"

"He's good. They're examining him right now."

"How about that woman? Do you know who she is?"

"She's not very well, I'm afraid. She's Jimmy O'Reilly's attorney. She called me this morning and said Jimmy had left a letter for me among his papers. He wanted me to have it tonight." He sighed and shook his head. "Terrible business. I'd better go. I'll be praying for all of you."

He slipped through the crowd. What was going on here? I started up to find Travis but he came back into the family room directing waiters carrying trays of steaming coffee. I motioned to him and he came over but his usual congenial expression had grown cold.

"Travis, is there something wrong?" I leaned forward. "You got so upset when Reverend Anderson came over—"

He cut me off. "Are you a member of that man's flock?"

His words pushed me back into the chair. "No, he's a client. Is that a problem?"

"I guess not." He shrugged, but his face still frowned. "I just don't like that man's religion."

Not everyone did. Reverend Anderson's detractors called him the P.T. Barnum of religion. He borrowed liberally from all faiths to create his own theological brand that had mass appeal. I didn't embrace all of it, but I knew he was sincere. I was simply too tired to argue.

Andre returned with Krystal leaning on his arm. He motioned for her to sit on the sofa and waved at Travis. "Get her something to drink. I could use one, too."

Travis didn't move. Krystal's gold bracelets jangled as she sniffed into a tiny scrap of lace and batted her eyelashes. "Please, Travis, I'm so upset."

Travis disappeared into the kitchen and a waiter returned carrying a bottle of Jack Daniel's and two glasses. Krystal's silicone-stuffed breasts heaved. "I don't understand why I have to stay and talk to the police. I've been through enough, first with Jimmy and now with this crazy man shooting people. For all I know, he's probably waiting for me at my house."

I leaned forward. "What makes you think that?"

Krystal eyed me as if I were a competitor in the championship race. Andre introduced me as a friend and Krystal's nose crinkled. "Well, that man shot Jimmy's lawyer and I'm Jimmy's widow. Maybe I should get that officer to take me home and search the house."

Andre patted her knee. "Don't trouble the police. I brought you; I'll take you home and check under the beds."

Krystal smiled. The self-centered bitch acted as if the entire world revolved around her. I wanted to ask her about the divorce settlement, but the mourners drifted back into the room to sympathize with her and joke about the interruption. Ryan lounged on the arm of my chair and I got up.

Stupid, shallow people. Jimmy O'Reilly was dead, a woman was dying, Jack was hurt and no one cared. I checked Mickey. Even using

Football Standard Time, Jack's five minutes were up. He was going to the hospital if I had to drag him.

10

7403809798274981798409197

Sometimes men are just too dumb. Jack sat in the front seat of the patrol car with electrodes stuck on his bare chest and a cell phone in his hand. An angry red welt covered the left side of his ribs, and he'd have to improve to look like shit. I snatched the phone.

"Liz, I'm talking."

"You can talk on the way to the hospital." I glared at the officer standing on the other side of the car. He was talking to Hal. "Are you driving this thing, or am I?"

The officer saluted. "I am, Ma'am."

I gave Jack the phone and picked up his clothes and that precious vest from the street while the paramedic untethered him from the monitors. Hal came around and put his hand on my shoulder. "His vital signs are good. The hospital's ready for him. There's a counselor from the department waiting to talk to you."

"A counselor?" I stiffened and made a face. Not again. "Why? I don't need a counselor. I need Jack in the hospital."

"Whoa, Liz. Calm down. The department takes care of its own. You know that. He's there to make sure you both come out of this okay. He'll see that the hospital treats you right, take care of all the

B.S., and answer your questions."

"I'll be okay as long as Jack is."

"It won't hurt to talk to him." Hal poked a finger at Jack. "Behave yourself. I'll be there."

Hal helped me into the back seat. I hugged Jack's things as the officer got behind the wheel and raced the engine. "Hi, I'm Eric. Fasten your seat belts, we're going to make time."

Officer Eric must have been a New York cabbie in another life. I hung on as we dodged through traffic on Newport Boulevard. The Emergency Room personnel had a gurney waiting for Jack when we drove up. They pulled him inside before Officer Eric could free me from the back seat. He took me by the elbow and led me to the examination room. By the time we got there, nurses and technicians surrounded Jack.

I sank in a chair, burying my nose in Jack's shirt and inhaled his scent. Officer Eric stood by my side. "Can I get you anything?"

I glanced at the nearly bare, white skin of my thighs. "New panty hose, maybe."

He studied my body. Any well-trained police officer could guess my height within an inch and my weight to five pounds and I squirmed. "Just joking. All I want is for Jack to be okay."

A sandy-haired man dressed in jeans and a sweater introduced himself as a counselor from the police department. His name sailed through my head. He seemed determined to explain how he would help me cope, but his words sounded like unintelligible gibberish as I studied the people hovering over Jack. I nodded to make the counselor feel better.

"Lizzie! Where are you?"

I jumped up, clutching his clothes, and plowed through the crowd, trying not to see the man sticking a needle into Jack's arm to suck out blood. "Are you okay?"

"Just didn't want you to leave."

I kissed his forehead. "After all the work it took to get you here?"

He wound his fingers in mine. Good genes and regular weight training had given him exquisitely sculptured shoulders and six-pack perfect abs, but muscle, bone, and skin were never meant to stop bullets. He had to be okay. Thank God he'd had on that vest and hadn't taken the bullet, but he looked so vulnerable lying there, flat on his back.

The nurse took the blood pressure cuff off Jack's arm and carefully examined the welt on Jack's ribs. It seemed larger and redder. He winced as she touched the area around it.

"How do you feel?"

"Like I got hit by a truck."

She covered him with a blanket. "You should."

"How's the shooting victim? I need to talk to her."

"She's in surgery."

I shook my finger at him. "Jack Black, give the woman a break. Why do you need to talk to her so badly?"

"She's O'Reilly's attorney. She said he left some important information for the police and she wanted me to have it."

The news hit me between the eyes. I couldn't remember what she'd said was in her briefcase, and I squinted. "What information? Why?"

"She didn't know. It was in his final instructions."

"But why you?"

He winced as he shrugged. "We've worked together before."

A bearded, balding man in green surgical scrubs entered the examination room like a king. A stethoscope and a pair of tortoise shell glasses on a chain hung around his neck. He took Jack's chart and put on the half-moon reading glasses.

"Let's see what we have here. Gunshot." He pulled down the blanket and peered over the frames of his lenses at the welt. "Damn good thing you were wearing a vest." He consulted the chart again. "This can't be. It took nearly thirty minutes to get you here. What happened?"

"I had work to do."

"I see. You took a hit in the chest, but you had work to do, so you made EMT personnel twiddle their thumbs?"

Jack didn't answer. He swallowed a groan when the doctor moved his arm and examined the welt. "Does this hurt?"

Jack nearly went to the ceiling. The doctor frowned and put his stethoscope against Jack's chest. I held my breath and tried to listen, too. He dictated a series of tests.

"Is he going to be okay?" I asked.

"I'll know more later, but I expect he'll survive if he can follow instructions and exercise better judgment."

We followed Jack's gurney to the MRI room but they wouldn't let me stay with him. Officer Eric got us coffee and the counselor insisted on chatting about the incident. I held Jack's things and humored the man.

When they finished the MRI, we returned to the examination room. Three off-duty cops were waiting for us and they greeted Jack like a returning war hero. They pumped his hand and examined the welt.

One handed me a paper bag; then they proceeded to compare scars. Before I saw something I really didn't want to see, I peeked in the sack and found a pair of black panty hose in the perfect size. I hugged Officer Eric and left him in charge of Jack's clothes. I scurried to the ladies' room while the scar search continued.

The silky panty hose transformed me from a bag lady to Liz Matthews, Wonder Woman. I ran my synthetically sculptured nails through my hair to fluff it and rubbed at the mascara under my eyes. With my equilibrium restored, I returned to the wound-comparison party in the examination room.

They wedged me in by the gurney and I held Jack's hand while they swapped war stories, initiating Jack into their special fraternity. Jack smiled at the appropriate occasions, but his heart wasn't in it.

The doctor interrupted the proceedings and laid the chart by Jack's feet. "I don't like the looks of your spleen. If it ruptures, you'll be dead in five minutes. We're going to monitor you overnight and do more tests in the morning."

Spleen? Dead? God, he hadn't even been shot. I almost forgot how to breathe. I glanced down at Jack but he avoided my gaze and stared at the ceiling. The counselor stopped the doctor and questioned him but all I processed was dead, five minutes. Jack was supposed to be safe now. Wasn't that what hospitals were for?

When the doctor left, the counselor stood by the bed. "There's no reason to worry—"

I interrupted. "But he said Jack could die any minute."

"He's not in any immediate danger. This is simply a precaution. These things usually take care of themselves without surgery."

"Surgery?" I nearly popped a blood vessel. "He's going to need surgery?"

"Liz, don't make a fuss."

Jack's cold tone worried me as much as the doctor's warning. I pressed my lips together and folded my arms while the counselor explained how normal this all was in the case of a gunshot, as if normal meant it was okay.

Officer Eric, the counselor, and the scar squad accompanied Jack's gurney through the maze of hospital corridors, joking to boost Jack's spirits, but he didn't pretend to smile anymore. When we got to the private room, I blocked them. "Sorry, guys, let me get him settled."

After the nurse and orderly left, I closed the door. Jack stared at the white sheets. I felt scared. "What's wrong?"

He didn't answer. As I folded his clothes and laid them on the chair, I glanced at his bulletproof vest. I slipped it on. It dwarfed my shoulders and weighed a ton, but every ounce made me feel macho. "What do you think?" I swaggered over to the bed. "It's the newest fashion."

He averted his eyes. "Someone might as well wear it."

"Tell me what's bothering you." I touched his cheek. "Please. I'm worried. You owe me this."

He took a deep breath. "The fucking son-of-a-bitch got away because I didn't fire."

If his jaw got any tighter, it would break. "Oh, Honey, it's not your fault. You didn't have time."

"I had time. I hesitated. The fucker shot me."

My chest ached. The bullet had bounced off Jack's vest, but it had left a scar deep inside him. It was as real as the scars his buddies had been showing off, and I clutched his hand. "He got lucky. That's all. It won't happen again."

His voice dropped below freezing. "You're right, it won't. I don't have any business being a cop if I don't have the balls to pull the trigger."

"But you're a good cop."

He shook his head again.

"If pulling a trigger was all it took to be a cop, I'd be one." I tossed my hair. "You know what that would be like."

"A fucking disaster. You're too wild-ass crazy."

"Well, I prefer impetuous, but you see my point. Trigger-happy cowboys end up dead. Dad told me that enough times."

A smile almost escaped from his grim expression. He reached up and caught a lock of my hair in his fingers. "Oh, Lizzie. I can't believe you'd want me to stay on the force after what happened tonight."

My jaw refused to work. I didn't want to go through this again but the alternative scared me just as much. My voice wavered and I took a deep breath to say what he needed to hear. "You have to do what makes you happy. You told me you didn't like being an accountant before."

"A man can change."

I squeaked my worse fear. "But if you change too much, you might not like me."

The smile broke loose. "Oh, darlin', that would never happen. But would you still love me if I wasn't a cop?"

"Of course." I swept my hair back and held his vest against my body, then pressed my lips against his.

"Jesus Christ! I thought you were a dying man." Hal Peters burst into the room like a freight train followed by Officer Eric, the counselor, and the scar squad.

"Any luck?" Jack asked.

Hal shook his head. "I don't know how the son-of-a-bitch got around us, but I had to find out how you were doing."

"How about the attorney?"

"She didn't make it."

Jack faded with the news; the little containers he kept his work stored in cracked and the ugliness seeped out. He shifted uncomfortably in the bed. "Look, fellows. I'm beat. I want to be alone with Liz. Do you mind?"

Jack's friends said their good-byes and we promised to meet with the counselor the next morning. Officer Eric paused. "I'll wait outside, Liz. When you're ready, I'll drive you home."

"You don't have to. I think I'll spend the night."

"No." Jack shook his head. "You need your sleep."

"But I want to be with you."

"No. That's final." He glanced at Officer Eric. "Just give us a few minutes."

When the door closed, I slipped off the vest and under the blankets, scrunching up against Jack's good side on the narrow bed and holding him. But Jack was stiff as wood; I could have gotten splinters.

"I'm sorry about that woman. Were you going to ask her what she had for you?"

"No, It was something Travis said."

I replayed the conversations. "Oh, you mean the laugh."

He frowned at me. "Who told you that?"

I propped myself up on an elbow. "It's the only thing he said that she didn't tell us or we didn't hear."

He blew out a puff of air. "Guess I might as well tell you so you don't go shooting off your mouth about it. But you got to promise not to repeat this."

"My lips are zipped." I moved my fingers across my mouth.

"I wish. Okay, a fellow wearing a mask jumps out, shouts boo, and laughs. Do you know who that is?"

My eyes widened. Understanding washed over me. "Oh, my God, it's the man who raped Nicola."

He nodded. "But rapists don't do armed robberies."

I got out of bed and paced while I searched my mental file on the psychology of sex offenders. Unfortunately, I'd majored in statistics and the file contained only a few random notes from safety lectures that Dad had delivered and I'd ignored. "Maybe he needs money? The heat's on. Maybe he wants to get out of town?"

"No, he's not worried about getting caught."

"Then that means Jimmy O'Reilly knew who the rapist was and told his lawyer, so the guy killed both of them."

Jack shook his head. "That doesn't necessarily follow."

"But two murders in three days roughly fifty feet apart have to be related and Jimmy died the morning the mask was in the paper. Willow couldn't be involved."

He pinched the bridge of his nose as if he'd been overtaken by a headache. "We can't go to court with that."

"What about my sister?"

"I'm sorry. I know you're worried, but this is so far-fetched, people will think Travis and I cooked it up for your sake." He held out his hand. "Get back in bed, please. I want to feel you."

He held me this time. I felt so warm and safe; I stopped being strong and almost choked swallowing the tears. "You scared the hell out me."

"Me, too. I won't put you through it again."

"Everything else is changing in my life. I need you to be my constant. Please, don't be different."

"Am I that perfect?"

I tousled his cop-cut to mask my fears. "Well, you could grow your hair a little longer." He grimaced as if I'd asked him to be an anarchist. I gave him a quick peck. "We'll negotiate that in the morning."

11

03809798274981798409197

I tried again to talk Jack into letting me spend the night at the hospital, but he said he wouldn't be able to sleep if he knew I wasn't. Like I was going to get any sleep at home worrying about him.

Officer Eric drove fairly sedately down the Peninsula to Jack's house. He helped me get Useless and took us around the corner to my place. He even walked the dogs for me. After he left, I lay in bed holding Puddles while Useless camped in front of the door waiting for Jack to return.

After a night of bloody nightmares, I woke before dawn could crack, dying to see Jack. I threw on some tight jeans and a blue sweater and took care of the dogs. Once I had them settled and the sun peeked over the horizon, turning the sky pinkish-blue, I raced to the hospital, tying Officer Eric's speed record. I felt warm and breathless after running in from the parking lot, expecting to be Jack's first visitor at dawn. But when a pair of nurses came out of his hospital room eating beignets, I knew Travis Tourville was serving breakfast.

Travis held a beignet in one hand and a cup of coffee in the other.

Powdered sugar dusted through his heavy mustache and across the chest of his green sports shirt. A large silver thermos and white boxes bearing the purple and gold Crescent City Café logo covered the top of the small chest beside the bed. A plate of half-eaten food sat on the tray in front of Jack.

If I hadn't been worried about Jack's spleen, I might have jumped on top of him despite the audience. I settled for a kiss. His lips felt warm and I brushed his forehead. It was hot and his eyes seemed even more tired and distant than they had last night. The dark stubble on his face added to his haggard appearance. His left arm still protected his ribs.

"You look like a narc. Are you okay?"

"I'm sick." He rearranged the food on his plate. "I have a fever and I have to stay till it's gone."

I sank to the edge of his bed. I'd hoped to bring him home, but at least he was alive and I could fuss over him here. "That's what you get for sitting out in that cold ocean air."

Travis passed me a beignet and a cup of fragrant coffee. The chicory-laced New Orleans blend opened my eyes.

"I told him that, too. And if he doesn't behave himself, I'm calling his mama. She won't need a plane to fly here."

He chuckled at Jack's expression while I took a bite of the light, fried pastry. "Mmmm." I licked my fingers. "This is delicious, Travis, but what are you doing up so early?"

"Early? Lord, I've been up for hours. But I got to thinking about poor old Jack and what they had to be feeding him, so I whipped up something and brought some beignets to honey up the nurses. Want them to treat him right."

At least Travis seemed in a better mood than he had last night. I speared some of Jack's eggs Florentine. "Did you ever find out what was in that letter Jimmy O'Reilly left you?"

"Lizzie, you have to stop snooping." Jack pointed a finger at me. "You had no business being at the wake last night. Now leave poor Travis alone."

Travis shrugged. "It's okay, Jack. I don't think it's a real mystery. I'm hoping he left me his share of the restaurant in his will. Then maybe I can scrape some money together and buy out Andre."

The eggs caught in my throat. "Andre is your partner?"

"He's the co-owner." Travis shrugged. "But he doesn't understand the restaurant business. Now, Jimmy understood good food, but Andre fusses over the bottom-line."

"Hey, buddy! Got your laptop and your files." Hal walked in with a briefcase and a computer. "We'll get you all plugged in and you can do your work right here."

Laptop? Files? He couldn't be serious.

Jack straightened up with a groan. "Thanks. Lizzie, if you don't mind, we need to talk." He motioned toward the door.

He was serious. I folded my arms and my blood pressure shot up. "Yes, I do mind. I took the day off to be with you. I'm not spending it in a hospital hallway."

It took about twenty seconds of motionless silence to convince them I wasn't leaving. Hal nodded toward Travis. "We'll take a walk."

When they left, Jack placated me. "Lizzie, be reasonable."

"I've gone way beyond reasonable. You made yourself sick last night because you didn't have the sense to stop working. One reason you're here is because that doctor doesn't trust you to take care of yourself, and he's right."

"I can't just drop things."

"And how long is this going to take?"

"Two, three hours." I tapped my foot and Jack looked at the ceiling. "Maybe four."

According to my Jack Work Estimation Study, he was usually low by a factor of almost fifty-percent. But his inability to gauge time wasn't the problem. I wanted to be with him. I needed to be with him. He'd stepped on my feelings too often lately and I would draw the line here. "Fine, but it may be the last thing you do, and I'm not going to be a party to it."

I stood. While my mother's disappearing act had left me with a closet full of insecurities it had also taught me to act calm and cool, no matter what. "I don't have a salary. If I don't work, I don't make money. We'll just consider this a regular day." I kissed him. "If you can squeeze me in later, I'll drop by."

I made myself walk toward the door.

"But, Lizzie. We have an appointment with the counselor this morning."

I shook my head, keeping my eyes on the corridor. "No. It's clear my feelings don't count. I'm not going to waste my time listening to some cop psychologist tell me that I should sit quietly and be proud while my man works himself to death."

Panic crept into his voice. "Lizzie. You can't cancel."

"Yes, I can. I haven't been here five minutes and you're ready to throw me out so you can tell police secrets. If I want my consulting business to work, I can't keep dropping my job to fit in your schedule." I glanced over my shoulder and fought the urge to crumble and run back into his arms. "I still love you and I'll see you later."

Before I weakened, I rushed to the elevator and pounded the button. Men! How did he expect to find a murderer from a hospital bed?

I only broke about four laws driving home. The phone rang as I rushed into my apartment. I nearly tripped over the dogs to answer it, but it was only Nicola checking on Jack. She'd heard the news and I assured her Jack was okay. We went for a run to clear my head, but it didn't help much. When I got back, Jack hadn't left a message. I switched on my computer but my eyes kept wandering from the numbers on the screen to toward the phone. Finally, I threw a volume of the *Transactions of the Society of Actuaries* across the room. It thudded against my vanity wall, narrowly missing my diplomas, but hitting a stack of papers sitting on the file cabinet. The papers drifted to the floor.

"Damn! Why did he have to turn into a man?"

Puddles sprang into my lap and kissed me. Useless shrugged and I argued with him. "I can keep secrets. And I can reason just as well as he can. It's what I do for a living. I could help him find the man who shot him."

Useless raised his eyebrows. He was on Jack's side. "I can. It can't be any harder than an actuarial exam, especially if this is the same guy who raped Nicola. All I have to do is find a man close to Jimmy O'Reilly who's angry and violent."

Someone like Viper. I pushed Puddles on the floor and went in the bedroom to shower and change into a little black power suit.

The police still had the dead-end street beside Jimmy O'Reilly's house cordoned off and everyone who passed by the barriers stopped and stared at the dark stain in the pavement where the woman had been killed. I paused, too. No matter what Jack said, the two murders weren't a coincidence. I'd find out. I walked up on the porch and rang the bell.

Any woman with half a brain would've run away screaming when Viper answered the door. His eyes looked like a map of the Mississippi Delta colored in shades of red, and his breath smelled worse than a landfill. Although he was only in his late twenties, the gray-green undertone of his skin and the baggage under his eyes made him seem older. His black silk pajamas had disappeared and his boxers revealed his malnourished and overly tattooed chest, arms, and legs.

He leaned against the doorframe. “What do you want?”

My smiled dazzled brighter than the Southern California morning sun and I chirped. “I was worried. You disappeared last night and I was afraid you’d sleep through the funeral.”

“Fucking cops kept me up half the night, then they woke me up this morning.”

“Well, they do that sort thing when there’s a murder.” I held up a bag. “I thought you could use coffee and doughnuts.”

He eyed me up and down and ran the silver stud in his tongue around his lips. Most people would consider walking into the home of a suspected rapist and murderer to be pretty damn stupid, but I had my pepper spray in my pocket. I put my right hand on the container and walked past him.

The beach house had a hangover to match Viper’s. The Arctic white carpet had grayed and showed indelible red wine stains. I could practically feel the sand and grit through my shoes and the air reeked of tobacco and alcohol. Even the paintings on the wall had a lopsided viewpoint. Viper lurched through the living room to the dining room and sprawled on a chair.

“Where’s this coffee?”

He almost got it in his crotch, but I gave him the bag and sat. He took a bite out of a cream filled doughnut. Frosting covered his lips. “So, what’s your scam?”

“There’s no scam.”

“Bullshit.” He leaned forward and grabbed my wrist. “You don’t like me. You’re only here because the cops think your baby sister killed Dad.”

Damn family resemblance. My grip tightened on the pepper spray and I jerked free. “I’m here because someone shot my boyfriend and I’m pissed. Why’d you leave the wake last night?”

“Because I was tired of fucking Andre treating me like fucking shit.”

“Well, duh. What do you expect when you act like an fucking asshole?”

He froze, and then cackled. “You’ve got balls.”

I got into his face. “No, it’s estrogen, and it’s out of control. Don’t push me.”

God bless PMS. Viper shrank at the thought of raging female

hormones. I sat back and crossed my legs while I brushed invisible lint from my suit. "What did you do when you left last night?"

"I walked to the end of the beach and sat on the rocks."

"Who do you think killed your father?"

Viper licked cream filling from his long, slender fingers. "I don't know. If I had to guess, I'd say it was Destiny."

I rolled my eyes. "You mean you think it was fate?"

"No, I think it was Dad's ex-wife, Destiny. The bitch." He made a face as if he'd just eaten bugs. "She's been flying around here on her broom ever since he died, wanting money."

"Why?"

"I don't know what goes on inside that slut's mind."

"You don't think much of women, do you?"

He smirked. "Why should I? They're all whores. Your little sister's a whore. What's your price?"

It was a damn good thing I didn't have the coffee in my hand. I got up. "I'm not going to take any crap from a grown man who sponges off his father. Talk about whores."

Between the adrenaline and estrogen, I was flying *without* a broom. Viper caught me as I grabbed the doorknob. I jerked away. "Don't touch me."

He backed off. "I'm sorry."

"Yeah, right." My fingers curled around the pepper spray in my pocket. "What's my sister doing that you're not?"

"She does whatever that prick Ryan tells her. She'd sleep with me if he told her."

I recoiled. "Have you?"

He shuddered. "God, no. She's a kid. But if you want to help her, keep her the fuck away from him."

His concern surprised me and I shook off my anger. "I'm trying. You'd better take a shower before the funeral."

He glanced at his dirty feet and shifted. "Yeah, the limo should be here soon." He drew in a lung-full of air as he continued examining his toes. "I've never been to a funeral before and I don't want to go to this one."

I understood this. "Viper, funerals only happen once. It's now or..."

He raised his head and I saw the face of a man grieving for his father. "I know you don't like me but I don't think I can do this thing alone. Do you have the balls to go with me? You can ask all the questions you want. You can even search the fucking place."

I glanced out the window. Freedom. I hated funerals; Peter's hadn't been that long ago.

Viper. The poor guy had to be desperate to ask me, a total stranger, to go with him. Common sense told me to leave but guilt combined with compassion and tugged at my conscience. "Do you have an alibi?"

"No. I was sleeping in my car."

"Then get cleaned up. I'll wait."

I stood at the bottom step until a door closed, then I took off my heels and tiptoed upstairs. The shower in the guest bath was running.

I went in the study. The police had taken the computer and left only a few pens and paper clips in the drawers. Damn their efficiency. I started on the book case, flipping through books. A micro floppy disk labelled 'checkbook backup' fell out of the financial planning software instruction booklet. Jimmy O'Reilly not only backed up his work, he used the same software Jack had given me for Christmas. I kissed the disk and slipped it into my suit pocket.

The doorbell rang as I stepped into the master bedroom and I dashed down the stairs, pausing just a second to smooth my clothes before opening the door. A trim woman with sleek, dark hair pulled back from her face and wearing a black suit stood on the porch. Emeralds and diamonds glittered on her fingers and she had a permanent tan like most Newport Beach matrons. She introduced herself. "I'm Sondra Ramirez, Mr. O'Reilly's neighbor. Is Viper in? I'd like to speak with him."

A neighbor! I nearly licked my lips. "That's so kind. Viper's really feeling down. Come in. He's changing." I played hostess and waved her to a chair.

We took matching white silk chairs and carefully tucked our skirts around our legs. Sondra Ramirez glanced around the room and shook her head at the filth. "I can't believe what they did to the house. Jimmy would be upset."

I nodded. "You weren't at the wake last night?"

"I was out all weekend and frankly, I wouldn't have come anyway. Those weren't my type of people." She scrutinzed me as if to determine what sort of woman I was and raised an eyebrow at my feet.

Oops. In my haste to answer the door, I'd left my shoes at the foot of the stairs. I sat primly with my best company manners and demurely crossed my ankles, confident that good posture and politeness would counterbalance my shoeless condition. "Yes, some of them were rather strange."

"If you'll excuse me, you don't look like one of Viper's girl friends."

It worked and I smiled. "Oh, I'm not. He seemed so alone last night and I was worried about him, so I stopped by. Did you know his father well?"

"We've been walking together every morning at seven-thirty since his heart attack. We were up to an hour."

An hour alone with Jimmy O'Reilly everyday. "That's great. The walking I mean. Did you two walk Saturday?"

"Yes, I'm probably the last person to see him alive, well, other than the murderer."

I knitted my fingers together and squeezed them to keep my hands quiet. "Oh, my. How was he?"

"He was very upset and late."

"Really? Did he tell you what was wrong?"

The older woman inspected me again. "You ask a lot of questions."

"I'm sorry. I didn't know Jimmy well, but he seemed like such a nice man. I can't understand how anything like this could happen. And poor Viper's just devastated."

She nodded. "The poor boy. I've wracked my brain, but I can't think of anything except for that girl who'd spent the night. She'd run away from home and Jimmy was afraid she was in some sort of trouble. I told him to call her mother."

"You didn't hear any shots or see anyone?"

"I took a shower as soon as I got home and left for Palm Springs. I saw a blonde woman walking away from the back door when I pulled out of the garage, but I didn't hear anything. Anyway, I can't imagine how a stranger could get in this house. Jimmy was so security conscious. He always kept the doors locked and the alarm on, even when he was home."

The picture of Jack kicking in French doors Saturday morning flashed into my brain. The alarm hadn't been on then. "I know I'm a dreadful snoop, but I'm worried about Viper. He's so angry and bitter. Had he quarreled with his father?"

She nodded. "Jimmy was worried because Viper couldn't hold a job or live within his means. He finally cut him off."

My head jerked up at the sound of footsteps on the stairs. Viper came down in something that actually appeared to be a dark suit and a white shirt. Although the shirt didn't have a collar and he didn't have a tie, he wore real shoes and socks and only one discreet earring. Plus the stud in his tongue. While his coloring hadn't improved much, he smelled clean.

"Wow, Viper," I gasped as I stood. "You look sharp."

He hung his head self-consciously. "It's for Dad."

12

103809798274981798409197

For a moment, I thought we were crashing a royal funeral when I glanced through the leaded glass door of the formal parlor at the Church of the Risen Son where Jimmy O'Reilly's family was gathering. Krystal O'Reilly sat regally on the edge of a mauve wingback chair, her ankles demurely crossed. She wore a tailored, black coatdress and her blonde hair was tucked into a smart, little black hat. A bit of veil covered her face. Gloves and a dainty lace hanky, too delicate to absorb more than six tears, completed her ensemble. All she lacked was the photographer to record her pose.

Andre Lefebvre, elegantly attired in a dark gray Italian suit, lounged on the crewel sofa with the grace of a panther. He drank coffee from a china cup, holding his pinkie out. His son, Ryan, slouched beside him, his hands shoved deep into his pockets. He wore a navy blazer and an expression that said he didn't want to be anywhere near here. I didn't either. All Peter's Feng Shui decorating principles couldn't overpower the hostility of the occupants.

Viper sighed. He'd behaved in the limo on the trip to the church, even if he had been semi-comatose. After his confrontation with Andre last night, I knew the situation could get ugly fast and I only wanted to find a murderer, not witness another death.

I touched his arm. "There are other places to wait."

"No, I have to do this." He set his jaw and opened the door. I crossed my fingers.

The temperature dropped ten degrees when we entered the room. Reverend Anderson must have cranked up the air-conditioning in anticipation of some hot tempers. Krystal sniffed and turned away, her nose up as high as it could get. Andre put his cup on the coffee table and stood to greet us. Ryan followed.

Andre shook Viper's hand. His voice sounded sharp. "Thank God you're here. I was worried. How are you doing?"

Viper matched Andre's tone. "I'm fine, Uncle Andre."

Andre fussed with the shoulders of Viper's suit. "Good. At least you dressed decently. And you brought the lovely Liz. That shows remarkable taste."

Andre stepped aside and Ryan moved into position in front of Viper. He stuck out his hand. "I'm sorry about your dad. He was great. Maybe I could stop by and we could hang out."

The thought of the eighteen-year-old prep doing anything with a burned-out punk ten years his senior almost made me laugh.

Viper grimaced. "Sure. But call first."

"There's coffee and croissants over there." Andre dismissed Viper with a wave at a silver urn and tray on a small Queen Anne dining table. "You look like you could use some."

The sound of Viper's nerves popping filled the quiet and mine were stretched. This had to stop now and I tugged his sleeve. "I'll join you for a cup in a minute, but I want a word with Andre first. Please?"

He eyed Andre, then me. "Cream or sugar?"

I ordered cream. Ryan smirked as Viper left but his father shot him a menacing glance that made Ryan flinch and slither to his corner of the couch.

Once we were alone, I folded my arms. "Why do you treat Viper like that? I mean, he's your godson and he's burying his father today. Can't you cut him a little slack?"

Andre paused. "I'm sorry. You're right. I guess we've all been under a lot of stress. Viper and I haven't been close the last few years. You know how it is when boys grow up. And I'm afraid I have my hands full with Krystal."

I glanced over Andre's shoulder. Krystal sat with her legs crossed jiggling her foot and glaring at us. I meowed. "How is the widow holding up? Did you check under her bed last night?"

"I never sleep with my friends' wives, current or ex. I made certain Krystal got home safely and once I deliver her there today, I've fulfilled my obligation to Jimmy."

His answer was too smooth and I shook my head. "Then why is she staring at us? I can almost feel the daggers."

"That's because she's staring at you. Krystal can't stand not being the prettiest woman in the room."

Vanity turned my head for another look and I flushed. "I'll give you a ten on that line. I fell for it."

"But it's the truth. You have an aura of self-confidence that appeals to men and annoys insecure women. Krystal needs constant reassurance. Frankly, I don't have the time for it."

That I could believe. "Then who is comforting her?"

"I'll tell you everything you want to know about Krystal if you'll let me help Willow."

"Just keep Ryan away from her." I walked away and joined Viper in the opposite corner of the room. He lay across a burgundy and cream striped armchair like a marionette without strings and I sat beside him. "Are you okay?"

He lolled his head toward me and flicked his tongue, the silver stud a glistening blur. He was as okay as he could be under the circumstances. The unseen puppet master pulled Viper to a sitting position, first one shoulder, then the other, and finally the legs. Viper nodded toward two gold-trimmed china cups and saucers on the piecrust table between us. "I got your coffee."

The rich aroma said hazelnut, but before I could raise the cup to my lips, Andre paused beside us. "Liz pointed out that I was very curt. I'm sorry. I miss your father. Stop by the office later this week, maybe I can find a position for you."

My eyes narrowed as Andre resumed his place near Krystal. He smiled at me and raised his coffee cup in a salute, his pinkie arched in the air.

Viper went limp from astonishment and almost slipped to the floor. "Jesus, he wants you bad."

While I agreed Andre wanted something, Viper's incredulous tone irritated me. "So, what part of that surprises you?"

"You're not his type. Chicks throw themselves at Andre, and he buys them with recording contracts or trips to Paris. But you seem like a high-maintenance woman."

"What makes you such an astute judge of character?"

"A lifetime of sitting on the outside looking in, watching Andre and Dad operate. When folks think you're too stupid to amount to anything, they don't think you know what they're doing."

Although he tried to sound flippant, the bitterness ran to his core. His hand trembled as he picked up the china cup and slurped the coffee. After he drained it, he closed his eyes. I touched his arm. "Do you have any family?"

He answered in a monotone. "My mom bailed on me when I was nine. Her new husband didn't want some snotty kid hanging around, but that was fine with me. I didn't want him either."

"So you went to your father?"

"No place else to go. He wasn't happy about it and that bitch Destiny made it clear she didn't like me."

While Dad and I had our differences, he all but smothered me with parental love and concern. Thank God, he cared. If he hadn't, I might have turned into something like Viper.

"My mother ditched me when I was a baby. She didn't bother to call for thirty years, so I know what it's like to feel unwanted and unlovable. If you ever want to talk—"

Viper scowled. "Like I'm going to confess I killed my father. I don't think so."

"No. Just talk."

The Reverend F. Wesley Anderson swept into the room in his flowing white robes, radiating his famous charisma. He spoke to Krystal first; then he shook Viper's hand and greeted him like a long lost son. Viper shifted and mumbled his responses, but he spoke respectfully. The Reverend arched an eyebrow as he took my hand. "How's Jack doing? I thought you'd be at the hospital."

I kept the explanation short. "He's working. Viper asked me to come."

Reverend Anderson greeted Andre and Ryan and then motioned to all of us. "Perhaps the family would like a moment of prayer alone with Jimmy before the service."

He escorted us to a small chapel at the end of the hall and held the stained glass door open. The small room held only six rows of pews with dusty-pink cushions. An empty cross was centered in a round rose window behind the altar. The window, lit from behind, glowed softly. The deceased lay in state at the end of the short, center aisle surrounded by flowers. Organ music flowed through speakers and the room smelled of death and lilies. Krystal led the way but faltered after four steps when she saw the open casket. Andre eased her into the last pew and sat beside her. Ryan glued himself against the back wall and stared at his shoes. The mortuary man in a black suit stood near the door like a sentinel. Viper and Reverend Anderson went to the coffin. The overpowering scent made me queasy, but I stood beside Viper.

Jimmy O'Reilly seemed like a wax figure surrounded by flowers and I quickly averted my eyes. I counted dead people, I didn't like looking at them and the only other time I'd seen this dead person, he had a hole in his chest and blood on his clothes. Since then, I'd witnessed a second murder and almost lost Jack. I hugged myself and wished I'd stayed at the hospital.

"Oh, Dad. I'm sorry." Viper dropped to his knees and prayed.

I'd come hoping to find a murderer, but this was too real. Jimmy O'Reilly was dead. He deserved some respect. Before I bought a one-way ticket to Hell for voyeurism and with the eyes of all the nuns from Catholic School watching me from Detroit, I crossed myself and recited the prayers they'd programmed into my brain. When Viper finished, he stood, but as he gained altitude, his blood drained to his feet. He fell into my arms. He was heavier than I thought and I braced myself against the pew.

Andre and Reverend Anderson pulled him off and Viper moaned. "I feel sick."

I followed them from the chapel, but my concern stopped at the men's room sign and the unmistakable sound of retching. Andre could clean up after Viper, and I turned back to find Krystal standing nearby and Ryan just behind her.

Krystal folded her arms and sneered. "He shouldn't of come here. If he ruins the service, it'll be your fault."

This was not a good time to pick a fight. I tossed my hair. "Well, excuse me, but I think a son outranks an ex-wife at a funeral."

"Jimmy and I are still married. In fact, we were reconciling. We talked about it Friday night."

"Oh, really? So what were you doing Saturday morning?"

"I had an appointment with my personal trainer, Georg."

Ryan leaned against the wall and smirked. Krystal noticed me staring at him and glared over her shoulder. "Ryan, go away. If you hadn't taken that girl to Jimmy's Friday night, none of this would have happened."

Ryan shrugged and sauntered back to the parlor. Krystal adjusted her gloves. A personal trainer wasn't much of an alibi and a neighbor had seen a blonde leaving Jimmy O'Reilly's house. "I'm really sorry about your husband. Andre didn't tell me that you'd gotten back together. And then with Viper staying at the house I thought, well, why is Viper staying at the house?"

She shrugged and wrinkled her pretty little nose. "When we separated, Jimmy got the house. It was in our prenuptial agreement, but since we never finalized our divorce, I'm certain my lawyer won't have any problem overturning the will and getting Viper out of there." She dabbed her eyes with the hanky. "My poor Jimmy."

Andre and Reverend Anderson helped Viper out of the restroom and back to the parlor. He looked as pallid as his father's body, but he was steadier on his feet. Reverend Anderson gave him a glass of ice water and sat beside him with his hand on Viper's back. Andre stood over them, shaking his head. "Viper, you're not well, you should go home. I'm sure Liz will take you."

Viper leaned forward, with his elbows on his knees and his head hanging down. "I'll be okay."

Krystal waited by the door, tapping her foot and practicing annoyed expressions. I sat beside Viper and held his hand. "Are you sure?"

"I have to." Viper stood and wobbled slightly. "I'm going back in."

Given the way he staggered toward the chapel, it seemed likely he'd collapse again. Then I could take him home. Reverend Anderson and I walked beside him supporting his elbows. Viper dropped to his knees in front of the coffin and bowed his head. Andre took a pew.

The doors burst open. "Where's the bastard?"

A small blonde woman in hot pink marched down the aisle, her cheeks flushed to match her revealing, skin-tight dress. She peered at Jimmy O'Reilly. "The son of a bitch really is dead."

Viper struggled to his feet, pointing. "Get out of here, Destiny!"

"I'll be glad to. I just have a little parting gift for the deceased." She bent over the corpse and spat in his face.

Viper turned purple and lunged at her. Andre and Reverend Anderson caught him, but Destiny went after Viper. Andre grabbed her and she bit him.

It was my turn. I tried to pull her off, but she took a swipe at me. Mistake. Although she was small, she was strong, but I'd been in catfights before. I had the weight and reach advantage and the best acrylic nails money could buy. I grabbed a hunk of her big hair and dragged her out by her dark roots.

13

403809798274981798409197

I'd heard of bitter divorces but this was ridiculous. I almost broke a fingernail dragging Destiny into the corridor. Thank God, Hal had come to the funeral. He came charging down the corridor from the sanctuary when he heard the commotion. "What the hell's going on here?"

"This bitch attacked me." Destiny lunged for my eyes when I let go. Hal grabbed her arms and held her back.

"She spit on the corpse and hit Viper."

Andre came out of the chapel examining his wounded hand and confirmed my story.

"There's nothing illegal about that." Destiny struggled so hard her non-bio-degradable boobs almost popped out of the confines of her hot pink dress, but the one hundred pound woman was no match for a cop the size of a grizzly bear.

Hal tightened his grip. "Ma'am, you'd better calm down fast. Assault is a felony."

A man, slightly younger than Viper with a skinny, blond ponytail came from the sanctuary. He'd chosen to wear a black Grateful Dead T-shirt and faded jeans to the funeral. "Mom, what's going on?"

Hal took Destiny and her son outside. I straightened my suit and pulled Destiny's blonde hair out of my nails before I went back into the chapel. Reverend Anderson had Viper sitting in the front pew and was trying to calm him, but diffusing a nuclear warhead would have been easier. The mortuary man bent over Jimmy O'Reilly, cleaning his face with a handkerchief.

Viper gestured wildly. "I'm going to kill the fucking bitch!"

I knelt in front of him and grabbed his hands. "Don't say stupid things! Someone's likely to believe you. Now come on, calm down, the police took her outside."

The mortuary man held his handkerchief by a corner. Blotches of California Tan skin color covered it. "We just need a little makeup. I've called for it."

Viper went to the coffin and stroked his father's face while Reverend Anderson patted Viper's back. I sank on the pew. I'd come here with the innocence of Nancy Drew, but things like this never happened to her. She lived in a nice, polite fictional world where she found secrets in old clocks. If real detective work were like this, I'd stick to solving actuarial mysteries where I didn't have to see the dead bodies I tallied.

Andre sat beside me and put his arm around my shoulders. He shook his head sadly as he watched Viper. "The poor boy."

"What's that woman's problem?"

"A life filled with disappointment, I guess."

Krystal rushed in with Ryan trailing behind her and shrieked. "How'd Destiny get in here?"

Andre shrugged wearily and extended his hand. She threw herself into his arms, burying her face in his shoulder, and sobbed. Her little black hat tumbled to the floor. As it fell, it pulled a few locks loose from her chignon.

Andre glanced at me. His face seemed worn. "It was so kind of you to come, but I'll understand if you'd like to get away from all this. I promise, I'll take care of Viper."

It was tempting. A second mortuary man entered the chapel with a black leather bag. He opened it on the foot of the casket and conferred with his colleague over small jars of flesh tone. Although I worked with mortality rates every day, dead bodies and the rituals surrounding them made me uncomfortable. When I died, I wanted to evaporate into celestial mist, so I didn't care to watch the men prepare Jimmy O'Reilly go into the hereafter with a healthy glow.

Reverend Anderson and Viper dropped to their knees and prayed while the mortuary men finished their touch-up job. Krystal sobbed. Tears left tracks down her cheeks. Andre rubbed his chest as he stared at the cross hanging on the wall behind the altar. Ryan just watched.

Viper wiped his face with his palms and stood. Reverend Anderson stood, too, and motioned. "Let's freshen up a bit."

The coolness of the parlor felt refreshing. I sat with Viper on the sofa while Krystal adjusted her hat and veil and replenished her makeup in front of an ornate gilt mirror. Reverend Anderson poured ice water and distributed the glasses on a silver tray. I found a bottle of ibuprofen in my purse and split it with Viper.

Slowly, the room polarized again. Andre and Ryan drifted to a corner and put their heads together. They spoke too softly to be overheard in the quietness. When Krystal finished primping, she joined them. Andre put his arm around her.

Reverend Anderson sat on the mauve wingback chair next to me. He folded his hands and pressed them against his lips as he observed the threesome in one corner and the lonely man in another. I wondered what Jimmy O'Reilly had told him about all of them, but asking was pointless, a minister never violated the pastor/parishioner trust.

Reverend Anderson raised an eyebrow at me and I glanced back to Viper. I knew what it was like to lose a loved one. If it hadn't been for Jack, Peter's funeral would've been unbearable. I wouldn't want to be alone at my father's funeral and I put my hand on Viper's arm and leaned near his ear. "I'm really sorry about your dad. May I get you something?"

He shook his head but my talents didn't include sitting still. I had to do something and food was my favorite panacea so I investigated the snack situation. While Andre had mentioned the coffee and croissants, he had neglected a vital bit of information: chocolate chip cookies. Everyone knew chocolate had enormous restorative powers. I made up a plate and put it in front of Viper.

"Eat! You need strength." I took one to encourage him. For store bought, it wasn't bad, and it made me feel better.

"I didn't kill my father."

I patted his hand. He wasn't the only suspect on my list. Jimmy O'Reilly's neighbor had seen a blonde woman at his back door on Saturday morning. Any person who would spit on a corpse could commit murder, so could an almost ex-wife with a pre-nuptial agreement.

Reverend Anderson rose. "I know this was a dreadful incident. It was the act of a disturbed woman and we must pray for her. But we must get on with the service. People are waiting to pay their final respects." He smiled at Viper. "Are you ready, son?"

Viper nodded but Andre stood. "I think Viper should go home. He was ill before Destiny got here, and he's simply too distraught."

"Andre, I'm not a child anymore." Viper squared his shoulders and grew an inch. "You can't order me around. Dad planned his funeral. I know there's something in it for me."

Reverend Anderson took control. "Of course you're staying. I know your father put a lot of thought and care into his plans. I think you'll find comfort in the service." He raised his arms, palms upward, toward heaven. "Let us pray."

I bowed my head, but I didn't close my eyes. While Reverend Anderson sought God's comfort and blessing, Krystal took a small gold compact from her purse and powdered her face. When she saw me watching her over the mirror, she slipped it back in the little black handbag and bowed her head.

Reverend Anderson escorted us as far as the massive carved cedar sanctuary door. Krystal led the way with one hand on Andre's arm, the other clutching her little lacy hanky. Viper and I followed while Ryan trailed behind.

Viper's eyes opened wide as he glanced around. "Holy, fucking, shit."

Most first time visitors had a similar, if less profane, reaction when they stepped into the sanctuary. Four-story tall stained glass windows on either side of the church rivaled those found in any of the Gothic cathedrals in Europe, as did the wood paneling in the chancel, but the pews upholstered in antique-rose velvet provided worshipers more comfort than their medieval counterparts enjoyed. At least one hundred white and gold organ pipes decorated the wall behind the choir loft in the front of the church. Angels, cherubs, and clouds drifted across the ceiling, however it was the larger than life holographic Jesus floating over the altar that made newcomers gasp.

My step faltered. Although I met with Reverend Anderson almost every week to go over the product development progress, I hadn't been inside the sanctuary since I buried my best friend. Coming here felt like a major mistake, but I couldn't run out now. I slipped my arm in Viper's and didn't look back.

Jimmy O'Reilly's friends and business associates seemed dwarfed by the cavernous, flower-filled auditorium. After waiting nearly thirty minutes for the funeral to begin, the mourners shifted restlessly in the pews and their voices could be heard over the organ music. As we passed, the congregation settled in, grumbling, rustling papers, and putting away cell phones. I focused my eyes on the back of Andre's neck until I glimpsed a woman with my own pale hair color. My head swiveled as we walked by. What was Ann doing here?

Jimmy O'Reilly's flower-covered coffin waited for us at the end of the aisle. Andre motioned Krystal into the front pew. I sat ramrod straight between him and Viper, with Ryan taking the aisle position. The scent of hundreds of blooms decorating the chancel nearly choked me.

Andre whispered. "It's nice of your mother to come."

I shook my head and stared at holographic Jesus in shimmering white robes hovering on the ceiling four stories above us. His eyes seemed to stare back at me. "She didn't even know him."

"Yes, she did. I introduced them at Ryan's eighteenth birthday party last fall."

I nearly got whiplash. "What? But she told the police—" What had she told police? I struggled to remember the conversation at the hospital on Saturday and cursed myself for not taking notes. "Did she know where he lived?"

"The party was at Jimmy's house. I didn't want all those teenagers at my place."

I glared over my shoulder at Ann and she ducked her head. Now I had a third blonde possibility, and I knew she'd been on the Peninsula Saturday morning. Had she gone to Jimmy O'Reilly's looking for Willow? Did she have the nerve to pull a trigger?

Would she frame her daughter?

14

40380979827498179840919 7

My thoughts were interrupted when the soft organ music was replaced by a rock tune I didn't recognize. Andre covered his mouth and groaned. "Good Lord, that's one of our songs."

Ryan leaned around Viper, brimming with sarcasm, and spoke in a stage whisper. "Way cool, Dad."

"Don't get smart with me." Andre scowled then sat back and shook his head. "Thank God, we only recorded one album."

Andre's discomfort amused me. Under the Italian suit, manicure, perfect hair and teeth, lived a man who was embarrassed by his youthful experiments. As for the song, I gave it an eighty-three. The beat was good and Andre had a nice voice, but it was too country for me.

Viper nodded to the rhythm. When the music ended, the trap door in front of the altar opened and Reverend Anderson, arms flung open, slowly rose on one of the sanctuary's hidden elevators. The spotlight made his silver-blond hair glow like a halo, and his spare, thin face carried his rich, amplified voice. He sounded like God as he blessed the congregation.

According to local history, Reverend Anderson had opened his first church in an abandoned legitimate theater, staging biblical plays and church services. As the money poured in, he built the present church for his religious extravaganzas. I prayed Jimmy's multi-media funeral wouldn't include an earthquake, lightening bolt, or flying angels.

The Reverend recalled Jimmy's time as technical engineer for the Church of the Risen Son, praising his work designing the high-tech audio and video systems. He glorified Jimmy for his return to the fold just a few months ago. Viper wiped his eyes when the Reverend told of Jimmy's love for his son. Krystal sobbed as the Reverend spoke of her life with Jimmy. Andre reviewed his eulogy, fingering the paper as he read the sixteen-point type—he obviously didn't wear glasses in public.

At last, Andre's turn came. He placed his notes on the pulpit and surveyed the auditorium. "You'll be happy to know I will not be singing." A polite chuckle rippled through the crowd. "Jimmy and I have been friends since first grade when his snake got loose in Mrs. Thibault's class. We enjoyed all the things little boys do." Andre's native Cajun accent grew richer as he recalled his childhood. "And one day, over forty years ago, Jimmy and I sat on the banks of the Mississippi River and made a pact. We pledged to be friends forever."

"And we sealed it with blood." Viper said the words with Andre, even catching the Cajun tones. He glanced at me and muttered under his breath. "Heard that crap most of my life."

Andre described his friendship with Jimmy as they grew into teenagers and then young men. "Nearly thirty years ago, we came to California to make our fortunes in the music business. Now that you've heard our music, you know why we didn't succeed. But we found we had other talents."

Viper leaned over. "Andre's only talent was marrying the boss's daughter."

Viper folded his arms and shook his head as Andre described his own rise from a gofer to an executive at the recording company. "But Jimmy was a technical wizard. He came to work here, at the Church of the Risen Son. When I took over the recording company, I stole Jimmy from Reverend Anderson, and he helped make the company the success it is today."

Viper's eyes narrowed. "Never heard him say that before."

"From his position behind the control panel, Jimmy could make a mediocre singer great. And he pioneered the music video. He became a master at special effects. Jimmy could put Elvis in the Eiffel Tower without leaving the studio."

Viper listened quietly and nodded. Krystal inventoried the floral arrangements while Ryan watched his father. I glanced over my shoulder and caught Ann staring at the sun glowing through the thirty-foot tall stained glass windows.

"Speaking to you now is the hardest thing I've ever done." Andre folded the papers and slipped them in his inner coat pocket. "I hope Jimmy knows exactly how I feel about him. How we all feel about him."

When Andre finished, the cross suspended over the altar rose and the walnut walls in front of the sanctuary parted, revealing a large movie screen. Although the pew and my posterior were padded, sitting quietly for so long made me fidget. I nudged Viper. "What now?"

"Dad's video. He made it after his heart attack. He said I was in it."

Andre resumed his place between Krystal and me as the lights dimmed. He straightened his tie as he glanced around looking for praise.

A photo of a chubby, freckled face boy about two- or three-years old filled the screen and soothing, New Age music enveloped us. Viper motioned at the screen. "That's Dad."

The series of still pictures that followed showed Jimmy growing older. Viper smiled as he pointed out the relatives in his father's video trip through the family album. When Jimmy was about seven, a second boy, slightly taller and thinner joined him. Andre grimaced and pressed his hand to his chest. Viper whispered in my ear, "And that's Andre."

I poked Andre with an elbow. "You were a cute kid."

"Yes, but I prefer to keep my childhood to myself."

Andre and Jimmy did everything together but Andre was always the one holding the trophy, or the bigger fish, or the prettier girl. I would have hated him in high school.

Then came the rock band and an 8mm camera. The early home movies showed them practicing in the garage. Viper watched in awe. "I can't believe the work Dad put into this. I saw all that old film. It was all but disintegrated, but look how perfect it is now."

I nodded. Jimmy was a technical genius. Except for the clothes and hairstyles, the film could have been made yesterday. As the band evolved from the garage to school dances, Jimmy and Andre traded the crew cuts and penny loafers for long hair, beards, and bellbottoms.

"I can't believe Dad dressed like that." Viper shook his head.

Ryan leaned around us with mock mortification. "Oh, Dad, tie-dye. How could you?"

The congregation laughed as Jimmy and Andre mugged their way through a song. When young Andre half-closed his eyes and crooned sexily into the microphone, Ryan and Viper chuckled.

"Oh, God." The sartorially correct Andre moaned as he slumped in the pew. "Don't let it get worse than this."

Fortunately for Andre, when the band era ended he disappeared from Jimmy's life. Jimmy married and Viper was born. Viper teared as he watched his parents display him as an infant and play with him as a toddler.

"I haven't seen these tapes in years." He swallowed as he viewed the restored old home movies. He turned to me, his eyes brimming. "We look so happy. Do you think we were?"

"Of course, you were."

He broke down. At first, I froze. In my world, big girls and real men didn't cry, and I'd worked hard at being brave to make Dad proud. But Viper's grief broke through the barriers to my feminine side. I put my arm around him and glared at Ann. She'd cheated me out of hugs and tears and family photos.

"You don't know how lucky you are," I said in a low voice. "You had two parents who loved you and you'll always have the memories. I wish I had that."

Viper took my hand. Reverend Anderson descended the steps from the chancel with a box of tissues and we scooted over to make room for him between Viper and Ryan. The Reverend rested his arm on the pew and bent his head toward Viper's ear.

"Your father locked himself in our studio for weeks while he worked on this. He wanted you to have it. You can see all the love he put in it."

Viper took some tissues and composed himself. The music changed and scenes from a wedding replaced the movies from Viper's childhood. Viper tensed as he watched his father wearing a rumpled suit as he stood in front of the altar of the Church of the Risen Son with a young Destiny in a white peasant dress. A small, blond boy stood beside her. Reverend Anderson presided over the ceremony. A woman with waist length hair sang.

Reverend Anderson stared at himself in amazement. "My goodness, I can't believe that was twenty years ago."

I poked Viper. "Who's the kid?"

"Rip, Destiny's son. I don't know why Dad had to put her in this. She wouldn't even have me at the wedding."

"I chased all Dad's girlfriends away before things got this far."

"You?" Viper scoffed.

I crossed my heart, but I didn't feel particularly proud. "Fear's a great motivator."

Andre tugged at his collar as he watched his younger self stand by Jimmy's side during the ceremony. Jimmy still sported long hair, a beard, and sandals, but Andre looked sleek and successful in an off-the-rack suit. At the reception, as Jimmy danced cheek to cheek with his bride, Andre performed something between a dance and making out with the lovely young singer.

"Is that your wife?" I asked.

"No. That's a friend of Jimmy's."

Reverend Anderson leaned around Viper. "That's Tara Jean. She was a soloist with our choir. God rest her soul."

Viper reappeared as a scrawny nine-year-old, but he stood to the side in most scenes. Behind us, papers crackled and people whispered as the video dragged on. At Jimmy's wedding to Krystal, she looked radiant, but it was the multiple-body-pierced Viper in black leather, chains, makeup, tattoos, and purple-spiked hair that caught my eye.

I studied the real-life Viper beside me. In the funky silk suit, he seemed almost normal by comparison. "Guess you really wanted attention."

His shoulders sagged slightly. I squeezed his hand and confided, "I drove the nuns crazy at school. I had a reserved seat in Sister Mary Catherine's office."

Mercifully, the video ended with picture of Jimmy holding a young Viper and a voice-over by the late Jimmy O'Reilly. "You have the answer in your hands. Look, and you'll find it."

The lights came back up and the walnut walls slid shut over the movie screen. The congregation murmured in relief and settled in for the finale. Reverend Anderson resumed his position in front of the altar with his arms widespread.

"Jimmy was right. The answer is in our hands and in our hearts." He finished with a short sermon of God's love and redemption. I wiped my cheeks, but my heart felt peaceful rather than sad. As the service ended, the congregation rose as a lone bagpipe played "Amazing Grace." Men in dark suits carried the coffin outside.

When we left the sanctuary, Viper disappeared into the men's room. I lingered by the door, but I only heard water running. The ushers opened the heavy bronze doors at the entrance and sweet, cool air flowed into the narthex. Andre took a deep breath and exhaled. He grinned as he brushed a fleck of lint from Ryan's shoulder.

I took refuge behind a potted palm, thankful the service had ended, and watched as the mourners filed out of the sanctuary. Andre played host, pumping their hands and taking their ribbing about his performances, live and on tape, with a strained smile. Krystal accepted condolences with a limp hand and air kisses, except for those from the young Teutonic God-in-training. I wondered when squeezing a widow's butt became an acceptable expression of sympathy.

Viper came out of the restroom freshly scrubbed. Although his eyes were still red, his expression was calm and his manner dignified. He moved through the crowd accepting offers of sympathy with more grace than I thought he possessed. I slipped beside him to check the size of his pupils. They seemed normal but something was different.

Destiny's son, Rip, wearing a The Grateful Dead T-shirt pushed through the crowd. I braced myself for violence, but he offered Viper his hand. "Sorry about Mom. Jimmy was the best stepfather I had."

Viper nodded. Above his white robe, Reverend Anderson's hair glowed like a candle beckoning a weary traveler as he worked through the sea of black-clad mourners. When he reached Viper, he handed him a videotape in a brown plastic case. "Your father wanted you to have this."

Viper beamed and held the tape against his chest as he thanked Reverend Anderson. That's when I noticed what was different. The stud in his tongue was gone.

15

403809798274981798409197

"Hey, Viper, wake up."

Viper snarfled and settled deeper into the gray leather seat of the limo. I shook him.

"Come on. You're almost home."

He blinked and gazed around the interior of the car as if he had wakened on another planet. We had laid his father to rest in a private service at a cemetery far from the ocean. As the only person present who hadn't known Jimmy O'Reilly in life, I backed out from under the green canopy sheltering his grave from the heat of the mid-day sun while Reverend Anderson comforted the true mourners. I nearly tripped over a low granite marker. The name on the headstone caught my eye: Angel O'Reilly, infant daughter of James and Destiny O'Reilly, buried nineteen years earlier.

I hadn't heard about her before and wanted to ask Viper what had happened, but he was too exhausted and upset after the interment. He'd crawled into the cool, dark stretch limo and fallen asleep wedged in a corner of the back seat as we pulled out of the gates of the cemetery. He'd snored for the last twenty minutes. If we'd known each other better, I would've suggested nasal surgery, but he needed rest and I wanted time to think.

Most people thought actuaries had morbid jobs. While we dealt with death every day, it was a statistic, the result of the roll of some celestial dice we couldn't control but we could predict. Facing actual rather than conceptual mortality was an entirely different matter and I struggled with my emotions while Viper slept.

When the driver turned off the 405 to the 55, I'd found a calmer perspective and was ready to get back to work. I searched the limo and found a Coke in one compartment and ice in another. I poured a glass for Viper. Viper drained it and poured more.

"I know this is a bad time, but I really want to know about your father, Destiny, and that baby's grave next to your dad's."

His tone was flat. "They had a baby. It died."

"But how? What happened?"

He rubbed his face and yawned. "I don't know. I was just ten. I think there was something wrong with it when it was born. Dad blamed Destiny. Destiny blamed everyone else."

He sounded as if his baby sister was some possession that had been misplaced. He didn't even call her by name. "Losing a child is rough on everyone. I mean, Angel was your sister."

He shrugged. "I guess. I never really knew it. Dad drank a lot after that and Destiny was always stoned. And they fought. I just hid under the bed."

"What about Rip?"

"He hid with me. Dad kept him awhile after Destiny left, but she came back for him. He ended up in a foster home."

"Why?"

He smirked. "It's hard to pass yourself off as twenty-one when you've got an eight-year-old."

I poured a Diet Coke over ice to get rid of the bitter taste. "God, my folks just had one fight and that was the end."

"You're lucky."

While I'd never considered myself lucky before, in comparison to Viper and Rip, I'd won the lottery. Losing a child had to be the most painful experience possible for a parent, and I wondered if Destiny still blamed Jimmy enough for their daughter's death to spit on his corpse.

The limo crossed the bridge over Pacific Coast Highway and we were back on Balboa Peninsula. In a few minutes, we'd be at Viper's. I tried another question.

"What's going on with Krystal and her personal trainer?"

"The Body Nazi?" Viper's eyes must have hurt from rolling so far into his head. "She was screwing him at the house while Dad was having by-pass surgery."

"And he found out."

"I told him."

While Viper actively tried to make Krystal's life miserable, I gave Viper a high five for protecting his father. "You should know her lawyer's trying to overturn the will."

Viper muttered obscenities. The driver opened my door and the sunlight bounced off the pavement and glared inside. After the prolonged period of soothing darkness provided by the heavily tinted windows, my pupils constricted. I popped on my mirrored glasses before emerging from the limo and took a deep breath of the salty ocean air.

While the funeral had provided Viper some closure, he was still dragging a heavy burden as he walked to the house. I followed him up the steps.

"Want to go to the pier, grab some lunch?"

He shook his head. "I'm not hungry. Just want to crash."

"Are you going to be okay?"

"Sure." He squinted past my right ear out at the ocean. "Thanks for coming with me."

"No problem. You're not a bad guy."

He frowned and shrugged. "I know how to behave. It was Dad's funeral. Dad's friends. No point scaring them."

"No, there wasn't. And I'm sure he's proud of you, especially taking out that horrible thing in your tongue."

"Do you really think so?" He shifted his gaze from the horizon to his feet and finally my face. "Dad and I had a fight Friday. He threw me out, said I disappointed him. He died thinking I was a nothing."

He seemed so forlorn; I threw my arms around him and squeezed. It surprised both of us and I backed off. "He's with you now, you know. It's not too late to show him who you are."

"Maybe." He swallowed. "If I leave the stud out, would you come back later? I'd like that talk you promised."

Viper bonding with me? A few hours ago I wouldn't have thought such a thing could happen. I smiled. "Sure. We can swap dysfunctional family stories. I'll stop by when I get free." I hugged him again. "Call if you need anything. I'm in the book."

He went inside. I had no doubt that Viper could commit rape or murder, but it was easier for me to imagine killing an ex-husband than a father. Both Krystal and Destiny had a motive and a young male accomplice who matched the rapist's description, but after a morning surrounded by bitterness, grief, and greed, I felt drained. I needed a break to regain my strength and I drove home to recuperate.

An overflowing mailbox welcomed me. A catalogue ripped as I pulled out the bundle. I shuffled through it, bill, bill, junk, junk, bill. Maybe I should start playing the lottery. An express package leaned against my door, my new assignment. At least that was a positive. I added the package to my untidy burden and let myself in.

Useless and Puddles greeted me as if I'd been gone for weeks and not just a few hours. I nearly dropped everything as I fought my way to the office and dumped the mail on my desk. Puddles jumped on her chair while Useless laid down in the doorway where he could keep me company and watch for Jack.

I picked up a fax from the machine. It had a simple message: "I fucked up. Please call. Jack." He'd left a voice mail, too, sounding appropriately contrite, so I phoned him.

"I'm really sorry, darlin'. Are you coming back?"

His plaintive drawl made me want to dash to the hospital and into his arms but my emotions were too near the surface, it wasn't safe. Until I had my feelings under control, he could hurt me again. I sank in the chair and closed my eyes. "I told you I'd come after dinner."

"Can't you come before that? I miss you."

I stared at the mountain of work on my desk and the papers scattered across the carpet from my earlier book-tossing incident. Jack put his job first and I needed to do the same. "I've got a lot to do. I'll be there later."

I slipped off my shoes, picked up the papers from the floor, and reorganized my desk. Once my office achieved a state of semi-neat tranquility, I grabbed a yogurt and some crackers and studied the data from my client, but my mind wandered back to Viper and the funeral. For Viper's sake, I prayed my theology was correct and he could posthumously make peace with his father. From all the mortality statistics I collected, I knew that life was unpredictable. I needed to do some emotional housecleaning of my own before one of my parents or I got hit by a bus or shot, so I put on my headset and hit speed-dial on my phone.

Dad's deep voice boomed, "How's my favorite girl?"

I crumbled the crackers into flour and began with the easy stuff. "Jack got shot last night. I saw it happen. He was wearing his vest but he's in the hospital. They're worried about his spleen."

Dad quizzed me about the caliber, distance, and point of impact. My answers were pretty sketchy.

"Does he have blood in his urine?"

"I don't know," I whined.

"Well, you should. Now, listen to me, Elizabeth."

Normally, this was the point where I tuned out his lecture, but I got out a pencil and took notes. Dad knew his stuff. When he finished, I'd filled one page of a legal pad.

"I'm not surprised the doctor didn't tell you more but the department should've had someone there to explain everything."

"They had some counselor guy there, but I didn't feel like talking to him."

"Honey, you're experiencing major emotional stress, you need to talk to a professional."

I pulled off the headset and stared at it. My father with his upper lip cast in concrete was telling me to see a shrink. "I'm okay."

"I've seen this before. Did you sleep last night?" He waited. I could hear him shake his head. "I didn't think so. How's Jack dealing with it?"

I bit my lip. Even now I wanted Dad to think my life was perfect, including Jack, but Dad had thirty years experience on the force and I needed to talk to somebody. "He's blaming himself for letting the guy get away."

Someday, I wish Dad would sugarcoat things a little more but he believed in total honesty concerning everything except my mother. While it was normal for a cop to question his actions after a shooting, Dad couldn't guarantee how it would come out. When he told me I needed to see a counselor with Jack, I almost went straight to the hospital.

"Okay, I'll do it." I braced myself for the bomb. "There's just one more thing. Ann called. She lives out here."

His voice was unusually quiet. "I'm sorry. Give me her number and I'll make sure she doesn't bother you again."

"I'm thirty-two years old. I can take care of myself but I need to talk to you about her."

"No. I've told you before; I don't want to talk about her. She's trash."

"Does that make me trash, too?"

"Of course not, you're my daughter."

"But she's my mother. Did you ever love her, or was I just a mistake you got stuck with?"

"You weren't a mistake. I wouldn't let anyone take you away from me. Just drop it."

"But did you love her?"

"I had a good job. I was ready to start a family and I thought she was, too."

"Dad!" I screamed from frustration. "You're evading my question. I have to know. She was pregnant when you got married. Did you love her, or was I just the product of some urge you couldn't control."

I almost thought I'd lost the connection. All I heard was my heart thumping and my knuckles ached from clenching my fists. Finally, he answered softly. "I loved her."

I threw my head back and squeezed my eyes shut. "Thank you, Daddy. I didn't mean to hurt you. I know she did."

"Then leave her alone. She only called you because she wants something." He paused to let me deny it. "What is it, money? I've already paid her enough."

"It's not money." I slumped in the chair and explained about Willow and the murders.

"Oh, Elizabeth. That's it. I'm flying out there to take care of things for you. The *nerve* of that woman."

I sat up straight. "No. Don't do that."

"Honey, I've been through your causes before. We're talking murder. It's not like liberating the frogs from biology lab. She's using you and you're going to get hurt."

"Daddy. I don't want you here. I can handle it."

"No, you can't. She's confusing you. I'll run her through the computer and show you what kind of woman she is. I'll call when I've made the arrangements."

"But, Dad. I don't even have a place for you—" the line went dead. "To sleep. Shit!"

I hung up and considered bashing out my brains but I knew from experience that my skull was harder than drywall. While I dearly loved my father, I'd never convinced him that I was an adult. The weekly call home, the emails, and the annual pilgrimage to Detroit were all I could handle. On a good visit, he made me crazy telling me how to do things.

Useless lifted his head and stared as I paced. The thought of having my parents within ten miles of each other made my insides curl up. If they got together—oh God, I had to stop him. I hit redial. No answer. I left a message and ran out to warn Ann.

16

4038097982749817984091 97

Ann lived on a quiet residential street just below the foothills in North Tustin. Little, neat stucco boxes lined both sides of the road, most with brightly colored toys and trikes in the driveways. Her bungalow was the smallest on the block.

I almost drove past. I didn't owe her anything and if I called Dad back and promised not to get near her again, maybe he'd stay in Detroit.

I stopped the car. This was not the time to get wimpy. The only way to rid myself of all this anger was to tell Ann how I felt as calmly as I could and go on with my life. What Ann did with it was her problem.

A battered white Subaru station wagon filled with empty fast-food trash sat in the driveway. Although the lawn was mowed, the shrubs had grown into a jungle and the brown paint on the wood trim around the doors and windows cracked and curled. Dad could drive down any street and pick out the houses without men in residence. He'd spot this one a mile away.

I took a deep breath before I rang the bell and repeated, "I will be nice. I will be nice."

Ann came to the door. Her red-rimmed eyes made her irises a brilliant blue. She was still dressed in the navy suit she'd worn to the funeral. I wondered what she had been doing the last two hours to set off a crying jag.

"Elizabeth. What a wonderful surprise. Come in." She dabbed her nose with a tissue and stepped to the side.

There was barely space for us to stand in the living room, and with the shades drawn, the darkness made me claustrophobic. I bumped into an easy chair. Ann opened the drapes and picked up tissues from the gold shag carpet. The small room was crammed with knick-knacks and the coffee table was filled with teen magazines. Dad could never live like this. He considered a stray book clutter. Since I moved out, his house resembled a marine barrack.

"I'm sorry the place is such a mess. I went to see Willow after the funeral. We had a therapy session."

"How is she?"

"Not good. She simply doesn't understand the trouble she's in. She thinks she's going to walk out of rehab and marry Ryan. I just don't know how to get through to her." She hid the balled-up tissues in her fists. "Would you like some coffee?"

I followed her as far as the kitchen door and watched her make it. "I was surprised to see you at the funeral."

"My boss gave me the day off to deal with Willow." She dried her hands on a dishtowel and joined me. We exchanged smiles and I glanced around in the hope of finding something to discuss politely before I got to the hard stuff. The china cabinet was filled with odd little clay figures and other mysterious things. I motioned toward them.

"What are those?"

"Oh, those are things Willow made. Let me show you." She opened the cabinet and took out a piece of notebook paper with a second, multicolored strip bent in an arch taped to it. She held it in her palm like a treasure.

"It's a rainbow. Willow made it when she was three. She thought it would bring me good luck."

I murmured politely and Ann brought piece after piece from the Willow Forrester art collection: clay animals and people, pinch pots, coil pots, brightly decorated Easter eggs, Halloween masks, mosaic coasters, even painted rock paper weights. The more Ann talked, the more she glowed, and the more I hurt. I wanted her to stop babbling about the daughter she'd kept and pay attention to the one she'd abandoned.

"Do you like art?" Ann belatedly asked.

My voice sounded frosty. "I like to look at it. I don't have any artistic ability."

"Oh, but you have so many other gifts."

"Yeah, everything but a loving mother."

The moment the words tumbled from my mouth, I regretted them. Ann wilted. She looked sadder than when I came in.

"I'm sorry. I shouldn't have said that."

"It's okay." She shut the door of the china cabinet and backed away. "I understand why you hate me."

"I don't want to hate you. I just want to stop hurting and I don't know how."

Her eyes searched the house for an answer, but it was the aroma from the kitchen that caught our attention. "The coffee's ready. I have brownies."

She darted about the kitchen, opening and shutting cupboards as if I were timing her. My manners kicked in. "May I help?"

"Oh, no. You're my guest. Sit down."

I took a chair and sat with my best posture, just the way Dad had taught me. Ann hurried so quickly to serve me, her wan skin flushed. After she brought out the brownies and poured the coffee, she sat and watched me. I put the paper napkin on my lap and picked up the cup with my tea party etiquette. Since she'd provided forks, I felt obligated to eat the brownie with one. Moist, chewy, chocolaty, right-to-my-hips-good.

"Mmmm." I swallowed. "Delicious."

Ann beamed. "Thanks. It's a mix. I'm a terrible cook."

I took another bite and waited. This seemed so civilized and made her so happy, I almost hated to ask questions, but I did. "Why did you have me? They had birth control back then."

She blushed. "I didn't think I'd get pregnant the first time."

I rubbed my temple and considered my parents' sexual stupidity. My fact-gathering actuarial side had dozens of questions concerning the exact circumstances of my conception, but my prudent and prudish self took charge. I didn't want the intimate details of how and why my parents did it. At least they'd done it quickly and weren't doing it anymore.

"So, why'd you keep me? There were options."

"We wanted you."

"Did you love Dad?"

"Oh, yes." Ann's eyes got dreamy. "He was so handsome in his uniform. And smart."

Just knowing that was comforting. "Why'd you stop sending the birthday cards?"

"Calvin, Willow's father." Ann hesitated over every word. "He made me. He didn't want to share me with anyone."

"Even your daughter?"

"Especially a daughter by another man."

"But how did he stop you?"

Ann stared at her half-eaten brownie. "Calvin always got the mail from the post office. When your father sent back your fourteenth birthday card, Calvin found it. He went into a rage. He tore it up and then he hit me."

When she said those last three words, she pulled her head into her shoulders as if she were a turtle hiding in a shell. I leaned across the table. "And you let him?"

She shrank away and nodded. "I thought I deserved it."

"No one ever deserves a beating."

She flinched at the harshness of my voice. "I know that now. But my father used to take his belt to me and my mother. I thought that's what men did."

"That's so wrong. Dad never hit you, did he?"

"Of course not. But he's the only man that didn't." Ann wrapped her arms around her breasts. Her eyes were moist. "I'm sorry. I knew if I ever wrote you again, Calvin would kill me. But when he went to work the next day, I got your baby things out of the trash and hid them so he wouldn't find them."

She spoke so rapidly; I nearly got whiplash when that last statement whizzed through my head. "What baby things?"

"Your baby book and a photo album. I know I shouldn't have taken them, but I wanted something to remember you by. I slipped back into the house when your father wasn't there."

I sucked in my breath. "Do you still have them?"

She led me to her bedroom. Folded laundry filled the top of the dresser and pieces of lilac-colored fabric with tan tissue pattern pieces pinned to them covered the cedar chest. Ann dug a key out of the dresser drawer. She moved the pattern pieces from the chest to the bed and knelt. As she opened it, the fragrance of cedar filled the room.

From under a pile of sweaters, she fished out a large gray metal file box marked 'Receipts' and unlocked it. I dropped to my knees beside her. She handed it to me and I felt a chill. After thirty years of thinking Dad had thrown out everything associated with Ann except me, here it was. I was afraid to look, afraid of how I would feel.

"Aren't you going to open it?"

I wanted to take it home and go through alone, but she seemed so anxious to watch me, I pulled back the lid and took out a book. The pink embossed leatherette cover read 'Baby's Milestones.' I ran my fingers over the raised letters and the ribbon running under them.

"Look," she said, turning the book to the first page. She pointed to all the statistics surrounding my birth. "And here's a piece of your baby hair."

With the professional distance of an archaeologist, I studied the tiny lock of reddish brown hair tied with a pink thread and wrapped in waxed paper. This was a trick to make me think she really cared. "I've always been blonde."

"Not when you were born. And here's your baby bracelet from the hospital and your first picture. You must have been about an hour old."

I tilted my head and examined the old photograph. It didn't look me. The baby's eyes were swollen shut, her face was smushed and lopsided, and she had a cone-head. The punk Mohawk hairstyle only accentuated the point. How could anyone love something like this? Could I?

Ann radiated happiness. "You were so beautiful."

Were we talking about the same baby? "I look like I've been on the losing side of a fight."

She smiled. "Well, it took forceps. The doctor said you had the loudest cry of any newborn he ever heard. In fact, the nurses always brought you out first because you were the noisiest."

Her maternal pride seemed so genuine; I scrutinized the photo again. Motherhood must induce myopia. "But how long did I look like that?"

"Not long. In a couple of days, you just blossomed. See."

She turned the page and showed me a picture of Dad holding me in the hospital. My arms and legs were still scrawny but my head had a more normal shape. I recognized myself and the parental love and pride in Dad's expression. I blinked to keep from crying.

"And here we are taking you home."

I swallowed as I looked at the happy young couple and their baby. I could see bits of myself in both their faces. The tears came. We had been a family once. I hadn't just sprung to life at age two. And Dad hadn't thrown my baby pictures away to get everything that reminded him of Ann out of the house.

Ann put her arm around me. "I'm so sorry."

"No, don't." I pushed her away and struggled to reason through this and regain control. "This isn't fair. You can't use my things to make me like you. You should have stood up to Dad. You should have been there when I needed you."

"You were better off without me."

"That's bullshit. I wanted a mommy to tuck me in and fix my hair and take me to the mall and buy me the right clothes. Do you have any idea how awful it was to buy bras with Dad? And when I got my period! I wanted to die."

My voice veered off the scale of human sounds at the painful memories and I sobbed. Ann bent over with her face on her knees and her hands over her ears and cried.

"Stop it! I thought Dad threw out all this stuff because it reminded him of you and I thought he'd throw me out, too."

I wanted her to stand up and fight, but she didn't. She couldn't. Dad told her to run and she had. Calvin beat her and she cowered. She was terrified of me, but I could say all the hateful things I wanted and she'd sit there and listen. The choice was mine and I had to make the correct decision for both of us.

I found a box of tissue on the nightstand and dried my eyes, then sat beside her and rubbed her back. "Please stop," I said quietly. "I'm okay now. I'm not going to hurt you."

Her shoulders gradually ceased shaking. She sat up, but kept her head bowed. "I won't bother you anymore."

She wasn't the mother I wanted, but I believed enough of her had loved me once and she hadn't ruined my life. She couldn't. It was my life. I stroked her hair.

"No, that wouldn't be right."

Her head snapped up. She almost burst into tears again.

"I don't know what I want right now. Things are pretty confused. Let's just play it by ear. Okay?" I held out the baby book. "Will you show me some more?"

She dried her eyes and we shifted to more comfortable positions, almost shoulder to shoulder. She told me everything.

"And this is when I left." She bowed her head when we reached the pages documenting my second birthday. "I'm afraid there's not much else."

I didn't expect anything at all, but she'd filled out pages from kindergarten through my senior year with bits of information, report cards, school programs, clippings, and a few photos.

"Where'd you get all this?"

"One of the sisters at the parish school sent this to me."

I paged through the book. Ann kept better records of my school years than Dad did.

"Your father did a wonderful job raising you." Ann glowed just as she had when she talked about Willow. "I wish I could have been there for you and for me, but I would've taught you the wrong things. Just look at me. I screwed up my life and I'm afraid Willow's going to do the same."

I glanced down at the program from my high school graduation. Ann had highlighted my name and the word Valedictorian. My life would have been different if she'd been around. My hair and clothes might have had more style. And maybe I wouldn't have run out on all my boyfriends before they could run out on me. Or maybe I would have turned out mousy like Ann, or worse.

"May I take these things with me? I'll scan them into my computer and make copies."

"No, they're yours. Keep them."

She sat on her hands to stop herself from snatching the things away. "Then I'll make you a copy. But I want to take them to the hospital to show Jack."

"Oh, God!" Ann put her hand to her heart. "Jack's in the hospital? Whatt happened? Is he okay?"

"He got shot last night at the wake. Didn't you read the paper this morning?"

"I don't get the newspaper. I haven't even listened to the news since Willow disappeared Friday night. Was he hurt badly?"

"He was wearing his vest, but they're worried about his spleen, so they kept him in the hospital."

"That's awful. You must be worried sick." She squeezed my hand and I didn't pull away. At last, I was getting the sympathy I wanted and I basked in it.

"Yeah, well. He's going to be fine. But it was scary."

"You poor thing. That's so frightening. You know, your father got knifed once right after you were born."

"Oh, the scar on his arm." I smiled. "He got a commendation for that."

"Yes, he did. But he didn't even bother to tell me when it happened. He didn't want to worry me, but when he was two hours late and then I saw the squad car pull up in front of the house, I thought he was dead."

"They didn't make you see a counselor or anything?"

She looked at me blankly. "Why would they do that? I was just his wife. I knew it could happen when we got married."

I checked my Mickey Mouse watch. Jack and I needed to have a long talk, but I remembered the other question I'd come to ask.

"Why didn't you tell the police you knew Jimmy O'Reilly?"

Her face twisted in confusion. "Didn't I? I thought I had. I told them he's Ryan's uncle."

"Well, why didn't you tell Jack and me where he lived? If we had gotten there earlier, we might've prevented all this."

"Oh, God. I stopped there on my way to see you and no one answered. I didn't think anyone was home."

My shoulders sagged. "Did you tell the police that?"

"No. I was so upset I just didn't think."

"You've got to start thinking sometime."

She cowered. "I'll call the police."

"No. Call your lawyer first."

17

103809798274981798409197

Ann flinched when the interview room door opened and Hal Peters walked in. Her lawyer, Ms. Provost, and I had prepped her. All she had to do was make a simple statement, answer a few questions, and shut up.

I tagged along so I could put my hand over Ann's mouth just in case the interview didn't go well and to see Ms. Provost in action. She wasn't on the list of lawyers I'd given Ann. While she appeared appropriately professional with a charcoal tweed suit and matching hair, she made it clear that providing the police with suspects was not part of her job, nor was she open to suggestions about Willow's defense. I hoped Ann hadn't confused competence with an unpleasant disposition.

We shook hands and took our places in ergonomically incorrect chairs, Hal on one side of the table, Ms. Provost and I flanking Ann on the other. Ann squeezed her hands together in her lap. Ms. Provost had an impatient air as if she was already late for an important engagement, but Hal didn't seem rushed. He pulled his seat out about three feet and leaned back.

"Mrs. Forrester, you have something to tell me."

"I forgot to mention I went to Jimmy O'Reilly's house Saturday morning. I was looking for Willow. No one answered the door. I'm really sorry I didn't tell you earlier."

Ann delivered her statement with the right combination of nervousness and apology. Hal's eyes narrowed. "When was this?"

"About eight-fifty."

"And why didn't you tell me this earlier?"

"You didn't ask."

Hal leaned forward. "And you didn't think this was important enough to mention."

Ann shrank and stammered. "I-I was so upset. I'm sorry."

"Detective Peters." Ms. Provost touched Ann's arm, signaling her to be quiet. "You must recall my client was overwrought at the time. Her daughter was in a coma. Mrs. Forrester did her best to cooperate under the circumstances."

I joined in. "And it wasn't just Willow. My mother and I had a really bad fight that morning."

Steam came out of Hal's collar. "Mrs. Forrester, just how did you happen to remember this today?"

Ann glanced at me. "Well, Elizabeth and I were talking today and it just came up."

I nodded. "I figured it was important, so we called you."

"After you called her lawyer."

"Detective Peters." Ms. Provost oozed legal indignation. "Mrs. Forrester is always entitled to counsel. If you don't have any further questions..."

"Oh, believe me, I have questions." Hal pulled his chair closer to the table, resting his folded hands on the smooth artificial wood-grain top. "Mrs. Forrester, why did you go to Jimmy O'Reilly's house looking for you daughter?"

"I'd checked everywhere else. It was my last hope."

"Did you phone first?"

"No, I called Friday night, but he said she wasn't there."

Hal frowned. "Where did you call from?"

"The mall. I'd gone there looking for Willow."

Ms. Provost stood. "I need to confer with my client."

The air in the hallway flowed more freely than it had in the small interview room. Ms. Provost wagged a finger at her. "Mrs. Forrester, before there're any more surprises, I need to know what contact you've had with Jimmy O'Reilly lately."

Ann's face screwed in confusion and she looked at me for help. "Did I do something wrong? I didn't think who I called Friday night was important."

"It's okay." I patted her arm. "But this is a murder investigation and the police probably checked all of Jimmy O'Reilly's incoming and outgoing calls for the last few days. Did you talk to him any other time?"

"Just Valentine's Day. I grounded Willow but she sneaked out to see Ryan. I was so angry." She ducked her head. "I found them at Mr. O'Reilly's house. I threatened to call the police if he ever hid her again."

If Willow had disobeyed me like that, I would've dragged her out by the hair. But given Ann's fear of conflict, her threat probably didn't carry much weight.

Ms. Provost checked her watch and lectured Ann as if she was an eight-year-old instead of a middle-aged mother. Ann listened intently. She wasn't stupid or evasive, but prying information out of her took enormous patience. Maybe she didn't think she could possibly know anything important or maybe she'd learned that if she didn't volunteer information she was less likely to get in trouble. Whatever the case, it certainly clashed with Dad's hit-them-between-the-eyes communication style and learning to talk to her was going to take practice.

We went back to the interview room. Ann told Hal about the visit to the beach house on Valentine's Day. He quizzed Ann about the argument but he focused on her search for Willow.

"Did you make any stops on the way to O'Reilly's?" She apologized to me. "I bought a pack cigarettes."

"But you didn't make any calls then?"

She shook her head.

He asked her for the location of the convenience store. "I'll be in touch. You two can go, but Ms. Matthews," he pointed at me just in case there might be some other Ms. Matthews in the room, "needs to stay and answer some questions."

Ms. Provost looked down her nose. "I'll be in the lobby. If you feel you need legal advice, get me. Do you understand?"

As Dad used say, "If you can't say anything pleasant, keep your mouth shut." I nodded, readjusting my skirt and trying to remember if I'd done anything illegal recently. When the door closed, I capitulated.

"Okay, I give up. What did I do?"

"Well, for starters, you witnessed a shooting last night and you got in the middle of a brawl this morning."

I gave him an animated account of the fight before the funeral. I felt the rush of combat as I gave him every detail. But when I relived the nightmare of watching Jack get shot, I couldn't remember anything but seeing him go down.

I sat on the edge of my chair, anxious to get to the hospital, and made a quick pitch for investigating Krystal O'Reilly and her boyfriend and Destiny and her son. "They all have motives and the guys fit the rapist's description."

He shook his head. "Let me give you a bit of friendly advice. When a cop's working a case, and he keeps running into the same person wherever he goes, he gets suspicious, or pissed. You're turning up too many places. Cool it before you get hurt or screw up the investigation."

I took his subtle reprimand and hurried out. Ann and Ms. Provost were waiting in the lobby and I motioned them to follow. Outside, the late afternoon sunlight hit me straight in the eyes and I popped on my dark glasses. Ms. Provost must have been a nun before she went to law school because she gave me that familiar glare as she asked for an explanation.

I briefly recounted my conversation with Hal and we made arrangements to meet the next day. Ms. Provost reminded Ann not to talk to the police without calling her. She glanced at me. "Remember, your daughter isn't an attorney."

I just smiled. But it couldn't be that hard to pass the bar. As she drove off, I warned Ann about Dad.

Ann inched back. "I don't want to hurt you or your father. I'll call him and promise to leave you alone. Give Jack my best, if you don't mind."

She turned and I caught her sleeve. "No, Mom, I'll handle Dad. Focus on Willow. Call if you need me."

Her face warmed. "No, I need to talk to him."

She gave me a kiss and hurried away. I obeyed every traffic law in the police station parking lot, but once I got a few blocks away on the Coast Highway, my lead-lined shoes took over. I whipped my Corvette down PCH to Hoag Hospital and squealed to a stop in a parking spot made even smaller by a Lexus and a Suburban encroaching over the lines on either side. I grabbed the metal file box containing my baby things and hurried toward the hospital, high heels clicking furiously on the pavement.

His floor was quiet this late in the afternoon. Two nurses sat at their station going over paperwork. One ambulatory patient in a bathrobe crept down the hall with baby steps. As I neared Jack's door an important rule flashed into my mind: Never jump into water or relationships without knowing the temperature or depth. I nearly toppled forward in my high heels when I stopped. Our relationship had been surprisingly cool and shallow in the last twenty-four hours. I cautiously stuck my nose in the room.

"Hey, Lizzie. Come in." Jack motioned. Two off-duty cops stood as I entered. A stack of greeting cards tucked in brightly colored envelopes lay on the tray beside the bed. Three floral arrangements crowded the chest and their delightful spring scent masked the hospital odors. Jack introduced me to his friends and I hesitated.

"I didn't mean to interrupt anything."

His friends took the hint and left. I froze about five feet from the bed, holding the file case in front of me as if it would protect me from getting hurt again, and tried to examine Jack with the same detachment I'd used on the room. It didn't work. After a day without shaving, his heavy dark stubble made him look like a derelict and accented the circles under his eyes. But even worse, the spark that animated my Jack had disappeared. His eyes were dull and he seemed a little smaller.

I scrunched my emotions into a ball. "You look awful."

"I feel worse. I'm sorry. You must be pretty pissed."

"Not pissed. Hurt." I conserved every syllable.

He sank against the pillow. "Don't blame you. I know your job's important."

I bobbed my head once.

"Spent most of the day with that psychologist fellow. All I could talk about was you. He said you had more sense than I did and he didn't blame you for walking out. I got to worrying that you weren't coming back."

I shrugged. "Just busy."

He stared at his feet. "Still haven't called Mama. She's always after me to come to my senses and get a real job. She makes me crazy, that's why I shut her out." He paused. "According to that psychologist fellow, I did the same to Allison. That's why she packed her bags."

"I know."

He looked at me with a question on his face. He'd told me the story. Once. His wife moved out when he was on patrol. Period. But I filled in the blanks. "You work too hard. You've got too many compartments. And your pager is more important than I am. When it goes off, I'm history."

Jack threw off the covers and eased from the bed. He held the back of his hospital gown together with his right hand and cradled his ribs with his left. I met him halfway.

"I don't want that to happen to us." He ducked his head. "I acted really stupid. I'm sorry. You're not like Mama or Allison. I promise I'll do better."

I put the file box on the floor and helped him to perch on the edge of the bed. We sat with our shoulders touching, Jack clutching my hands in his. "I'm scared, Lizzie."

My voice cracked. "Me, too."

We threw our arms around each other and squeezed until we almost burst. Before we ruptured his spleen, we repositioned ourselves under the blanket and whispered our fears. We grew stronger comforting each other and clinging gave way to kissing.

Jack tangled his fingers in my hair. "Would you talk to that psychologist fellow with me? You really help me think."

God only knew what would happen if I opened my thoughts for public evaluation but I nodded. "Dad says I should. I talked to him today. He gave me a list of questions."

I wiggled out of bed and reached into my pocket. My fingers felt the computer disk and pepper spray along with the legal-sized paper. Damn, the disk would have to wait until later.

I fluffed the pillows and sat beside Jack, demurely crossing my legs at the ankles. Jack unfolded the yellow sheet and rested his head on my padded breasts. He had positive answers about his physical condition but he grumbled as he read Dad's comments on his mental health. "I don't like having your Daddy inside my head, but he's right. I shouldn't make any decisions here. I can't think in this goddamned dress." He put the paper down. "He must think I'm a real asshole."

"Not really, but you may get a chance to ask him that yourself. I told him about Mom and Willow and he says he's flying out here to chase her off."

"He going to chase me off, too?"

"Only if you run."

"I'm not running." He pulled himself to my lips for a kiss. "Anyway, it's time your Daddy and I talked."

I stroked the stubble on his jaw. "Well, Mom's supposed to call and stop him. I'm going to try later."

"Tell me about this 'mom' business. Never thought I'd hear you use that word."

"I went to see her. I want to show you what she gave me." I slipped out of bed again and retrieved the metal file box. Jack stuffed the pillow behind his back and sat up. I sat beside him, taking out my baby book with the same reverence I'd use for the Dead Sea Scrolls. I held my breath when I showed him my first picture.

"You surely were a pretty little thing."

I smiled. "But my face is smushed."

"All babies look smushed. But you're beautiful."

He oohed and aahed as I showed him everything at high speed, then he took the book. "Lizzie, I wish you could see yourself. It makes me feel better just looking at you."

"Excuse me, Jack?"

My head turned in the direction of the voice. A woman wearing a navy blue suit and carrying a brief case stood in the door. I tugged at the hem of my skirt as I evaluated her: short hair, perfect posture, cop. Jack introduced her as Detective Rivera. "She's taking over some of my caseload."

Detective Rivera gave me a firm handshake and the proper pleasantries, but I had the impression I was in the way.

"But you're only going to be off your feet a few days."

Jack shrugged, more fatigued than before. "We've got a rapist loose. We can't let the investigation slip."

Detective Rivera held out her briefcase. "I have some questions. I thought we might be able to go over them now."

I braced myself to get bounced, but Jack shook his head and slipped his fingers through mine. "No, Lizzie and I need some time together."

He'd put me ahead of his job. I glowed.

"I really need to go over this today."

Before I got a ticket from the time police for obstructing justice, I returned Jack's kindness. "Look, Honey, if I don't eat soon, I'm going to faint. I could come back in an hour."

He lowered his eyes. "You sure you don't mind?"

I pulled his chin around and gave him a deep kiss. "No. Thanks for putting me first. Can I get you anything?"

“A robe and a pair of pajamas.”

Detective Rivera laid her briefcase on the foot of the bed. As the locks snapped open an idea clicked into my brain. Hal wasn’t interested in my theories about the rapist and Detective Rivera would never listen to me, but I knew how to get some evidence that would change their minds.

18

403809798274981798409197

Twilight doesn't linger in Southern California. Once the sun hit the water, day fizzled into night. It was dark when I got to Carl's Jr. and bought a Western Bacon Cheeseburger. I ate it on the way to Jack's place. I groped for the keyhole and let myself in, flicking the switch by the door.

The living room lamp illuminated enough of the hall to get me to his bedroom. I hit the lights. A vulture's mask stared me in the face and I screamed.

"Jesus." I put my hand over my heart as if that would slow its beating. Jack had taped a copy of the rapist's mask to the mirror over his dresser. No doubt about it, this guy pissed Jack off big time. My photo had only earned a coveted position on Jack's dresser next to pictures of his parents and Useless's mama. Except for his weapon and other police paraphernalia, Jack never brought work into his bedroom.

I gathered Jack's things and drove to Nicola's. She wore jeans, a rust-colored sweater, and a big smile when she opened the door of her apartment.

"Liz. Come in. I'm glad you're here."

Nicola locked the dead bolts. Law books and books about rape covered the coffee table along with printouts from the Internet. As she forced the sheets of yellow legal paper strewn across the sofa into a stack, she motioned me to sit.

"How's Jack?"

"Better. I think he'll come home tomorrow."

She settled on the couch. "Good. I was worried when Detective Rivera called this afternoon and told me she was taking over the case."

"He'll just be off his feet a few days. They don't want to let the investigation get cold."

"I guess I understand that. But he'll be back, won't he?"

She ran her fingertips lightly over the scabs on her chin. The abrasions and scratches on her face and neck were healing and the visible bruises had faded to yellow-green, but I didn't want to burden her with Jack's internal turmoil.

"I don't know. How are you doing?"

"Better. I only took one shower today and I went to work. But I came home early. I couldn't concentrate after Detective Rivera phoned. I left a message on your machine."

"I'm sorry. I've been out. What can I do?"

"Nothing really. It's difficult to put into words, but changing detectives is like starting over." She shook back her thick, red hair. "It's so frustrating. I don't know how to explain it, but I'd rather wait and have Jack handle it."

"I think Jack would, too." I paused to wrestle with my conscience. It was a quick, but painful victory. "You know I'm good with secrets. There's something you should know, but if you tell Jack, he'll kill me. There's this lawyer-client thing. Could I retain you?"

Her back went straight. "Liz, don't insult me."

I raised my hands. "I think the guy who shot him and killed that attorney last night is the same man who raped you."

Her fair skin lost more color. "Why?"

I told her about the laugh and the boo. She closed her eyes. Me and my bright ideas. "I'm sorry. I shouldn't have mentioned it."

"No. I'm glad you did. But why would he do that?"

"I think Jimmy O'Reilly knew who the rapist was and he told his lawyer. I mean, the odds of having two unconnected murders in Newport Beach roughly fifty feet apart in two-and-a-half days must be a million to one."

"I agree it's strange, but legally speaking, statistics aren't worth much with juries. If the attorney knew the rapist's identity she wouldn't have withheld that information after her client was murdered."

"I know." I rubbed my forehead to get my brain going. "But sex offenders don't do armed robberies. There must have been something in her briefcase he wanted. The attorney called Jack and told him Jimmy O'Reilly left something important for the police. She was going to give it to him at the wake." I leaned forward. "I want to find out what was in the briefcase. That attorney must have a partner or an assistant who would know. I figured that since you're an attorney, you might have more luck making the initial contact than I would."

"The police will look into it."

"But they aren't going to tell me anything."

Nicola pressed her fist to her lips. "Please, Liz, you can't find this man yourself. It's too dangerous. He's evil."

Growing up Catholic, I'd heard a lot about evil, but Nicola had seen it and I respected her enough so that her words sobered my enthusiasm. "I'm not doing anything silly, just a little research. We've got to catch him before he hurts anybody else."

She lowered her eyes. God, what was I thinking? We were strangers. I stood up. "I'm sorry. I shouldn't have asked. Just don't tell Jack or Detective Rivera about this, please. I've got to get back to the hospital."

"Oh, Liz, sit down." She folded her arms. "You're too impulsive and I don't want you to get hurt on my account. I'll check it out provided you promise you'll tell Jack and you won't do anything foolish."

I raised my right hand. "I promise. Do you think you could find out about Jimmy O'Reilly's will and prenuptial agreement, too?"

The pillow came hard and fast. Thank goodness it was soft. Nicola chided me for being incorrigible and pumped out more information. After additional promises to be careful, I hurried home to the dogs and let them pull me around the block, then I called Jack. "Is she gone?"

"She just left, but I'm mighty bushed. Would you mind if I shut my eyes for a couple of minutes?"

"No problem. You're in the hospital to rest. I'll give you an hour. I've got your clothes, do you need anything else?"

"If you could smuggle in a burger and some fries, I'd be eternally in your debt," he drawled. "You wouldn't believe what they try to pass off as food around here. Ought to be illegal."

He was feeling better. I agreed and checked my messages. They could hold until morning, but I had one more outstanding obligation, and I drove the half-mile down to Jimmy O'Reilly's beach house.

Every light blazed inside the place. Viper answered the door. His jeans and sweatshirt had earned their rips and frays honestly. At least he was sober and relatively polite. He stepped aside to let me in. Although the red wine stains remained on the carpet, it had been vacuumed, and the pictures and lampshades had been straightened.

"Wow, the place looks a lot better."

"I cleaned it."

He walked back toward the family room and plopped on the leather sofa, putting his bare feet on the coffee table. He aimed the remote at the television. "I was watching the video Dad made for the funeral."

Lucky me. Despite Viper's violent temper and my promise to Nicola, I didn't view him as a safety risk. I needed to learn more about Jimmy O'Reilly if I wanted to find his murderer and the only risk I faced tonight was getting bored to death.

The tape played his toddler years on the big-screen TV. I sat on the other end of the leather sofa and listened as Viper described the scenes. When the tape reached his father's second wedding, he pushed fast-forward and the wedding party moved around the screen in a manic procession.

"Oh, slow it down and tell me about it. Did Destiny always hate you?"

Viper frowned and clicked the remote. The wedding party danced at normal speed. The bride and groom seemed glued together. Andre slowly gyrated with the beautiful singer. Her long brown hair almost hid his hand on her butt.

"The only thing she was interested in was her fucking singing career. She made it clear I was a pain in the ass. If anything happened, she went after me with a hairbrush."

"And your father didn't do anything?"

"He worked."

The home movies progressed to the ultra-punk teenaged Viper in leather and chains. "I guess when your father's in the music business you have to go to extremes to get attention. I lived with the hemline police. Say, maybe you should've tried drag." He shuddered. "Or told him you were going to be a priest."

He almost grinned. The video ended with Jimmy O'Reilly's voice-over: "The answer is in your hands." Viper hit rewind.

"What do you suppose he meant by that?"

"I don't know. Probably his religion thing. Ever since his heart attack, he's been into that junk, saving his soul."

"But if your father was this born-again Christian, why did he hide my sister from my mother Friday night?"

"He did it for that asshole Ryan. He was always doing things for him."

"Why?"

"I don't know." Viper shrugged. "Sometimes I think he felt sorry for Ryan for having Andre for a father. Sometimes I think he just wanted to piss off Andre."

"But he had this whole blood brother thing going with Andre, why would he want to make him mad?"

"Andre treats us like white trash. He hated the Uncle Jimmy crap and he shits when I call him Uncle Andre. It's the only reason I do it."

"Then why does Andre let Ryan hang out here?"

"It keeps his house clean."

Viper pressed play again. When the tape ended, he pointed the remote and rewound it. It would be quicker to get out my old Ouija board and ask Jimmy O'Reilly what his mysterious message meant, but I was afraid Viper would take a suggestion like that seriously. I slid across the leather couch and took the remote from his hands.

"Talk to me, please. Tell me what's bothering you."

"This is all my fault." My breath caught short of my lungs as Viper's face contorted. Oh God, don't let him confess to me. He choked out the words. "If I hadn't had that fight with Dad, I would've been here Saturday morning and he'd still be alive."

I blew the air out and tried to keep Viper from crying. "No, you can't blame yourself." It didn't work. His grief made me squirm and I shook him. "Come on, look at me. Who ever killed your father wanted him dead. If you'd been here Saturday morning, he would've waited for another time. Unless you knew someone wanted to murder him and you stuck by him every moment, there wasn't anything you could've done."

He rubbed his face and squinted. "Maybe you're right."

"Of course, I'm right." My panic calmed as Viper regained emotional control. "Your father knew the person who killed him. He let him in the house and stood right there," I pointed at the dark stain in the grout, "and looked him in the eye."

He stared at the spot. "If Dad let the murderer in, how did he get Dad's gun? He keeps it upstairs by his bed."

I slumped against the sofa. Willow was in Jimmy's bed Saturday morning, the reasonable solution was to have Willow bring the gun down and blow him away to keep him from calling Ann. But I didn't want that answer and I compiled a list of people Jimmy might let go upstairs in his house unattended: Ann to drag Willow out or Viper or Krystal to retrieve something.

"Did Rip ever come over here?"

"Yeah, I got this band. He plays bass. He was over the other day, we were writing songs. But he wouldn't kill Dad."

I shrugged. Telling Viper about my rapist theory didn't seem like a wise move. "I think your father's murder is connected to the shooting last night. Whoever killed your father's attorney knew she was coming. Who knew?"

"Whoever was in the will. He wanted to make a production out of it."

The doorbell rang. Viper got up grumbling. "Ryan, what do you want?"

Ryan? I scrambled up and peeked into the living room. A young girl with maroon hair stood beside Ryan. He had his arm around her shoulder and his hand inside her tank top fondling her perky little teenaged breast. Big sister got pissed.

"Hi, Ryan." I flew to the door and struck my Valkyrie Bitch Goddess pose. "Who's your little friend?"

Ryan's hand popped into the air. Someone needed to tell the girl makeup should never be applied with a trowel but since her pupils were the size of dimes she probably wouldn't understand. I smiled and spoke slowly. "I'm Willow's sister."

Ryan backed up. "Oh, Liz. Magenta's just keeping me company. I thought she'd like to see Uncle Jimmy's house."

Viper pushed Ryan out. "You're welcome to visit, but call first and leave the chick-lettes home." He closed the door and walked past me to the family room. "I need a beer." The rubber seal on the mini refrigerator behind the walnut bar glupped as he opened it. "Want something?"

"Ryan's balls. Was Willow that stoned when she came here?"

"She didn't need to be. She's a carpet when she's sober."

Viper's insight didn't comfort me but Ann had balked when I suggested statutory rape because she didn't want to cause any trouble. I'd have to think of some other form of revenge as soon as I got Willow out of the murder mess. I glanced around the room and my gaze fell on the telephone.

"Could I look at your caller ID?"

Only one call had come in Saturday morning, a local exchange at eight-ten when Jimmy was out walking. Viper cleared his throat. "Excuse me, but what the fuck are you doing?"

"The police are trying to figure out who called Saturday morning. Recognize it?" I showed him the phone number.

"No, but there's one way to find out." He picked up the receiver and punched the buttons. "Hello, is Scorpio there? Oh. I'm sorry. He left this number. Where are you?" He scrawled the name and address of a convenience store on Newport Boulevard not far from the beach house. He hung up. "That didn't seem useful."

"I don't suppose there was a message on the machine?"

"The police still have it."

I scrolled back to Friday. "What about these calls?"

"The first is Andre's number. The other one is Krystal's."

I rubbed my chin. "Does Krystal have a key?"

19

4038097982749817984091 97

Detective work takes a lot of time. Viper confirmed that Jimmy hadn't changed the locks after Krystal moved out, but no one answered the door at the Widow O'Reilly's house, just three blocks away. I checked Mickey; the hour I'd promised Jack was up, no wonder he was always chronically late. I headed for the hospital, making a slight detour to drive through Jack-in-the-Box.

While I waited in line, I phoned Dad. Ann had called him and unleashed a torrent of emotion. Even with the phone on the passenger seat, I could hear him and the tension made me nauseous. When he slowed down I picked up the phone. "Dad, I love you. It's not a contest. Please don't make me choose."

I managed to make the five-minute trip to the hospital without crashing. From the way Jack wolfed down the food, he was feeling better. A nurse offered to give him a sponge bath, like I was going to let that happen. I took the bath-in-a-bag from her and did it myself, nice and slow. Since Jack didn't like the idea of me holding a razor to his throat, he shaved himself, but I helped him slip into his baby-blue pajamas. And when we made out in the bed, I stopped worrying so much about his health. Even getting shrunk by the cop psychologist wasn't too bad, and then the night shift of visitors arrived. At nine-thirty, when my stomach complained and the stories got blue, I kissed Jack and went out for my own celebration.

Arguing with a lawyer takes energy, but I'd studied debate with a master. If I could persuade Dad to let me go to the all-night post-prom party when I was seventeen, I could coax Nicola into changing from jeans to nice slacks to go out for dessert so we could plot revenge on Ryan.

We paused under the forest-green awning that covered the sidewalk from the parking lot to the door of the Crescent City Cafe. The cool February sea breeze ran up my short skirt and I was anxious to go in, but Nicola stared at the entrance as if it housed a chamber of horrors.

"I can't do it."

"Nicola, I dragged you up a sand dune. I'm tired and hungry and you're going in that restaurant one way or another."

"But it's ten o'clock."

"And I haven't had a curfew in years." I slipped my arm in hers. "Come on. We're wild, powerful women and I want to party. Anyway, the valet's taken my car."

While Nicola let me guide her in, each of her steps seemed to require a conscious decision to go forward instead of fleeing. Once inside, she stopped to absorb the warmth and the delightful smell of food mixed with fresh flowers. I nudged her forward. The maitre d' tucked two menus under his arm. "Ms. Matthews, how nice to see you again. This way, please."

Nicola's eyes widened at his personalized greeting. Even I was impressed and I strutted in with my most regal bearing. Nicola ducked her head and squeezed herself together as she threaded her way through the candle-lit dining room to avoid touching anyone.

Jack's phone call for reservations netted us a prized harbor-view table. I took the chair with my back to the window to spare Nicola from facing any curious looks from other patrons. The waiter swooped by with water and took our drink orders. Within minutes, we were enjoying Irish coffee while we studied the dessert menu.

I raised my glass. "Tell me the truth, wasn't it worth coming out for this?"

"Yes." Nicola returned my salute. "I've been dying to eat here, but I'm on the waiting list. You must be a regular."

A little envy crept in her voice that I seemed to be so familiar at a place noted for turning away movie stars and millionaires without reservations. I hid a smile behind my Irish coffee mug and tried to drink it without getting whipped cream on my nose. I failed, but, God, it was worth it.

"Not really." I casually brushed my napkin across my nose. "Travis Tourville is one of Jack's best friends. Now, the only rules here are that we enjoy ourselves and you don't make me look like a pig by only ordering fresh berries. All I've had today is a yogurt and a Western Bacon Cheeseburger."

We celebrated indecisiveness and ordered three chocolate desserts to share and another round of Irish coffee. Although I thought Nicola was rather contained and repressed with her proper Boston upbringing, when she flagged down the waiter to order a third drink, I revised my opinion.

"How are you ladies doing this evening?" Travis Tourville leaned over and gave me a bristly peck on the cheek. His chef's whites smelled of the holy trinity of New Orleans cuisine.

"Everything is perfect. Thank you. Won't you join us?"

Travis pulled up a chair and I introduced him to Nicola. When he took her hand, she stiffened but she didn't pull away.

"So, how's that ol' rascal?"

"He's complaining so much they'll probably throw him out tomorrow. I'll have to keep him for awhile."

The waiter placed a gold-trimmed coffee mug and a plate of chocolate truffles in front of Travis. Travis offered one to Nicola first. "Well, you tell that son of a gun he's lucky to have a pretty lady like you to nurse him back to health."

"I'll remind him." For a moment, I considered declining the chocolate confection but it had my name on it. At least, it looked like an 'L'. As soon as I touched it, the fat raced through my arm down to my thighs and I resigned myself to another six-mile run. "But how are you doing after last night?"

"It shook me up." He stroked his bushy mustache and stared. "That poor woman. And Jack getting hit. I'll never forget it. From now on, I plan to stay in my own kitchen and leave murders to the police."

Nicola leaned forward. "You really saw the man."

"Just a glimpse. I thought it was prank at first, the way he laughed."

She nodded. I jumped in to avoid any troubling reminders. "You know, this is Nicola's first time here."

"Oh, really? I hope you'll be back to dine with us soon."

"And I have reservations in three months."

He handed her a card. "Call this number and give the man your name. It should shorten your wait."

She cradled the card and thanked him. He offered her a tour of the restaurant and I tagged along. Since she'd never visited New Orleans, Travis showed her everything with a full description of the Crescent City and Mardi Gras. She flinched slightly at some of the purple, gold, and green masks and necklaces as she made the connection to the man who had raped her. Her questions sounded like cross-examination as she tried to get all the facts on Krewes. Travis enjoyed the intelligent and appreciative audience.

When we got to the entry, he proudly pointed to a photo. "And here's a picture of us when Daddy was king of his Krewe. That little fellow's me and those are my sisters Teresa and Tara. Tara was his queen."

My eyes felt like tennis balls when I saw his older sister with her waist length brown hair. "Tara Jean the singer?"

"Yes. Did Jack tell you about her?"

"No. She was in the video they showed at Jimmy's funeral."

His jaw fell. "What? Why? He didn't know her."

"She sang at Jimmy's second wedding. They were both working for Reverend Anderson at the time."

Travis shook his head and I touched his arm. "Reverend Anderson said she died. I'm very sorry."

Travis exploded with pain and fury. "It was his fucking fault. She was murdered in his church." He shook off the emotions and put on his man face. "I'm sorry, ladies."

Nicola gasped. "My God. Murdered! How awful. What happened? Who killed her?"

"The police never solved it. That son-of-a-bitch Anderson has them in his pocket. He's kept it quiet for twenty years." He struggled to maintain his composure. "The hardest journey I ever made was to take her body back to New Orleans."

"Oh God, I had no idea. I didn't mean to bring up anything to hurt you." I looked from him to the picture. Jimmy O'Reilly said the answer was in our hands, but had Viper and I been asking the wrong question?

"Travis, you really need to see this video. Can you be at the hospital in twenty minutes? I want Jack to see it, too."

He glanced at the grandfather clock. It was nearly eleven. Then he studied the dining room. Two-thirds of the tables were empty, and most of the remaining guests were having dessert. The maitre d' standing behind the podium sorting receipts gave a single nod that everything was under control.

By the time we collected our things, the valet had my Corvette waiting under the green awning. We slipped in, but before we left, I got out my cell phone and called information. Jimmy O'Reilly's number was unlisted; I had to go to his beach house first. I pressed down the clutch and threw the car into gear.

"Liz, what's going on?"

I gave her the condensed version of the funeral and Jimmy's mysterious message at the end of the video while I hugged the speed limit. This was not the night for a ticket. "A twenty-year-old unsolved murder can't be another coincidence. I want to show Jack the tape. Here." I handed her my cell phone. "Call the hospital." I recited the number.

When she finished punching it in, I took the phone and told Jack to get Hal there. I turned off the phone and tossed it in my purse. "This might get late. I'll drop you at home."

Once she was safely locked in her apartment, I drove to Viper's and parked illegally next to the house. The place was dark except for the glow of the doorbell button. I pressed it, praying Viper was home and sober. In my anxiousness, I pressed it again. A light came on.

Viper opened the door wearing nothing but boxers. I recoiled at the sight of the underfed, overly tattooed, nearly naked man, but I was thankful he wasn't drunk.

"Viper, get dressed. I think I know what the message on the tape means. We have to take it to the hospital."

He yawned and his breath carried the scent of beer. "Liz, what the fuck are you talking about?"

"The woman who sang at your father's second wedding was Travis Tourville's sister. She was murdered twenty years ago. It's never been solved. Now get dressed."

Viper dragged up the steps cursing. I wanted to get behind and push, but in a matter of minutes, he slapped down the stairs wearing flip-flops and the frayed jeans and sweatshirt he'd worn earlier and carrying a small combination TV/VCR.

"I got this for Dad when he had his bypass."

He grabbed the videotape and followed me to the hospital. Travis met us in the waiting room. He'd changed from his whites to a blue sweater and slacks. I led the way toward the elevators, but hospital security intercepted us. The man explained that visiting hours had ended long ago. By now, my tolerance for explanations had dropped below zero, but Hal came up and flashed his badge. A few moments later, we were in Jack's room.

Jack sat up in his bed reading. He'd gained color and dimension since I'd left. Simply getting him out of that 'goddamned dress' with its ventilated backside and into blue cotton pajamas made him appear healthier. The doctor would have to hog-tie Jack to keep him in the hospital much longer.

The floor nurse regarded us like a gang of hoodlums and spoke in a low voice. "I don't care if this is police business. If you wake any patients, I'll throw all of you out."

She closed the door behind her. Hal took up his position beside it. I moved the flowers and cards from the chest and squeezed them on the nightstand. Viper set up the portable television and slipped in the tape. Travis fidgeted by the set.

"Where's the part with Tara?"

"It's later." I sat on the bed. "Jack should see all of it."

Jack made an annoyed face. "But, Lizzie, what am I supposed to be seeing?"

I shushed him as the music began. When the tape reached Jimmy's and Andre's singing career days, Jack frowned. "This had better be good."

I shushed him again. A lovely soprano replaced Jimmy's and Andre's voices as Jimmy and Destiny exchanged vows.

Travis stopped pacing. "That's Tara."

Travis stood transfixed by her image. His eyes glistened, but when the dancing began, his expression changed to surprise. "What the hell is she doing with Andre?"

When the wedding scene ended, Travis pressed rewind. The wedding party danced frantically backwards to the beginning of the scene. Jack eased out of bed and put his arm around his friend's shoulder.

I pressed fast forward after the wedding until I reached Jimmy's cryptic message. Jack and Travis sat on the bed. Travis shook his head, dazed. "I don't get it. What's this all about?"

Jack ran his fingers through his cop cut. "That's a good question, Lizzie. What is this about?"

It seemed so obvious; I didn't know how to explain. "Well, the only women on the video are Jimmy's wives and Tara Tourville. And besides Jimmy, she's the only one who's dead. And then there's the message at the end."

The room got so quiet; I could hear the nurses whispering down the hall. Jack held my hand. "Lizzie, you've been under a lot of stress the last few days."

Heat crept up my face. "I'm not crazy."

Hal spoke from his post at the door. "Everything you said is perfectly true but it doesn't mean a damn thing, unless you think this is some sort of confession."

Viper's cheeks flamed and he took a step toward Hal. "My father didn't fucking kill anyone."

Before Viper got himself arrested I jumped in front of him. "Viper, no, I don't think it's a confession. Just stay cool."

"Then what the fuck is it? If you're setting up Dad—"

"I'm not." I glanced at the set and the heat crept up to my scalp. Had I just performed the ultimate actuarial joke, providing totally correct and perfectly logical information that was absolutely meaningless? I faced Jack and Travis. "Maybe Jimmy knew who did it."

Jack exhaled. "Why didn't he come forward before now?"

"I don't know." I raised my hands and whined. Even I had to admit my argument was weak. "But don't you think it's odd that Tara pops up in the video Jimmy O'Reilly made for his funeral twenty years after she's murdered? And isn't it a weird coincidence that Jimmy financed her brother's restaurant?"

Jack frowned at me and turned to his friend sitting beside him. "Okay, Trav, how did you meet Jimmy?"

"It was about six years ago, not long after I moved to California. I was working in Beverly Hills and I got the write-up in the *Times*. Jimmy came in the restaurant late one night and asked for me. He said my food reminded him of home." Travis stroked his mustache. "He wanted to know why I didn't have a restaurant of my own and I told him money. So he asked how much it would take. I gave him a number and he said okay."

"See?" I said. "That doesn't happen every day."

"Liz, hush!" Jack shot me a look that pushed me back a step. "I'll admit that's peculiar. So you went into business with him, Trav?"

"Not right away. I checked to make certain he was legitimate. Had an attorney and an accountant look over everything and I met with him and Andre several times."

Despite my efforts, my mouth wouldn't stay shut. "And Jimmy never told you that he worked with Tara?"

"Liz! Let me handle this!" Jack's voice grew sharp.

Travis raised his hand. "It's okay. I don't mind." He glanced at me. "Jimmy never mentioned Tara and I don't remember her talking about him. Maybe he didn't make the connection. She changed her name to Taylor when she came out here."

Jack put his hand on Travis's shoulder. "What happened?"

"She was practicing in the sanctuary. Someone bashed in her skull.

No witnesses, they said."

"You want me to look into it? I can't guarantee anything."

Travis nodded. "Even if it doesn't help us find the son-of-a-bitch that killed my sister, I got to hear her sing." He got up and stood by Viper. "Could you make me a copy of the tape, Viper? It's important to me. Come by the restaurant sometime and I'll fix you up something special."

"Lizzie." Jack patted the spot on the bed beside him that Travis had just vacated. I sat with my arms folded. "I know you mean well, but I'm beat. Why don't you go home? I want to talk to Travis and Hal before I turn in."

I glanced around. Everyone, except for maybe Travis, thought I was out of my mind. I'd show them. Viper picked up the TV and shuffled down the hall. I hurried after him.

"I'm sorry, Viper. I'll talk to Reverend Anderson, see what he has to say."

He sneered. "What good will that do if there weren't any witnesses? Unless the walls there have ears, what would he know?"

I sucked in my breath. Reverend Anderson had built the Church of the Risen Son for theatrical performances. He could stage an earthquake in the sanctuary or make a thunderstorm. He could make a person disappear. And he taped everything.

"Yes!" I gestured with my fist. "That's it. The walls there have ears and your father made them work. He was the sound engineer. Viper, you've got a job to do tomorrow."

20

4038097982749817984091 97

Detective work was going to kill me. At least I'd remembered to set up the coffee maker last night and put it on auto-start. I crawled out of bed Wednesday morning and stumbled down the hall to the kitchen with my eyes closed, following the scent of caffeine. One eye opened enough to enable me to pour a cup without scalding myself.

Jack thought I'd lost my mind and so did everyone else. That was depressing. I'd had the same trouble in math class. I could just see the answers, but the stupid teachers made me show all the work. Jack was so cranial-rectally inverted; I couldn't bring up the subject again until I had every piece in its place.

My eye opened a little more and I shuffled to the study to warm up my computer. The disk containing Jimmy O'Reilly's electronic check register sat on the mouse pad. I'd been too tired to look at it last night, but I had to do it before I brought Jack home from the hospital and he had a hissy fit about it.

I double-clicked on the financial planner icon and slipped in the disk. When the file opened, my eyes did, too. The man brought home money in a truck and never left home without his credit cards. Krystal received a nice sum, but not nearly as much as she could spend as Mrs. O'Reilly. I scrolled back and stared at the screen. Destiny got as much as Krystal. No wonder Jimmy had a prenuptial this time. I did a search on Viper and wished I could've been on the family payroll, too.

I closed the file and hid the disk in with mine before I called Jack. He moaned about having to pee in another cup then wait until eleven for his doctor. Since he didn't apologize for doubting my reasoning, I promised to arrive at eleven-fifteen.

Viper grunted intelligibly when I called to remind him we were going to see Reverend Anderson at nine o'clock. I didn't quite catch all he said, but I think he agreed. Useless came into the study and glared at me. The sun had risen and he had to go out.

With my doggy audience watching impatiently, I threw on bike shorts and a sweatshirt, then took them around the block, spending most of the trip untangling leashes as Puddles insisted on taking a random walk. We had to do obedience school soon.

When we got back to my apartment, Useless stopped at the foot of the stairs. Apparently, a morning person's dog needed his morning exercise more than I needed another cup of coffee. I put Puddles inside and headed for the beach with Useless.

While I loved watching the sun set into the Pacific, nothing compared to a California morning at the beach. The sweet scent of perfect air, the sound of the ocean rushing on the shore, and the sight of sea gulls and pelicans diving for fish was almost enough to get me up earlier.

The view on the sidewalk was pretty good, too, although none of the guys running really compared to Jack and I wondered how long it would take him to recover. Jimmy O'Reilly's neighbor and walking companion sat on her patio drinking coffee and reading the morning paper, like many of the other lucky people with beach front property, except for Viper. I'd have to ring the bell on my way home to make certain he was awake.

Useless trotted easily at my side as if I was just creeping along, the rude dog. As we passed Krystal's place, my blood finally circulated up to my brain. The poor widow probably needed a little consoling. I could stop on my return trip.

Half an hour later, I walked across the patio to her door. While Krystal's beach house had a spectacular view of the ocean, anyone walking by had an equally good view inside. I glimpsed her through the window and rang the bell. She answered carrying a barking dust mop in her arm. Useless sat motionless by my feet, uninterested in any creature smaller than a mouthful.

My smile mirrored the sun and my mirrored sunglasses hid my

eyes as I scanned her. Her sports bra and tiny stretch shorts didn't hide the large bruises on her shoulders and upper arms the way her dresses had.

"Hi. I was just out running and I thought I'd stop by and see how you were doing. Maybe you'd like to go out for coffee."

"I'm fine, thank you, but I'm busy."

"Then tomorrow. Losing a husband is so hard."

Georg, her Germanic boyfriend came to the door wearing a lot of muscles and a Speedo. Although he strutted about displaying his physique, I thought he looked silly without body hair. A low growl rumbled in Useless's throat as Georg glared. "Who is this?"

"One of Viper's friends."

He pushed in front of Krystal. "We don't want you here."

"I'm just trying to be neighborly."

He took one step too close. The Rottweiler snarled, barring his teeth. Georg jumped back. "Get that animal out of here before I call the police."

"I will, but my boyfriend's a cop and his dog's a good judge of character." I tugged the leash. "Come on, Useless."

It took a couple of minutes for Useless and I to get our hackles down. Maybe Krystal had a kickboxing accident, but her muscle-bound boyfriend needed to be neutered. We stopped at Viper's to make certain he was awake. He answered the door in his boxers, but I was getting used to sight of that skinny, mostly naked and tattooed body. Viper knelt in front of Useless, stroking the Rottie's glossy black coat.

"What a cool dog."

"Yeah, he is, but we have to be at the church in less than an hour."

Viper grumbled but went inside to dress. I waved at his neighbor and the dog and I dashed home. I set a new record for showering and putting on my make-up. The early morning exercise and wonderful spring weather inspired me to escape the aura of death that had filled the last few days. I chose a beige linen suit for my meeting with Reverend Anderson instead of my usual more formal and powerful dark ones. Even my panty hose cooperated. I double-checked to make certain the report was in my brief case before I raced to the Church of the Risen Son. Viper was waiting and we slipped into the studio where Reverend Anderson taped his daily inspirational television show.

Viper followed the morning-fresh aroma to its source and bonded with the silver coffee urn. At least he was dressed in unripped jeans and a short-sleeved shirt with a real collar. Socks would've given his ensemble a more professional look, but I wasn't complaining. I fixed myself a cup of coffee, too, and settled into a chair in the area reserved for guests.

Reverend Anderson wore his normal television blue shirt and suit combination. He sat behind his desk in one corner of the set between takes while the makeup woman in a pink smock smoothed his silver hair. In the other corner, a young woman with a heart-shaped face stood in front of a stained glass window flanked by cascades of flowers. She wore a simple, yellow dress. As she warmed up, running through scales with a sweet, silky voice, Viper stood beside the control panel and watched the sound engineer tweak levers and knobs.

The makeup lady buzzed across the set and ran a large, fluffy brush across the singer's nose and cheeks to douse the shine. The young woman closed her eyes and giggled.

This scene had been repeated five days a week for nearly three decades. Twenty years ago, Tara Tourville would've been the ingénue standing in that spot hoping to warble her way into a recording contract. Jimmy O'Reilly would've been behind the console. Since I couldn't turn back the clock, I had to make do with a second hand feel for the world Tara lived and died in.

The director quieted the set. When Reverend Anderson's segment ended, the young woman with the heart-shaped face sang a pop-gospel song. Reverend Anderson closed his eyes and nodded along, his expression serene. He ended the broadcast with a homily and a blessing. The electrician killed the lights and the studio cooled off.

"Viper, Elizabeth." Reverend Anderson smiled and extended his hand. "How nice of you to come. How can I help you?"

Viper let me talk. "I was hoping we could have a few minutes of your time before our meeting. We've been trying to figure out what Jimmy meant by the message at the end of the video. We thought it might have something to do with Tara Jean Tourville."

He knitted his brows and tilted his head. "Tourville? I thought Tara Jean's last name was Taylor."

"I guess she changed it. She's Travis Tourville's sister."

"The chef? I had no idea. What do you want to know?"

"What happened? How did she get killed in the church?"

He took off his gold-rimmed glasses and rubbed the bridge of his nose. "I wish I knew. It was a terrible thing. In the early days, I used to leave the sanctuary open so our members could come pray whenever they felt the need. Tara liked to practice her solo on Saturday nights. Sometimes I'd come down to run through my sermon and have a little chat with God and I'd find her here. She worked so hard."

He polished his lenses with his handkerchief. "I came down about midnight that night. It had been a troubling day at the deathbed of a young mother and I needed solace and guidance. I found Tara's body by the altar. She'd fallen and hit her head." He put on his glasses and exhaled. Even after twenty years, it still bothered him. "I don't know what happened. The chalice and candlesticks were missing. They certainly weren't worth a human life. I locked the church after that."

"And no one else was in the building that night?"

"To the best of my knowledge, no. The police conducted a very thorough investigation. I'd be happy to help, but I don't know that we can unearth any new evidence."

"Well, can you at least tell us how she was practicing her solo alone? Didn't she need someone to accompany her?"

"It's probably easier to show you. Come along."

He led us down a short corridor and through a hidden door by the pulpit. The sunlight filtered through the stained glass windows and cast a warm, peaceful glow over the sanctuary. We followed him up the steps to the choir loft. At the podium where the conductor directed the choir, Reverend Anderson pointed out the sound system. Viper investigated the set-up.

"Every week, the music director gives the soloist a cassette tape of the song for practicing. The formal rehearsal is Thursday night, but for informal practices, the soloist can play the tape here."

"Where does she stand to sing?"

"That depends on the piece and the service. She usually stands over there." He pointed to a raised platform to the right of the conductor's podium.

"But she was killed by the altar?"

He nodded. I stepped up on the soloist's platform and gazed at the cavernous auditorium with its ranks of antique-rose-cushioned pews. Even empty, it was an awesome sight but when it was filled with two thousand people with their eyes focused up here, plus the television audience, it had to be a rush.

"Where are the cameras?"

He pointed to cameras mounted on either side of the balcony and a third up in the center back balcony in front of a dark glass booth. "The cameras and all the other electronic equipment are operated from the control room up there."

I tried to imagine the warmth of the spotlight on my face and the cameras sending my image into thousands of homes. For a young woman like Tara, searching for stardom, it must have seemed like the answer to her prayers. If God had given me the voice of an angel rather than a brain like a calculator, I might've tried it myself.

"Travis said Tara was hoping to get a recording contract."

Reverend Anderson nodded. "Most of them want that. Tara had talent, but she was so sheltered. She didn't know a thing about the recording industry. Jimmy helped her."

"Then she and Jimmy O'Reilly were close?"

"Like brother and sister. Since they were both from Louisiana, I think they were drawn together. God rest their souls."

I glanced back at the electronic equipment at the podium. That alone was worth more than a pair of brass candlesticks and a goblet. It could be carried off with very little effort, and the video cameras in the balcony couldn't take that long to detach. A real pro wouldn't let a dead body stop him from snatching big-ticket items.

But then, a real pro wouldn't come into an occupied place. Even a novice would hesitate. The murderer would've seen Tara through the back windows in the sanctuary when he entered the church and Tara would've seen him from her perch in the choir loft. So why had he come in and why had she come down to meet him? Was she helping a stranger or greeting a friend?

"Did Jimmy work here a lot after hours?"

"Yes, the equipment was one of the attractions of the job. He was always making short movies of his own and experimenting with different techniques. The man was a genius."

"Where was he when she was murdered?"

"At home with his wife. He was stunned when he got the news. He quit not long afterwards."

We walked down the stairs from the choir loft and I paused by the massive altar. "Did Tara have many friends?"

"Everyone loved Tara. She was very sweet and generous."

"Was she happy?"

Reverend Anderson hesitated. "When she sang, she was in heaven. But I think she was homesick and the last few weeks of her life, she seemed distracted. I asked what was troubling her, but she wouldn't talk."

We left the sanctuary through the hidden door by the pulpit. "Do you have any tapes from when Tara Jean sang here?"

"In storage, yes. Why?"

"We think Travis would like a collection of her solos. Viper can make it."

"Oh, that's so thoughtful." The Reverend's face lit up. "If I'd known, I'd have done it years ago. Viper, you can use whatever you need. My staff is at your disposal. And I'll call on Travis Tourville later and talk to him."

"I wouldn't do that just now." I shook my head. "He blames you for Tara's death. He's so upset, he wouldn't hear anything you said."

Reverend Anderson stopped just outside the studio door and his expression grew somber. "The poor man. I understand, of course. He must've been devastated by his sister's murder. But maybe you'll find the clues you're looking for."

He winked and I checked my skin to see if it was as transparent as my motives obviously were.

21

40380979827498179840919 7

My business meeting with Reverend Anderson didn't take long. As soon as he blessed my numbers, I hurried out to my car. The closer my Corvette got to Hoag Hospital, the stronger the magnetic pull became, and the needle on the speedometer climbed. I landed in the parking lot just before eleven and practically flew into Jack's room.

He sat on the edge of the bed shuffling through a mass of papers and photographs strewn in front of him. Except for the jumble on the bed, the room had been straightened to military precision after last night's video presentation. Only one person I knew would take the time to perfectly align the flowers, phone, and green plastic water pitcher and cup. If Jack felt up to doing that this morning, he'd probably alphabetize everything in my apartment during the next few days of his convalescence.

When he heard me, he glanced up and smiled. He was showered, shaved, and dressed in nice, tight jeans and a blue knit sports shirt. His color had improved and his shoulders seemed broader. There was still a little pain around the edges, but my old Jack was almost back. I swooped down for a kiss. Jack tasted as good as he smelled. I sighed and went for seconds, hoping all his equipment was in proper working order. From the way he kissed back, it was.

"I was beginning to think you were going to stand me up," he drawled with his wonderful Alabama accent.

"But I'm twenty minutes early." I tapped my watch as I slipped onto the bed beside him. "And you knew I had a meeting. Ready to go home?"

"Almost. Want to show you something first."

He handed me a sheaf of eight-by-tens. The top one showed Tara Tourville sprawled on the floor by the altar; her eyes open but very dead. I stared at Jack. He never discussed cases with me or showed me police files. This behavioral aberration concerned me.

"Well?" He lifted his eyebrows. "You're the detective. Tell me what you see."

So this was some sort of test. I studied the photo. Tara wore a low cut evening dress, high heels, and makeup. "It looks like she was going on a date. Something special. Not just practicing her solo at the church alone."

"Keep going." He motioned me to continue through the photos. I stopped at a close up of her face. "Okay, now what?"

Any woman could recognize the source of the smeared mascara and tear tracks. "She was crying."

"You're on a roll, Actuary. Don't stop." The next few pictures showed the body from various angles, then came close-ups of the crease in the back of her head. "So, what happened?"

"I guess she either fell or was pushed and hit her head on the altar."

He nodded. "Good. Go on."

I continued through views of the wound until I came to the autopsy photos. Seeing Tara's naked body on a stainless steel table with the incision was enough to put me off food for a month. I covered the picture and laid the pile on the bed.

"What's wrong?" He cocked his head.

"That's what I was going to ask. Are you mad at me?"

"It's my new theory." He smiled pleasantly as if he were dealing with a lunatic. "If you want to be Nancy Drew, I'm not going to stand in your way. But you've got to do the whole thing, complete with autopsies." The smile vanished and he stared at me. "Murder's not a game or an actuarial exercise. Tara was a real person. People loved her."

I hung my head. "Look, about last night. You have to admit there's something strange going on with that tape with Tara and with Jimmy O'Reilly's message at the end."

"Yes, Ma'am, it's strange, but next time, just come to me. Don't go dragging innocent people along with you on one of your little excursions." He took my hand and entwined his fingers in mine. "Travis is my best friend. He loved Tara and he was real torn up about her death. I don't want him hurt again."

"I didn't mean to hurt him. He enjoyed hearing her sing."

Jack gave a half-hearted shrug. "But I still have to deal with this." He gestured at the papers and photos on his bed.

"I'm sorry. Does this mean you've reopened the case and you're going back to work?"

"Shit, I don't know what it means." An invisible weight pulled down his shoulders. "This is totally unofficial and has nothing to do with my career. I promised Travis I'd take a look." He picked up the photographs. "I knew Tara. I liked her. I really didn't want to see her like this, and I really didn't want to open up this case. If I can't find the son of a bitch who killed her, it's going to hurt Travis all over again."

"Guess there weren't any leads?"

He shook his head.

"But she was all dressed up like she was meeting someone."

"But we don't know who. She wasn't dating anyone at the time. Her old boyfriend had an alibi."

"Maybe he had one, but no woman goes to that much effort to get dressed up on a Saturday night to stand alone in a church and sing. There's a man behind this."

"Oh, there's a man involved, all right. She was three months pregnant."

"Damn." I exhaled. "Reverend Anderson didn't mention it."

"Liz, what the hell have you been up to?"

I extracted my size ten foot from my mouth. "Ah, well, Viper and I went to see him this morning. We thought Travis would like a tape of Tara's solos. Reverend Anderson said Viper could make it."

He buried his face in his hands. "Oh, fuck. Now you've got Viper in on this, too, going through the poor Reverend's tapes looking for clues."

"Reverend Anderson said it was okay."

"Does he know why you're doing it?"

"Yeah, he figured it out."

He jabbed a finger between my eyes and they crossed. "You've got to think before you do these things. I don't want Viper or you or anyone not connected to the department touching those tapes. What would happen if Viper found evidence that his father killed Tara?"

I tried to shrink. "I'm sorry."

He pulled the telephone on his lap. Three calls later, he hung up, and grinned through clenched teeth. "I've got an officer going down to the church to collect all the goddamned tapes. And if you don't stop interfering, I'm going to handcuff you to a chair and make you watch every single one, start to end, over and over. Is that clear?"

I nodded.

"Good. Now tell me what you told Reverend Anderson."

"It wasn't much. I just asked him what happened to Tara. He thinks it was a thief. He didn't mention she was pregnant."

"Good. I'm not sure Travis knows and I don't want to tell him. It's bad enough."

"Would her being pregnant be that awful?"

"Tara went to convent school. How would you have felt if you had to tell your daddy you were pregnant when you were twenty?"

I pulled my head between my shoulders. "I wouldn't have told him."

"And you've got twice the backbone Tara did. She must have been worried out of her mind."

"Reverend Anderson said she seemed distracted the last few weeks but she wouldn't talk about it."

"Not surprised. She was probably worried about her job."

"You don't really think he'd fire her over that?"

"Oh, Lizzie." He rolled his eyes. "Don't you ever watch his services? We're talking Christian Fundamentalists. Reverend Anderson's not a man to throw stones, but he's still mighty conservative. He'd hide her back in the choir. There wouldn't be a record career."

I studied the picture of Tara's body. Twenty years ago, good girls got married when they got pregnant. If Tara were anything like me, she'd arrange everything before she told her parents or Reverend Anderson.

I leaned my head against Jack's shoulder and thought aloud. "I'd guess she was going to tell the guy that night. And she got all dressed up to make it special. But it didn't turn out right. He probably refused to marry her and she started crying. They must have had a fight and he pushed her into the altar."

"Probably." Jack put his arm around me. "But why did she meet him at the church?"

"Neutral ground?" Jack shrugged and I went for the obvious answer. "Maybe the baby's father worked at the church. It'd be the natural place to meet."

"Uh-huh."

I twisted a strand of hair and considered the men she worked with at the church. "Reverend Anderson said he was with some dying woman."

"Yes, Ma'am. According to the file, he was right here at Hoag all night."

"There's the music director and the men in the choir."

"And Jimmy O'Reilly."

Posthumously condemning a man for murder based on a video he made for his funeral didn't sit right with me and I got up and fingered a floral arrangement. "Yeah, but they didn't accuse him before and Reverend Anderson said they were like brother and sister."

"But Jimmy O'Reilly put a lot of cash into Travis's restaurant. That much money could ease a shit-load of guilt."

I faced Jack. "What about Andre? He was on the tape a lot and he invested in the restaurant, too."

"Somehow, I can't imagine Andre feeling guilty about anything." Jack snorted at the thought. "But they never questioned him. Hal's talking to him this morning."

I walked over to the window and stared at the ocean and the washed-out blue sky. Jack got up and stood behind me. I sighed. "It's like I've got three or four jigsaw puzzles and the pieces are all mixed up."

Jack turned me around and pulled my chin toward him. "Darlin', I need you to raise your right hand and focus for a minute." I made a face but I raised my hand. "Promise me that you will not, under any circumstances, bother Travis about this anymore."

"I promise."

"Or mention anything I told you about Tara to anyone."

"I swear."

"And you will stay away from Viper." I lowered my hand and he snapped. "Liz! Viper's a crazy son-of-a-bitch. If we accuse his daddy of killing Tara Tourville because of something you brought up, God knows what he might do to you."

22

4038097982749817984O9197

Sometimes, Jack worries too much, but a nurse with a wheelchair interrupted my protest and I was more anxious to get him home than to continue the discussion. Jack gathered the photos and papers from the bed into a neat pile and laid them in his briefcase while I grabbed his other things. Although he moved slowly and kept his left arm close to his ribs, we cleared out of the room in two minutes. It took a little imagination to get him and his plants and flowers in my Vette, but we managed and I drove down to my place, taking each corner and each stop smoothly.

He winced as he walked up the steps to my apartment, but once I got him installed on the couch, I knew he was finally safe and my spirits brightened. While he relaxed, I whizzed around organizing everything and fixing him something to eat while I stuffed down some yogurt.

"How can we have so damn' many channels and nothing to watch?" Jack aimed the remote at the television and clicked it like an Uzi.

"I don't know, I don't watch daytime TV, but I think most stations have the news on at noon." I put a tray with a steaming bowl of canned chicken noodle soup and a plate of grilled cheese sandwiches on the coffee table in front of him. I don't make gourmet lunches either.

"Oh, Lizzie. That smells good." Jack, with a goose down pillow under his head, smiled up at me as he lounged on the couch in my living room, wrapped in a burgundy afghan. The curtains flapped gently as the ocean breeze flowed in through the open sliding glass doors. Useless and Puddles sat up and stared at the food.

Leaving him alone half an hour after he'd checked out of the hospital made me feel guilty, even though I'd assembled every conceivable item he might need during the afternoon. I squeezed beside him, pointing out each one. "Okay, you've got lunch, a pitcher of water, the remote, my cordless, your cell phone, your laptop, your files, and your brief case, all within reach. You think you can manage for a couple of hours while I'm gone? Maybe I should stay home. Ann can handle the meeting with her lawyer."

"Oh, darlin', I'll be fine. It's sure a whole lot better than that hospital and you'll just fret if you don't go. Hope you and your mama get along okay."

"We will. I'm trying to think of each nice thing she does as a bonus." I paused. "You didn't happen to talk to Hal about her? She's not a serious suspect, is she?"

"Don't know. I'm staying out of it. Just remember, you've manufactured enough problems for Hal. He's going to get real pissed if you come up with anything else."

"But she couldn't have made the phone call from the convenience store Saturday morning."

"Lizzie!" He wrapped his right hand around my throat and pretended to strangle me. At least, I think he was pretending as he rattled my neck.

I giggled and braced myself against the couch so I wouldn't fall on his bruised chest. "Okay, okay."

He released me and shook his head. "I don't know. Maybe you ought to stay home, take care of me. I feel mighty weak."

"Liar." I fluffed his pillow. "Remember, the doctor said bed rest. Now, you can let the answering machine screen my phone so you don't have to take messages. I'll call your cellular if I'm running late. Take care of yourself."

Jack gave me directions to the courthouse area of downtown Santa Ana. Although his instructions were accurate and precise, he insisted on using compass points when all I wanted to know was when to turn left or right. It was a Y-chromosome thing, the same one that inhibits men from asking directions because they can't follow them. By the third step, my mind went dead, so I nodded. As soon as I got to my car, I pulled out the *Thomas Guide* from under the seat and mapped out the route.

An ocean of red brake lights greeted me as the Newport Freeway crossed the 405. Welcome to Southern California where an accident or construction could make a ten-mile trip take an hour. I worked my way across five lanes of traffic and got off at MacArthur Boulevard.

The major surface roads in Orange County were broad, flat, and straight, built to handle hundreds of cars. The scenic route up Main Street took me past stucco strip malls and small businesses, separated by fast-food restaurants and gas stations. Palm trees or yucca plants occasionally broke the monotone color of the low buildings.

All the Spanish I knew came from driving down streets like this. By the time I reached downtown Santa Ana, my Spanish vocabulary had almost doubled. I found the lawyer's office a block down from the county courthouse and squeezed my Corvette into a tiny space.

The waiting room at Ms. Provost's law office was empty except for Ann, or rather, my mother. I still didn't know what to call her. The receptionist had disappeared, leaving behind a half a cup of stale coffee on her desk. Ann sat stiffly on the colorless sofa. She held her purse on her lap just in case someone might wander in to snatch it. She wore a sensible navy suit with a white blouse and appeared even more faded and shorter than yesterday, as if the pressure was wearing her down.

Ann's mouth opened, but she waited for me to speak first. I tossed back my hair and tried the mechanics of a mother-daughter relationship. "Hi, Mom."

She smiled and lifted herself slightly, as if she wanted to come greet me, but an invisible seat belt kept her on the sofa. "Elizabeth. It's so good of you to come."

I sat beside her. "No problem. Most people call me Liz."

Her face blossomed. "I think I could get used to that. How's Jack?"

"Better. He's at my place."

"Oh, how wonderful. You must be so relieved." She put her hand on mine, then withdrew it as if she expected me to slap it away. She ducked her head and her voice was tentative. "I know it's none of my business, but does he live with you?"

"No, Mother." My voice sounded like a whiny teenager's. "It's just while he's recuperating. I have enough problems with relationships thanks to you and Dad." Ann flinched and I reined in my tongue. "Look, it's okay. I'm trying to work out this thing with Jack, but trusting people is kind of scary. At least you haven't criticized me for sleeping with him the way Dad does."

She nodded. "I can imagine."

"How did your phone call go with him?"

"It went okay." She twisted the handle of her purse and sniffed. "I told him I'd leave you alone. Willow and I will move once we get this straightened out."

Why did I bring out tears in everyone when I couldn't stand to see people cry? I grabbed a box of tissues off the receptionist's desk and handed them to her. "Mom, you have to stop running away. At least he's not flying out here today. I'll talk to him again once he's had a chance to calm down. Has Detective Peters been in touch?"

"Yes. I'm meeting with him when I get off work. You don't think there's a problem, do you?"

"Of course not." I flicked a blonde hair from the skirt of my beige linen suit and tried to act as if daily interviews with the police in the middle of murder investigations were perfectly normal. "He's probably just clarifying things."

The door opened at twelve-thirty and Ms. Provost waved us into her office. Her humor hadn't improved overnight. I scanned her diplomas as I sat in the dark red leather chair, but refrained from asking for her transcript. She was Ann's lawyer and I was determined to let my mother run her own life.

Ms. Provost sat behind her mahogany desk with a folder and a legal pad in front of her. Her mood seemed as black as her suit. She started with: The Burden of Proof is on the Police lecture, the one she probably delivered to juries. While that was theoretically correct, once the police had a good suspect, they didn't waste much time looking for other ones. The murder weapon practically had Willow's name engraved on it.

When Ms. Provost got to the: I'm the Attorney and We'll do things My Way portion of the sermon, it took all my Catholic-school training to keep quiet; my frequent visits to Sister Mary Catherine's office had taught me the virtue of silence. I sat stone-faced, reminding myself Ann was paying for this, not me.

"Our immediate problem is the probation violations." Ms. Provost folded her hands and laid them on the desk. "We'll have to appear in front of the judge on Monday after Willow gets out of the hospital, and we drew a hard-liner. We're in a difficult situation. The evidence is irrefutable. It would help if Willow appeared contrite, but from what I can tell, that may be impossible. But perhaps you can persuade her to be cooperative. I spoke to her doctor and she's still refusing to participate in any therapy. Unless she makes some progress and shows some indication of wanting to change her life, I can't do anything."

"I'll talk to her as soon as I leave here."

"Good." Ms. Provost smiled gently at Ann. "And as for our meeting with Detective Peters, don't worry. Just answer his questions truthfully unless I tell you to be quiet."

I leaned forward. "When is this meeting?"

Ms. Provost gave me a sharp look. "We don't need you. Now, if you'll excuse me, I need to get to the court house by one."

I nearly bit my tongue in half. Sister Mary Catherine would have been proud of my restraint. But if that woman charged us for more than fifteen minutes, she was going to hear from me.

Ann stood, clutching her purse. "Well, maybe we should go and talk to Willow." She glanced at me and I nodded.

I followed Ann's Subaru wagon to the hospital. I hadn't seen Willow since she'd come out of the coma Sunday and she wasn't particularly grateful that I'd saved her life. To her, I was a threat, a nerd twice her age who was going to back up Ann in her quest to get Ryan out of Willow's life, as well as a rival for our mother's love and attention.

It took less than ten minutes to drive east on Fourth Street to the hospital near the 55 Freeway. Ann knew the magic words to get us through the locked doors of the psychiatric unit. An aide left us in a plain but cozy room, decorated for psychological counseling. It held a comfortable sofa and chair, a large recliner for the shrink, and several boxes of tissues. Ann was too nervous to sit, and although the two of us were alone, she spoke in a hushed voice as if she feared the room was bugged.

"I don't know what to do." She hung her head. "I just can't get through to her. I need your help."

Willow came in wearing jeans, a plain gray T-shirt, and a bad attitude. Ann rushed to embrace her, but Willow brushed her off. She sneered at me. "What's she doing here?"

The sting in her words stiffened my resolve. Ann tried to make peace. "She's your sister. I want you to get to know one another."

"Whatever." Willow's voice had the inflection of scratching on a blackboard, a tone cultivated to irritate adults. She turned her nose up and flopped across a chair. To make certain we understood her reluctance to see us, she folded her arms and stared at the ceiling, jiggling a foot impatiently, waiting for Ann to kowtow.

Ann wilted onto the couch and leaned forward to placate Willow, but I waved her off. The little brat's attitude was going to land her butt in jail. I folded my arms and stared at her. Willow squirmed and turned her head away, but she could still feel my eyes. Her foot jiggled frantically.

"Mom." Willow whined in a singsong tone. "She's looking at me."

"Wow, it really works. I'm going to like this sister thing." I sat beside Ann and smiled brightly. "Mom and I need to talk to you."

Willow gasped and sat up with a look of pure horror on her face. Her worst fears had come true; Ann and I had formed a team. I lounged beside Ann with my arm on the back of the sofa behind her. Ann smiled. "Sweetheart, I talked to your doctor and lawyer today. They said you weren't cooperating in therapy."

"This place sucks."

"I know how you feel, but you tried to kill yourself."

"And you're punishing me for it by making me stay here. If you really loved me, you'd see that I need to be with Ryan."

"Willow! You know the trouble he's been in. And look where's he gotten you."

Trouble? Before I could ask Ann to clarify, Willow burst out angrily. "You know that's all lies. I love him and we're getting married when he graduates."

"Time out!" I made a 'T' with my hands. "Delusional girl, you're only fourteen. You can't get married without your mother's permission and you're not going to get it."

Willow raged at me. "You stay out of this!"

I shook my head and beamed angelically. "Sorry, but Mom asked me to help."

Willow's jaw fell and she turned to Ann who nodded and tried to stay out of the line of fire. Willow threw her nose in the air so violently, I thought she'd get whiplash. She faced me. "Fine! But I'd rather die than live without Ryan. It'll be just like Romeo and Juliet and it'll be your fault, too."

Damn Shakespeare. Why did he have to fill silly little girls' heads with the notion that killing themselves over boys was the ultimate romantic gesture? I laughed. "Oh, Willow, if you think Ryan's going to want a little wife around while he's at college, you've been snorting some really bad stuff."

"Oh, you think you're so smart!" She screeched in my face.

The gloves came off. I stood and towered over her. "Don't take that tone with me. I know I'm smart and you want to know why? Because I can walk out of here any time I want, and you can't. You can't even make a phone call. And a June wedding's a moot point, because you're going to be spending the rest of your teen years with the California Youth Authority."

"You don't know anything."

"Want to make a bet? My boyfriend's a cop. The deal is done. They're just waiting for Mom's insurance money to run out before they lock you up."

Her eyes widened. "No, I'm not going anywhere! Mom!" She pleaded to Ann. "Tell her I'm not!"

Ann bowed her head. "It looks bad."

Willow wrapped her arms around herself. "You're both lying. Ryan won't let me go to jail. He promised."

I knelt on her eye-level. "Just what exactly did he promise? Did he know you were doing something that was going to land you in jail?" Willow pressed her lips together and twisted her head away from me. "Willow! You have to cooperate."

"Mom! Make her go away."

Ann stood beside me. "No. She's right."

Willow pulled her feet on the chair and hugged her knees. "She's lying. Ryan's going to get me out of this and when he does, I'll get pregnant, just like you did with her." She pointed at me. "Then you'll have to let us get married."

For the first time, Ann showed some backbone. "I'm not going to let you ruin an innocent baby's life like I did. If you get pregnant, we'll move and you'll give up the baby. It's what I should have done myself."

"Mother! You wouldn't!" Willow protested.

No Dad? The thought shook me. "Oh, shut up!" I snapped at Willow so fiercely, she pressed back against the chair. "No, Mom. Getting pregnant with me was a mistake. But leaving me with Dad was right. I'd rather have him raise me alone instead of a couple of happily married strangers."

"Really?" Her eyes glistened.

"Yes. He's a pain in the ass, but he's my dad and you're my mom."

"Oh, baby." My mother threw her arms around my neck and cried.

Willow ran out of the room, slamming the door.

23

403809798274981798409197

Willow strengthened her lack of competency case by throwing a screaming fit in the middle of the psychiatric unit. She hurled every epithet she knew at us when we caught up with her and her range of profanity impressed me. Mom crumbled and I pushed her behind me to protect her from the verbal attack and to keep her from groveling for forgiveness. The angry words of a hysterical teenager bounced off me. I felt badly for pushing Willow to the edge, but she had to face facts and she had to treat our mother with respect in my presence.

I stood up cool and firm. “Calm down. You’re acting like a baby. We can’t talk to you like this.”

Willow shrieked, “I never want to see you again!”

“I don’t care. We need to talk about what’s happening before you go to jail.”

“I told you. Ryan won’t let me go to jail. He promised.”

I grabbed her shoulders. “Willow, listen to me! Ryan can’t do a damn’ thing about a murder charge.”

A look of terror filled her face. She wrestled with me. “You’re lying! I didn’t kill anyone! Mom!”

Two staff members pulled Willow off and dragged her to her room for a time-out. I wanted to follow and finish our conversation, but

Willow's doctor rushed into the hall. She eyed me as if *my* sanity was in question. I smoothed my hair and brushed invisible lint from my suit to regain my composure and explained Willow's violent reaction when Mom hugged me. The doctor thought we should let Willow cool off and scheduled us for a family therapy session in the morning.

The family therapy idea didn't thrill me, but I had no choice. We weren't a family at this point and it would take years for that to evolve. Willow's future was the immediate issue. She was spoiled, willful, and wounded, but she wasn't as emotionally fragile or despondent as she wanted us to think. We had to make her realize the seriousness of her situation.

"Come on, Mom, let's go." I put my arm around my mother's shoulders and nudged her out of the ward. She dragged her feet and dabbed at her tears with a tissue.

We stopped outside the hospital entrance under the shade of the concrete canopy. She glanced back over her shoulder. "Do you think Willow's okay?"

"Oh, yeah, she loves you. But she's always had you to herself. She's afraid I'm going to come between you. And she knows I'm not going to put up with any of her bullshit or let her treat you like dirt when I'm around."

"You were such a help in there. But why are you defending me to her?"

"Because you're our mother and part of this family business is treating each other with respect. But you've got to help me and step up and do the mom-stuff."

She shredded the tissue. "I don't know if I can."

"You have to, for her sake. It's not going to be easy, but you didn't let her cross streets alone when she was a baby, did you?" For a moment, I worried I'd picked a bad example, but thank God she shook her head. "See, you did the parent-thing then. Willow's not emotionally mature enough to be given *carte blanche* to make all her decisions."

"You're right. I'll try. But what about us?"

I took a deep breath. I'd accepted the idea that my parents conceived me in love, even if it'd been irresponsible, and that they had no business being married. Their actions for the next thirty-two years would always bother me. But if my mother had put me up for adoption or divorced Dad the normal way and taken me with her, my life would've been entirely different. I didn't even want to think about it.

"Oh, Mom. We're grown women. We can make our own rules. We could go out and howl at the moon or sit home some night and make chocolate chip cookies and talk. We'll figure out what works best for us."

The smile she gave me proved I could find joy in being wanted and loved. She stuffed the shredded tissue in her pocket. "Were you ever so obsessed with a boy?"

"God, no." I shook my head. "Dad and I argued about boys that didn't meet his standards, and that was most of the boys I dated. But I've always had this rule about breaking up with guys before they break up with me."

Ann touched my hand. "I'm sorry, Sweetheart. That's my fault."

"Yeah, well. How about you?"

"I guess I was obsessed with your father. I knew my parents wouldn't approve because he was Catholic, but I had to be with him."

We stepped out from under the protection of the canopy into the early afternoon glare. The brightness made my eyes hurt and I put on my mirrored lenses. Ann slipped on her sunglasses, too, and we strolled toward our cars.

I leaned toward Ann. "You know, Mom, we need to talk to Willow about Ryan and this marriage thing. He's filling her head with all sorts of silly ideas. It wouldn't surprise me if he planted that Romeo and Juliet nonsense, too."

"But why would he do that?"

"I don't know." I thought about Ryan's reaction when I'd asked him why he thought Willow had swallowed a handful of sleeping pills. His prideful answer made me uneasy. "There's something in his twisted little male ego. He seems to get off on having a girl who would kill herself over him. It's sick."

"I've never liked that boy." She shook her head. "He's only in public school here because he was kicked out his fancy prep schools."

I stopped in the parking lot. "Why?"

"Forcing himself on girls."

It took a moment to translate Ann-speak and another moment to make my mouth work. "You mean he raped them?"

"No. He was dating these girls. He just went too far."

"Mother!" I threw my hands in the air. I couldn't believe her attitude. "No means no. Even on a date. Are you sure about this?"

"Yes." She rubbed her forearms and glanced around to see if anyone was listening. "I'd heard rumors about it, and when Ryan started dating Willow, I got worried. There's this private investigator that handles inspection reports for the insurance agency I work for. He's a nice man. His daughter goes to school with Willow." She smiled apologetically.

I wanted to pull out my hair. “Mom! Get to the point. Did you have him check out Ryan?”

“Yes. I tried to show it to Willow, but she wouldn’t listen and she told Ryan. His father called. He was really upset that I had a private investigator pry into Ryan’s life. He threatened to do the same to me.”

“The son-of-a-bitch! Do you still have the report?”

“Well, yes, but I promised Ryan’s father I wouldn’t show it to anyone. I mean, I never wanted to spread vicious rumors.”

“Oh, Mom, I’m not just anyone. I’m your daughter. Come on, I’m following you home.”

We got into our cars and took the 55 north one exit to Seventeenth Street. Mom drove the speed limit. Dad must have loved that quality in her, but life in the slow lane made me mental. By the time we got to her house a few minutes later, I had the shakes.

She went through box after box on the top shelf of her closet. I was practically running in place out of frustration. She handed me the report and I sat on her bed.

The first time sex got Ryan in trouble, he and three of his Beverly Hills prep school buddies had bought booze and a hooker to celebrate his sixteenth birthday. They got wild, left some bruises, and then tried to stiff her. She turned them in. Their rich daddies bailed them out and compensated the woman. The school suspended them.

A few months later, Ryan took a Beverly Hills Princess on a date. He treated her royally until after dinner and vodka straight from the bottle. Then he collected what he thought was due him in the back seat of his Beemer. The Princess protested and he hit her. Her father wanted it kept quiet and Ryan was packed off to the East Coast.

The next time, the girl’s father ran the local deli and the girl fought back. Ryan got physical. It made the papers and Ryan flew back to Orange County where Andre rewarded him with a new Mercedes convertible. It didn’t take long for rumors to get around the high school that Ryan was a big spender but he collected at the end of the evening. Girls who didn’t want to get laid knew better than to go out with him.

And then he found Willow, a stupid little girl who’d been raised by a passive mother and an abusive father. She probably thought she was something, landing the richest boy in school.

“You let Willow date this little pervert!”

“I tried to stop her.”

“Dad would’ve locked me in my room.”

“She says he’s different. He’s very sweet.”

"Oh, I'm sure he's real sweet." I swallowed the next words. Willow had learned that behavior from her mother, our mother, and I'd insulted Ann enough.

Mom read my mind. "It's my fault."

"We don't have time to assess blame. We've got to keep her away from him. May I take this report to make a copy?"

"No, don't. There'll be trouble if you show anyone."

"There's trouble now. Let me handle it. You'd better get back to work. Why don't you come over for dinner tonight? We usually eat about seven-thirty. You can get to know Jack and tell me about your talk with Detective Peters."

My mother smiled as if the Publishers Clearing House van had just pulled up. We walked outside. She hugged me and hurried off. I tossed the report in my car and I dug through my wallet until I found Andre's business card. I memorized the address and stuck the card in my pocket.

24

03809798274981798409197

Andre had a lot of explaining to do and I set a new land speed record on the 55 Freeway from Tustin to Newport Beach and his office. Thank goodness there weren't any cops around to record my feat or I'd never drive again.

The four-storied, mirrored glass building perched on a hillside overlooking Newport Bay shimmered in the sunlight. The futuristic atrium lobby filled with exotic plants and strange metallic objects that were most likely meant to be art made me feel as if I'd been beamed onto a mall in another galaxy. Even the inhabitants of the place looked like barely disguised aliens.

The receptionist sat behind a curved granite desk built to deflect hordes of music hopefuls. She wore a tight little silver-gray dress over her anorexic little body and the pissed-off sneer that super models use on the catwalk. If I starved myself to look like that, I'd be bitchy, too. The receptionist was dismissing a young woman who appeared to be living one of my recurrent nightmares and had found herself in a public place dressed in her nightgown.

The young woman pleaded, cajoled, and whimpered to gain admittance, or at least leave her demo tapes, but the receptionist only shook her head and threatened to call security. The wannabe pop tartlet stomped out as quickly as her four-inch platform shoes would allow.

I took my place in front of the receptionist with my most professional manner. "I'd like to see Andre Lefebvre."

The receptionist eyed my beige suit as if I'd just arrived from Planet Geek. "Do you have an appointment?"

"No. But I'm sure he'll see me."

"Sorry. No one sees Mr. Lefebvre without an appointment."

"Well, could you phone him and check?"

"It's not my job." She buffed her silver fingernails.

"Fine." I got out my cell phone and pulled Andre's card from my pocket. He'd claimed this was his personal line and he only gave it out to special people. This seemed like a good time to find out how special he considered me.

A woman answered and I went straight to the point. "This is Liz Matthews and I need to speak to Andre about his son, my sister, and their June wedding."

The receptionist stared. I smiled and counted in my head: one Mississippi, two Mississippi. Andre picked up at six Mississippi. "Liz, what's this about a wedding?"

"I just came from seeing Willow and she told me all about their plans. I think it's something we really should discuss in private, but I'm down in your lobby right now and the young woman guarding your entrance won't let me in without a hall pass. Could you talk to her?"

I handed the phone to the receptionist and almost meowed. She returned it with a clip-on badge and a suspicious frown that was destined to leave her with a V-shaped wrinkle between her finely plucked eyebrows.

Andre greeted me at the door of his penthouse executive suite in his Armani suit and his usual overabundant charm, taking both my hands. I turned my face just in time to catch his kiss on the cheek. "Ah, the lovely Liz." His secretary lingered as he played the gracious host. "Would you like something? Coffee? Wine? Soft drink?"

"Diet Coke."

He flashed two fingers at his secretary and closed the door. The average American family with one and four tenths children could live comfortably in Andre's spacious office. He had the normal executive amenities: a bar, private washroom, and a panoramic view of the Pacific, but it was the rich sound of absolute silence surrounding us that caught my attention and I drew in my breath. "Wow. It's like a concert hall."

"Better than that." Andre preened. He pressed a button and Vivaldi's *Four Seasons* surrounded us. He led me to an L-shaped couch big enough for an orgy. I took a chair.

Andre sat on the sofa, leaning back and crossing his legs in a pose of casual elegance and success. "I'm really sorry about the misunderstanding with the receptionist. We get dozens of people in every day trying to audition and if I saw every one of them, I'd never get any work done."

Given the décor of his office, I wondered if he did any work at all. Instead of a desk, he had a large glass table supported on the heads of marble caryatids. It had the requisite telephone and gold desk set, but the surface was bare. The coffee table in front of us had the latest issues of *Rolling Stone* and *Billboard* magazines, as well as two demo cassettes.

Like most actuaries, I decorated my office in computer printouts and my in-basket routinely overflowed with technical publications that I really intended to read someday. I considered clutter the badge of a brilliant, busy person.

"Now, what's this about a wedding?"

"I went to see Willow today and she told me that she and Ryan were planning to get married in June after he graduates."

"Kids. They get such strange romantic notions. But you agree they're much too young to get married."

"Yes, but I thought you should know that Willow threatened to get pregnant."

"Oh, my." Andre stroked his sculptured chin. "I'll warn Ryan but I can assure you he uses condoms."

"Good. From what I've just read, he's been more sexually active than most boys his age."

Andre leaned toward me. "Did your mother show you that private investigator's report?" I nodded and his knuckles turned white as he clenched his fists. "I told her if she showed it to anyone, she'd answer to my lawyer."

I returned his temper with interest. "I'm not just anybody. And as far as I can see, that report doesn't contain anything that isn't already common knowledge at school."

"But she had no right investigating my family. How would you like it if I looked through the skeletons in your family's closet and spread them out for the world to see."

Andre's tone left no doubt that he would investigate Ann. My gut reaction was to shriek, but I clamped my teeth together and gave him an icy smile.

"Oh, Andre, threats are so unbecoming for a man of your stature. I'm sure you don't want to start slinging mud in public. You never know what might land on your Armani." Andre's eyes narrowed as I folded my arms. "My mother only did it for Willow's sake. She knows boys like Ryan don't marry girls like Willow."

Andre tried to gasp. "Liz, I'm stunned an intelligent woman like you would worry about class distinctions."

"Don't give me that. You've been patronizing me since the moment we met and I'm tired of it. I'm not some dumb blonde. I can put two and two together and I don't like what I'm getting."

He appraised me. "And what are you getting?"

"To start with, I resent Ryan for even talking marriage to Willow. He's stringing my sister along and I want to know why."

"Ryan's young, he's in love, he isn't thinking about the future." He dismissed the idea with a wave of his hand.

I shook my head. "The young man in that report isn't capable of love."

"That's because the facts are twisted. Ryan loved those girls. He'd dated them before and they wanted to have sex. It was only afterwards that they had a change of heart."

Andre could give Tom Sawyer a lesson on whitewashing. It took an effort to keep my eyes from rotating one hundred and eighty degrees. "That excuse might work once, but not twice."

"That was my mistake. I paid the first girl's family to keep things quiet. I didn't want Ryan's reputation to suffer, but now," Andre shrugged wearily, "I'm afraid he'll be a target for greedy young women forever."

My poor feminist heart couldn't take any more. "Oh, give me a break."

A soft knock at the door interrupted us. Andre's secretary entered carrying a tray with two Diet Cokes in large wine glasses. As she served us, Andre tugged his cuffs and pulled his plastic façade in place, becoming the gracious host again. He handed me a glass and saluted me with his. "To an improved relationship between our families."

I didn't return his toast. "Why do you care about Willow?"

The ice tinkled as Andre idly swirled his glass as if it were a fine cabernet instead of a diet soft drink. "She's a nice girl and she's been a good influence on Ryan. Since he's been home and found her, he's turned his life around."

"But her life's gone down the toilet."

Andre put his hand on my knee. "If you'll just let Ryan talk to Willow, I'm sure he can use his influence with her."

I moved his hand. "The last time Ryan talked to Willow, she swallowed a handful of sleeping pills."

"But you can't blame him for that."

I shrugged. "He seems pretty damn' proud of it."

"I'm sure you misunderstood. He's been very upset. This suicide attempt only happened because Ann told Willow she couldn't see Ryan again."

"What do you suggest?"

"Let it run its course. If you'll let Ryan see her, I'll send him to his mother for a month and things will cool off."

"I don't think it matters. Willow has to appear before the judge Monday on the probation violations and he's a hard-liner. And then, barring a miracle, the police will probably charge her with murdering Jimmy O'Reilly."

Andre stood. "No. I won't allow that." He walked to his glass desk. "I'll call my attorney."

The thick cream-colored carpet caught my high heels and slowed me, but I got to the glass desk in time to put my hand on the button to disconnect the telephone. "Andre, no. It's nice of you to offer, but Ann has an attorney."

"Yes, but my lawyer has the right contacts. He can change judges. And he'll squash this murder nonsense. The police can't possibly have a case against her."

"Actually, they have a good one and Willow's not cooperating."

Andre took my hands. "You must let me help. Just talk to my lawyer and let Ryan talk to Willow."

Andre could teach the devil about temptation. He certainly knew which buttons to press with me. I jerked free. "We don't want to owe you anything."

"You won't owe me. Letting Ryan see Willow won't cost a thing. As for the attorney, money's not important." Before I could protest, he held up his palm. "If you feel you must repay me, all I'd like is the private investigator's report and your promise not to tell anyone about it."

God, he was good. I edged back. "Let me think about it."

"Wonderful. We can discuss it over dinner. I'll book a table at the Crescent City Café."

"I can't. Jack's staying with me."

"Really?" Andre frowned. "I know it's none of my business, but I can't believe you'd live with a man who doesn't trust you. Can you do cocktails after work, or do you have to ask permission?"

He sounded so snide, the words jumped from my mouth. "I don't need to ask anybody's permission."

"Good." The corners of his mouth curved up. "Then I'll meet you at five-thirty."

I wanted to wipe the smirk off his face. He never stopped manipulating people to his advantage but he wasn't going to trap me. "I can't make it today. But speaking of the Crescent City Café, how did you happen to invest in it?"

Andre raised his eyebrows. "Now isn't that a coincidence. Detective Peters asked me that very question this morning."

"Did he?" I gave my hair a blonde toss. "Well, there certainly have been a lot of coincidences lately, don't you think?" His brows sank into a continuous line. "What did you tell him?"

"The truth. Jimmy came to me with the idea. I had to agree that Travis was an excellent chef and Cajun cooking was becoming trendy. The investment is paying off."

"Did you know Travis's sister was the girl you danced with at Jimmy and Destiny's wedding? The one in the video."

"My goodness, Liz." He wagged his head and stepped so close his designer cologne almost overpowered me. "Did you figure that out yourself or did your boyfriend tell you that?"

My nose went up. " I recognized her photo last night at the restaurant. It's hanging in the entry."

"Really?" He paused and squinted over my shoulder as if he were trying to bring the picture from across town into focus. "I never noticed it, but then Travis has so many photographs. I didn't make the connection until this morning when Detective Peters brought it to my attention."

"So you think it's just another coincidence?"

"Hmmm." He folded his arms. "Now that I think about it, maybe not. Jimmy never mentioned that Tara Jean was Travis's sister, but he must have known. They were very close."

"You seemed pretty close to her at the wedding."

"I was only doing my duty as best man and entertaining the unattached women. I never saw her again."

"So, why do you think he included her in the video?"

"Well, I hate to speculate, particularly when it means speaking ill of the dead." Andre glanced about as if someone might be listening and leaned toward my ear. "Jimmy had a very personal interest in Tara

Jean. They worked together lots of nights."

"You mean you think they were having an affair?"

He lowered his voice. "I know they were. He told me."

"But he was a newlywed."

"Oh, Liz. You're so naïve, it's rather refreshing. Jimmy never let fidelity stand in the way of fun."

The thought of Jimmy O'Reilly and Tara Tourville as lovers made me uncomfortable, but why? I didn't know either of them. It certainly worked with my videotape theory: Jimmy had documented his wives and his lover. The next logical step was that he had fathered Tara's baby and it didn't take an actuary to jump from there to murder. His investment in Travis's restaurant could've been his way to repay Tara's family.

"But if you knew they were lovers, why didn't you go to the police after she was murdered?"

"Jimmy was my best friend. Why would I cause him trouble? I had no reason to believe he was involved in her death."

"You know, for a man who couldn't remember Tara's name on Monday, you certainly remember a lot now."

Andre seemed almost melancholy as he bowed his head. His New Orleans accent deepened. "Memory is a funny thing. Maybe when you're as old as I am, you'll understand. I've met so many young women who wanted to be singers in the last twenty years, I can't remember most of them. It was only after Detective Peters talked to me that it came back."

"Then Tara talked to you about a recording contract."

"Jimmy mentioned it and I listened to her as a favor. She had a lovely voice, but she didn't fit our needs."

I folded my arms and walked to the window. "But what kind of man kills a woman like that? How could he live with himself all these years and *then* go into business with her brother?"

"Who says it was a man?" I spun around. Andre swaggered toward me. "Mind you, I'm not saying Jimmy was a saint. He cheated at cards and on his wives, but you know what they say." He stopped and held up his hands. "*Cherchez la femme*."

I grabbed my purse. Andre's message was clichéd but true. It was time to meet Destiny.

25

4038097982749817984O9197

"Liz, that's fucking stupid." Viper's voice grated in my ear.

An awning of palm trees in the atrium lobby of Andre's building shielded me as I talked on my cell phone. A fountain made of musical instruments bubbled beside me. "Oh, Viper. I'll be fine. I just need to know where Destiny works or lives. Can you give me a clue? Or at least a last name."

"Shit, she still uses Dad's last name. She sings in some band. If she's working, she works nights. I think she lives in Costa Mesa. You *are* coming by later, aren't you?"

I separated the fronds with my free hand and peered at the receptionist. She conferred with another too-skinny young woman and pointed in my direction. Andre obviously didn't pay his female employees enough to afford food or to keep their minds on their jobs. "Yeah, sure. I'll see you. Thanks."

I slipped the phone back in my purse and strolled over to the receptionist's granite desk, with a sassy grin. "Could I borrow your *White Pages*?"

She handed me a massive volume and craned her neck as I leafed through it. When I found the listing, I jotted down the address and phone number, and passed the book back to the receptionist along with my security badge. "The caterer. For the wedding, remember?"

By now, I'd lost track of the number of times I'd driven the 55 Freeway, but the scenery was all a blur as I pushed the gas pedal. To the outsider, Southern California appeared to be one continuous city sprawling across the basin. Only seasoned veterans could tell where one town ended and another began, but after eight years, I only knew the borders of Newport Beach. The rest of my geographical knowledge was based on the location of theme parks and malls.

Destiny's apartment complex was about a mile south of South Coast Plaza, a moderate walk if anyone walked in the land where the car was worshiped more than in Detroit. The complex consisted of more than a dozen identical two-story stucco buildings with weathered wood-shake shingle roofs clustered around a pool and recreation center. Man-made jungle streams babbled between the buildings to mask the street sounds.

After circling the parking lot once looking for Destiny's building, I gave up and parked in front of the clubhouse. Red, white, and blue plastic pennants fluttered in the breeze in front of the rental office and a large sign described the amenities found in the one- and two-bedroom apartments. The sign all but promised the perfect single life with built-in microwaves and parties, but it wasn't my idea of home.

A 'You are here' map stood near a block of stainless steel mailboxes. I carefully studied it, memorizing the turns: left, left, right. Even then, I wanted to leave a trail of breadcrumbs to find my way out again as I followed a stream and twisted through the maze of indistinguishable buildings.

Despite the size of the complex, the place seemed like a ghost town in the early Wednesday afternoon. The curtains were drawn at Destiny's apartment and I didn't hear any sound of life. I checked Mickey before knocking and wondered how late a day sleeper would sleep, especially one with the temper of a pit bull. Spitting on a corpse certainly showed a lack of breeding and waking her might be stupid, but I needed answers and I didn't have much time.

Destiny opened the door wearing a short red kimono draped over a skimpy pink chemise and a snarl. Yesterday at the church in full war paint and big hair, she could've been a candidate in a Dolly Parton look a like contest. This afternoon, she reminded me of the Bride of Frankenstein. It would have helped if she'd taken off her makeup before she'd gone to bed. She squinted at me through puffy eyelids and fluffed her lop sided matted blonde mop with dagger length blood-red nails.

"You're the bitch from the funeral."

She tried to slam the door but I caught it. "Please, Destiny. I need to talk to you."

She leaned all her weight against the door. "Which one of those assholes are you sleeping with, or were you Jimmy's slut?"

I put my back into the door and held firm. "None of the above. The police think my little sister killed your ex."

"Hell. She deserves a medal for that."

"Well, they're more likely to put her in jail. I just want to ask you a few questions about Jimmy and Tara Jean."

Destiny stopped pushing so abruptly, I almost fell butt-first into her apartment. The place reeked of tobacco, cat, and burned rope. I'd have to drive home with the top of my car down to blow the odor from my hair and clothes.

When my eyes adjusted to the darkness, I thought I'd wandered into an apartment occupied by six very sloppy female impersonators instead of one small woman. Dresses, mostly sequined, high heels, and wigs were scattered around the living room. Ashtrays overflowed across the pseudo-wood end tables and six months worth of unvacuumed cat hair, lint, and other debris covered the earth-tone carpet. Dirty dishes were stacked everywhere.

Dad and I had fought many battles over housekeeping issues, most of which I felt I'd won, but glancing over Destiny's apartment, I realized the ultimate victory belonged to him. While I couldn't live up to his military cleaning standards, I paid someone to do it for me. Filth made me uncomfortable.

Destiny walked to the dinette set and threw pizza boxes on the floor until she uncovered her purse. A seal-point Siamese cat wrapped itself through her ankles and purred. Destiny groped through the purse and pulled out a pack of cigarettes. The cellophane cover crinkled as she struggled to open the pack, handicapped by her two-inch claws. She popped a cigarette into her mouth. Her hand shook slightly as she held the lighter to the tip. She inhaled deeply and expelled a lung full of smoke. "So how did little Miss Tightass Tara Jean get into this?"

I waved the smoke away. Now I'd have to wash my hair. "Jimmy made a video for his funeral documenting his life. Your wedding was in it. Tara Jean sang."

"How touching." Destiny flicked ash onto the carpet and shuffled into the kitchen. The cat jumped on the counter. Destiny sniffed a pot of stale coffee, poured a cup, and stuck it in the microwave. The grounds in the pot swirled as she waved it at me. "Want any?"

"No, thanks." I smiled to cover the gag reflex and tried to establish some rapport. "You had a lovely wedding." She stared at the microwave as it hummed. Stroking the cat, she remained completely oblivious of me. I cleared my throat. "How did you two meet?"

"I was singing at a club. He was a regular."

"It must be fun singing at clubs."

"It sucks. No one listens." She took the cup from the microwave and slurped the coffee.

So much for friendly chitchat, it didn't work for me, either. "You're pretty bitter about your ex. What happened?"

"Son-of-a-bitch lied to me." She marched into the living room and threw a black spangled dress on the floor, then plopped on the couch. The cat sat on her lap and stared at me with crossed blues eyes.

I plucked a blonde bouffant wig from a chair using the tips of my thumb and first finger, and laid it on the coffee table. "All men lie."

"That's true." Destiny nodded. "But we were going to be the next Sonny and Cher. I had the talent. I could do it. But after the wedding, Jimmy decided he needed to manage Tara Jean's career. He said there was money in it for us. Easy money."

"Andre said Jimmy was having an affair with her."

Smoke shot out Destiny's nostrils as she coughed. "Andre should keep his mouth shut. Like he should talk. I begged him for a year for an audition, but Tara Jean earned hers on her back. And that asshole Jimmy sang with her. He even wrote her song."

"But she didn't have a contract."

"Jimmy said it was a sure thing. She was taking my place. My career. My husband." She filled her lungs with smoke and exhaled the words, "The bastard."

I folded my arms. Destiny's jealousy of Tara went beyond mere marital infidelity issues, she thought Tara had stolen her chance at stardom. "So what happened?"

"She died. Served the bitch right." She flicked the ash on the carpet and stuck up her chin. "Always walking around with her nose so high in the air, she couldn't see the shit she was stepping in."

"What shit?"

Destiny shook her head and complained to some invisible third person floating just beneath the ceiling. "She thought she was better than all of us, she just had a different price."

"Where were you the night she was killed?"

She startled as if she'd forgotten me, and sucked on the cigarette. "Minding my own fucking business."

"Where was Jimmy?"

She crossed and recrossed her legs. The cat jumped to the floor and sniffed my feet. "With me. Why all the questions?"

"Just curious." I shrugged. "The police reopened the case. They talked to Andre today."

"Andre?" She drew in a raspy breath and spat out her words. "He doesn't know anything."

"He thinks he does."

Her hands trembled as she scratched through an overflowing ashtray like a frightened mouse trying to dig its way to freedom. What did she think Andre knew that he hadn't told me? She found the end of a joint and lit it off her cigarette. My nose crinkled as the acrid smell of hemp hit my olfactory nerves. Jack could name all my perfumes; he'd recognize marijuana as soon as I walked in the door.

She inhaled deeply and held it in her lungs. When she exhaled, a hemp haze veiled some of the fear in her eyes. "What's wrong?" she sneered. "Never smelled grass before?"

"I went to school in Ann Arbor. It was everywhere." My internal actuary took over. "But all this smoke can't be good for your voice and it's taking years off your life."

"Who cares?" She shrugged and inhaled again.

"So, what happened after Tara died?"

"Andre gave us a contract, but I had to sing the song Jimmy wrote for her. It wasn't right for me and Andre didn't promote it. He booked us in some real dives."

"That's more than most people get."

"Oh, cut the Pollyanna crap. You know what that bastard did next? Instead of offering us another record, he offered us jobs. Like I was going to settle for being a backup singer."

"But Jimmy did okay."

"He did more than fucking okay. He knew more about the business than Andre did."

"That's great."

"For him." She dragged on the joint. "He promised me we'd be set for life and look at me. Just look at me." She waved the joint at the room. "He lived like a king and this is what I ended up with."

"But he was still paying you alimony."

Her breasts nearly popped out of her chemise as she leaned forward. "How the fuck do you know all this? Did Andre tell you or was it that asshole Viper?"

It didn't seem like a good time to admit I'd gone through her ex-husband's electronic check register, so I just shrugged. "Neither. I found it out all by myself. From the amounts it seems to me that you got a pretty good deal."

She got up, pointing the smoldering joint in my face. "It's none of your fucking business how much he paid me. He promised me half of everything, but he didn't give me shit."

Before she burned me, I scrambled over the arm of the chair and stepped behind it. "I'm sorry. Couldn't your lawyer have done something?"

"Lawyers! Jesus!" She threw her hands in the air. "Lawyers couldn't do anything. Not for me." She paced back and forth muttering under her breath to her invisible friend. "I trusted him. I helped him. And he cheated me. Viper and Krystal got everything they wanted and there was nothing left. Nothing left. What's going to happen to me?"

"Didn't you have any insurance on him from the settlement?"

She rubbed her eyes and smeared her mascara until she looked like the loser in a prizefight. "Some. But not enough, not what I deserved. He promised to take care of me forever."

"How much?"

"About fifty grand."

I blew the secondary smoke from my lungs. It wouldn't go far in Southern California, but people had killed for less. "Fifty grand of found money ain't bad."

"But it's not right. It won't last. Then what am I supposed to do?"

"Grow up and get a real job like the rest of us."

"Bitch." She blew smoke at me and I grabbed a sofa pillow for protection as she approached waving the joint. "You don't know shit. I'm a singer. And in this business, if you're not a star at twenty-five, you're through. Look at me. Just look at me!" She pulled back her hair so I could see every line and pore. "I'm thirty-nine. I might as well slit my wrists."

Her theatrics didn't impress me, especially since she'd seen thirty-nine about half a dozen times, and I held my ground. "That would be pretty damn stupid."

"What the fuck do you know? You don't care. No one cares. They all hate me. I was going to be famous."

She emptied the ashtray on the end table and poked through the butts until she found another small joint. The phone rang as she lit it. She complained all the way to the kitchen.

"Hello." She frowned and tapped her foot. "What the hell do you want, Andre?" The frown melted into an open mouth expression of disbelief. “Really? But I don’t have anything special prepared.” She smiled and twenty years fell from her face as she ran her claws through her tangled and teased hair. “You think so?” She gushed and checked her reflection in the microwave door. “Oh, yes. I can be there in half an hour. Thank you. Thank you.” She hung up, higher than a weather balloon. “I’ve got to get dressed. Andre wants me to audition.”

26

4038097982749817984091 97

One of us was smoking some really great dope and it wasn't me. Destiny emptied her purse on the dinette table. Matchbooks, crushed soda crackers in plastic wrappers, blue artificial sweetener packets, and other assorted purse trash tumbled out.

"Are you sure Andre said audition?"

She riffled through the pile. "I need to wake up. I've got to be sharp." She found a small brown vial, emptied something in her palm and slapped it in her mouth. She washed it down with a swig from an open bottle of beer.

Uppers and old beer, the breakfast of champions. "But don't you think it's a little odd after all these years? You just said your career was over."

Destiny dug through the dresses on the sofa. She held a little red number to her chest, then flung it over her shoulder and reached for another. "Andre heard me sing a while back. He told me my voice had matured." She paused as she held up a translucent black dress and smiled. "He said I had a sultry, torch-singer quality now. Like a female Tony Bennett."

A laugh bubbled up and I choked it back. Andre had spread the excrement so thick, he must have been using a shovel. Destiny rejected the see-through black dress, dropping it at her feet, and examined a blue spangled one. "The audition is just a formality. He's picked out a song."

"But why now?"

She held a black dress covered in black and silver bugle beads against her body and gyrated slowly, her lips pouting as if Andre was standing in front of her. I felt it was a little daring for afternoon wear, but the imagined affect pleased her and she draped the dress over her arm.

"Andre said he would have done it sooner but Jimmy objected. The son-of-a-bitch. I always knew it was his fault. He didn't want me to be a success. It was always him, him, him. But now, I'll show everyone."

"Well, I hope it works out, but I'd really like to talk to you some more."

She picked up a pair of black and silver shoes with four-inch stiletto heels and waved them at me. "Look, I don't even know who the hell you are. But that bitch Tara Jean is dead and so's Jimmy. They got what they deserved and now I'm going to get mine. I just have to change."

"But where were you when Jimmy was killed?"

She held the shoes over her head with the heels pointing at me. "Get the fuck out of my apartment."

"But I need to talk to you about your son."

I know when to leave. The shoes thudded against the door behind me and I drew in two deep breaths to clear my lungs. Even on a smog alert day, the air outside would be fifty times cleaner than the haze inside Destiny's apartment. A quick whiff of my suit sleeve told me it was time for the cleaners. Too bad I didn't have a fresh one in the car.

I shook my head and glanced back at Destiny's door, recalling Andre's parting words to me: *Cherchez le femme*. If sour grapes could be bottled and distilled, Destiny could make a fortune in vinegar. She knew something about Tara's murder and it scared her. But had Jimmy provided her with an alibi or had she given one to him?

I started walking down the path along the man-made jungle stream and tried to reason it out. Why would Jimmy protect Destiny if she'd killed Tara? Did he love her that much? Maybe, but after the divorce he could have said something, or at least used the alibi as leverage to reduce the alimony payments. I stuffed my hands in my pockets. The logic didn't work.

But what if Jimmy had killed Tara because of the baby and then bribed Destiny with promises of half of everything to keep her mouth shut? That certainly explained why he was still paying her alimony after all these years. But if he had murdered Tara, would he have exposed Destiny's son, Rip, as the rapist? Maybe, or maybe he just threatened to stop the money.

But just because I aced Logic 101, could I convince the police? Could actuaries fly? My shoulders sagged and I continued down the path and stepped into an unfamiliar section of the parking lot. Damn. Somewhere in the maze of identical buildings, I must have taken the wrong turn. At least no one had witnessed my navigational mistake.

I glanced to the left and right. With only two choices, I had a fifty-fifty chance of picking the correct direction. My instincts took me to the right. At the next corner, I saw the clubhouse with the red, white, and blue banners fluttering in the wind and my Corvette waiting out front.

As I fastened the seat belt, my cell phone chirped from the depths of my purse. I checked the time and hissed. Three-twenty and I'd promised to be home by two to take care of Jack. He probably thought I'd dropped off the face of the earth. I answered brightly, "Hello."

"Lizzie, darlin', where the hell are you?"

He sounded neglected and I sighed. "On my way, Honey. Sorry I got held up. Be there in twenty minutes."

Before he could ask what I was doing, I clicked off, punched the clutch, and popped the car in reverse. While I felt guilty about abandoning him so soon after he checked out of the hospital, Jack needed more important things to worry about than where I was.

My stomach grumbled that a carton of yogurt didn't equal a real lunch and my car tried to turn into every fast food restaurant we passed, but I kept it on the road and made it home with two minutes to spare. As soon as I walked in the door, my canine welcoming committee started sniffing the exotic smells on my clothes. They followed me to the living room, Puddles with her nose to my shoes and Useless pressing his snout against the back of my short skirt despite my efforts to brush him off.

Jack lounged listlessly on the sofa, one hand clutching the burgundy afghan covering him, the other holding the remote control. His brief case gaped open, and his black leather binder lay on the coffee table, but it didn't appear he'd done any meaningful work in my absence other than carry his lunch tray to the kitchen.

The poor man didn't know what to do without a crime to solve. He had to get back on the job before he withered into an invalid. I squeezed in beside him and pushed away the dogs. They sat at my feet and watched us. When I bent over to kiss Jack, he sniffed me, too, and his nose crinkled.

"Where the hell have you been?"

"It's a long story." I brushed at the Siamese cat hair on my skirt, but it clung to the fabric like glue. "Remember, I told you I was meeting my mother and her lawyer." I gave him a condensed version of the discussion, including my lack of rapport with the attorney. "I think Ms. Provost would like me to disappear. And she can't seem to get Willow to cooperate, so Mom and I went to the hospital to talk to her. God, that girl is such a brat." I related the story complete with gestures and facial expressions. "And she's got this stupid idea that she's going to walk out of that hospital and marry Ryan."

Jack nodded. "That would be damn' stupid."

"Well, I tried to talk her out of it, but she said she'd just get pregnant. At least Mom stood up to her then." I explained how the argument progressed and how it had helped reconcile my feelings toward my mother. "But now I've got to go into family therapy with them."

"That's probably a good idea."

"Yeah, but that could take years. The immediate problem is to keep her away from Ryan. That's why I went to see Andre."

Jack pulled himself to an upright position with a groan, nearly dumping me on the floor on top of the dogs. "I want you to stay away from that man."

"Oh, Jack! Don't be so primeval." The dogs ran to the safety of the rug in front of the hearth. I stood until Jack got settled, then plopped back down beside him with my arms folded. "I don't like being told who I can and can't see."

He folded his arms, too. "But I don't like the way that fellow leers at you."

"Neither do I, but have you ever noticed that I'm not looking back?"

He frowned and gave a half nod.

"Then why don't you trust me?"

"I trust you." He ran his hand through his hair. "It's just that cops have this sixth sense. It's hard to explain, but something about Andre Lefebvre just doesn't sit right. I want to protect you. Is that so bad?"

"Only when you smother me. I don't like being around Andre either, but this is important. I need his help to keep Ryan away from Willow so she doesn't get pregnant."

"Did it work?"

"I think so. He's going to send Ryan to France."

"Good. I don't like the boy any more than I do his father." He ducked his head and brought my hand to his lips. "I don't mean to smother you. But have you ever loved someone so much you just want to wrap them up in cotton and keep them safe?"

His eyes were so gray, and his lashes were so thick, and his Southern accent was so warm and sexy, my body temperature shot up ten degrees and my voice got all steamy. "Well, I'd like to wrap you in a bullet-proof body suit."

"I've got an easy solution for that? I'm still a CPA. Bean counters don't get shot at."

"But you're a cop. And cops don't get shot at everyday."

"But accountants have lower divorce rates."

"Maybe." I sighed dramatically. "But being married to an accountant probably feels like an eternity."

"Oh, Lizzie." He leaned back and chuckled. "What would I do without you?" He patted the empty place on the couch to his right. "Why don't you sit on my good side so I can hold you."

"Okay, but it's my turn to hold you."

A more modest woman might have walked around the coffee table, but I took advantage of my long legs and stepped over Jack instead. His grin said he enjoyed it. As soon as I situated myself in the corner of the couch, he laid his head on my lap and closed his eyes.

"Oh, Lizzie, I know I've been a pain in the ass the last couple days. I'm glad you stuck with me."

Small worry lines creased his forehead and I massaged them with my fingertips. "It's okay. Just don't push me away again. You're supposed to be the stable one in our relationship."

"I just put on a better show." The worry lines deepened. "I still don't know what to do about my job and all."

I massaged his scalp. "Well, I think you ought to get your butt back on duty. If it doesn't work, then quit. It's better than quitting now and regretting it later."

He closed his eyes and smiled while I ran my artificially extended nails through his cop-cut hair. The worry lines on his face relaxed into an expression of pure contentment. Taking care of him made me feel content, too. I could do this forever.

His breathing deepened. Useless and Puddles snored in unison as they lay in front of the hearth. Sam the Cleaning Man had come early this morning and polished my condo until it gleamed and smelled clean. The mid-afternoon sun glittered through the sliding glass doors to the deck. Both doors stood open a few inches, permitting the ocean breeze to flow in and mingle with the fresh spring scents from the floral arrangements Jack had brought from the hospital. I was the only thing that didn't smell good.

After nearly a week of stress, I smiled as I contemplated the domestic tranquility surrounding me. The only way to improve on it would be to go to bed. As I played with Jack's hair, I closed my eyes and considered the possibilities.

Jack shifted and yawned. "Would you feel smothered if I told you I missed you while you were out?"

"No." I bent over and kissed his forehead. "I want you to miss me all the time."

"Would you be angry if I told you I figured you were out chasing some more wild geese?"

My hand froze on his forehead. My tongue stumbled over the words. "Ah, no. It's okay. I don't blame you. Honest."

"Well, it was wrong of me and I'm really sorry. I should've realized you were tending to family business and not interfering in the investigation."

My cheeks felt warm. I swept my hand through my hair and let it fall over my face. Damn. Now I was going to feel guilty about not telling him what I'd learned, but it would only lead to another argument. I didn't want that. Things were finally peaceful between us. With Jack's tolerance for my investigations below zero, at most, I had one more chance to present my case. I needed solid evidence before I told him.

"It's okay, Honey. I understand why you feel that way."

"Good." His nose wrinkled as he rubbed against my suit jacket. "So could you tell me why you came back smelling of tobacco and marijuana?"

"Oh, that," I said blondely as my brain scrambled for an excuse. "Well, I told you, I went to Andre's office. There were some musicians there who were smoking. I don't know who they were, but you know how rock stars are. I couldn't breathe."

My stomach twisted as the lie poured out. It sounded plausible but I'd babbled way too fast. And I felt like a jerk.

Jack snorted. "Told you that man was trouble."

Before another argument erupted, I put my finger to his lips. "I know, and I don't want to talk about him anymore. I was thinking we might go to bed." I ran my hand over his chest. "You need to collect your reward for wearing your vest."

Jack squirmed. “Don’t know if everything’s working, yet.”

“Don’t worry about that.” I put my hand between his legs and stroked his ego. “I’ve got hot fudge and whipped cream.”

He sucked in air and his ambitions rose. “How long would it take to heat that chocolate?”

27

4038097982749817984091 97

Men are such babies.

The hot fudge and whipped cream was a big hit and helped satisfy my hunger, but it left us and the bed pretty sticky. After we showered and changed the sheets, Jack needed food. I fluffed his pillows, and tucked the blankets around him. Then I made a heart attack omelet loaded with bacon and cheese and brought it to him on a tray. He ate like a starving man.

As I put the dishes in the dishwasher, Jack called me. "Lizzie, where's the clicker?" Every three minutes after that it was, "Lizzie, could you get me some water?" Or "Lizzie, I think I left my book in the living room." And "Lizzie, is there any ice cream?" until this Lizzie was about to lace the ice cream with painkillers to make him sleep.

When I came back to get his ice cream bowl, he grinned. "Hey, Lizzie, why don't you get your butt back in bed."

With a romantic invitation like that, how could I refuse? I stopped halfway in the room and put my hands on my hips. "Because as soon as I do, you'll be asking me to run get something else."

"Promise I won't." He traced an X across his broad, hairy chest, then held his right hand in the air. "Please? Just watching you walk around all naked like that gets me all excited."

I sashayed over to the bed and posed with my chest up. At least he'd noticed. "You sure you're up to it?"

He admired my body and swept off the sheets to prove he was. "Yes, Ma'am."

My heart still ached a little every time I saw the large, ugly bruise on the left side of his ribs, but the rest of me ached for him. I slipped across to the empty side of the bed and pressed my mouth to his. When I came up gasping for air, Jack pulled me closer and covered my neck and breasts with healthy, hungry kisses. I threw my still damp hair behind my back and straddled him. We made love, and when it was over, I nestled on his right shoulder.

He kissed the top of my head. "Darlin', I'll wear that vest everyday if you'll keep doing that."

"It's a deal. But I'd better go do some work."

"Oh, just lay here for a minute. I love feeling you against me."

He talked me into it. I closed my eyes and listened to him breathe. I hated lying to him about Destiny, but the result was worth it.

A deep rumbling sound brought me back to consciousness. Jack was on his back, his mouth wide open, soundly asleep with soundly being the operative word. A noise halfway between a growl and the droning of a two-ton bee started in his throat and echoed through his sinuses.

The LCD of the clock radio glowed five thirty-three. Oh, well, a fifteen-minute nap was better than nothing. Outside the window, the brilliant blue sky had grown dusky as late afternoon clouds rolled in off the ocean. I slipped from under his arm and tucked the blankets around him. He snargled and snorted and clutched the comforter, then settled back into his snore.

As clouds obscured the low sun, my apartment chilled. I hurried into jeans, an oversized sweatshirt, and a pair of big, floppy socks for warmth. After I closed all the windows, I switched on all the lights.

Since I was entertaining my mother and famished boyfriend tonight, I pulled a pork roast from the meat drawer of the refrigerator. As I got out the pan, the phone rang. The caller ID displayed Nicola's number. "Hi, Nicola. What's up?"

"Outside of the fact I hate caller ID? I just met with the senior partner in the law firm that handled all of Jimmy O'Reilly's divorces and wills."

"Great! Tell me about it." I tucked the phone under my chin and grabbed a pen and notepad.

Nicola insisted on presenting the facts as if she was summarizing them for a jury. When I tried to speed her along, she shushed me, so I seasoned the roast as she related the history of Jimmy O'Reilly's divorces and wills.

He made his first will shortly after his marriage to Destiny with the usual terms to provide for his new bride and his son by his first marriage. But, when he appeared in the law offices to sign the document, he announced that his life was in danger. He said that, in the event of his unexpected death, an unnamed third party would forward a package to the attorney, and he instructed the attorney to immediately pass it on the police.

I put down the pepper and scribbled on the pad. "Wow. Who's this third party and what was in the package?"

"I don't know. But there's more."

Only a lawyer would be fascinated by the details of dividing a man's estate. While Nicola described the evolution of Jimmy O'Reilly's last wishes, I turned on the oven and popped in the pork roast. But when she mentioned Travis Tourville, I picked up my pencil again and took notes.

Shortly after Jimmy went into partnership with Travis, Jimmy not only bequeathed his share of the Crescent City Café to Travis, he planned his own wake. The plans included a guest list: Travis Tourville, The Reverend F. Wesley Anderson, Andre Lefebvre, Destiny, and a representative of the Newport Beach Police Department.

"Why?" I asked, jotting down the names.

Nicola couldn't answer. Travis was the only guest on the list mentioned in that will. It wasn't until a few months ago, after Jimmy O'Reilly's spiritual rebirth, that he added a codicil leaving a large sum to the Church of the Risen Son.

"But last week Mr. O'Reilly talked to his lawyer about changing his will in favor of the Church of the Risen Son, cutting out his son, but he didn't sign anything."

I wrote down Viper's name and drew an X through it. "Any clue how much money we're talking about?"

"Enough. Mr. O'Reilly owned about one third of the recording company and he had some other investments."

I drew dollar signs on the notepad. Based on the building and décor, the recording company had to be worth a mint. "What about Krystal O'Reilly?"

"Krystal O'Reilly's share in the estate is limited by the prenuptial agreement. The majority of the estate will pass to Viper but Mrs.

O'Reilly is contesting the will."

I stopped myself before making a disparaging remark about lawyers and litigation, wrote Krystal's name and circled it twice. Money would no doubt ease her grieving process. "What about Destiny?"

"There's no provision for her. They divided their assets at the time of their divorce."

"But he was still paying her alimony."

"The court didn't grant her alimony."

Then why was he paying her all that money? I scribbled Destiny's name on the pad followed by three exclamation points. "But you didn't find out what was in the briefcase that was stolen at the wake?"

"I'm afraid not. The senior partner was out of town for the President's Day weekend. Evidently, the package arrived Monday morning and his junior partner took charge of everything. The poor man feels very badly about it being stolen."

I thanked Nicola and we made plans to get together in the morning. After I hung up, I glanced over my notes. Viper had the most to lose if his father executed a new will. And then there was Krystal, contesting the will just twenty-four hours after burying her estranged husband. I wondered what the odds of winning that case were compared to the probability of getting away with murder. But I wasn't ready to give up the Tara Tourville connection, and the guest list for the wake intrigued me. All four named guests had close links to Tara. Destiny was the only invited guest who hadn't attended the wake and she wasn't getting alimony. The payments had to be blackmail and I had to talk to her about it.

I tiptoed into the bedroom. Jack made Rip Van Winkle look like an insomniac. It was only five-fifty. I could drive to Destiny's apartment and question her, and be back in under ninety minutes. Before Jack missed me and the roast finished cooking. I'd have the wine open and the table set before Mom arrived. During dinner I could present my case and apologize for the little lie. Jack would be angry, but he'd understand, and with my mother there, well, he wouldn't say too much. More importantly, I'd solve Tara Tourville's murder *and* Jimmy O'Reilly's. I slipped into my crummy but comfortable loafers and a jacket then left a note on my pillow that read 'Back Soon'.

During my conversation with Nicola, dusk had changed to the inky darkness of a cloudy night. The trail of red taillights stretching out in front of me pulsed brighter and dimmer in the stop-and-go traffic like lights on a Christmas tree and gave the trip a festive air. I felt exhilarated. I was getting close to finding out who'd murdered Tara Tourville and

Jimmy O'Reilly.

Destiny's apartment complex appeared barely more alive in the early evening than it had in the early afternoon. Lamps glowed behind closed curtains in about a third of the units but not a soul could be seen. Of course, it would be difficult to see a soul in the darkness. Dim oriental-style lights spaced at six-foot intervals shone on the curved pathway through the man-made jungle. The low-intensity beam created a romantic ambiance perfect for trysting or for mugging and I wondered about the burglary rates.

It had been difficult enough finding Destiny's apartment in daylight, doing it in the dark added a challenge. The curtains were drawn but the lights were on. I knocked at the door.

No one answered, but from inside I heard a wailing, an unearthly sound like an infant or an injured person. I listened at the window and called Destiny's name. The wailing persisted. I knocked again and twisted the doorknob.

28

103809798274981798409197

I peered inside Destiny's apartment and wrestled a dilemma. Dad's version of Grimm's fairy tales usually included references to the Michigan Penal Code. He used to quiz me afterwards and we could put Goldilocks in jail for years for all her infractions. But he always reminded me that Goldilocks was damned lucky Papa Bear didn't blow her away with his shotgun. A paranoid single woman like Destiny probably kept a loaded pistol on her nightstand and she'd shoot first.

The cross-eyed Siamese cat howled mournfully. I put my hand to my heart and exhaled. "Stupid animal."

The cat meowed again. Risking prosecution for illegal entry and possibly getting shot in the process all because of a noisy and no doubt hungry feline seemed incredibly stupid. I called out, "Destiny."

I glanced around. Destiny had cleaned the place, or at least straightened it. It still needed vacuuming but all the dresses, shoes, and wigs had disappeared from the living room, and she'd emptied the ashtrays. She'd removed the trash from the dinette table and placed a bottle of white wine on it. Soft music flowed through the small sound system.

I tried again. "Anyone home?"

It seemed odd that she'd go away and leave the lights on and the door open. I stepped in. The cat ran down the hall and meowed. "It's Liz Matthews. May I talk to you?"

Still no response. The wine bottle was open and half-empty. I checked the label. French. Expensive. The audition must have gone very well.

I peered down the short hall. The bedroom door was open. The room was dark but there was enough light from the corridor to show the empty unmade bed. The cat slipped through the partially closed door into the bathroom and wailed again.

I knocked lightly on the doorframe to the bathroom. "Destiny?"

I pushed the door open. It appeared Destiny was bathing in tomato sauce. But instead of the healthy, fresh smell of tomatoes, the bathroom smelled like the bottom of my meat drawer. She'd slit her wrists.

Chocolate and whipped cream don't always stay down. I bent over the sink and vomited. When I glanced up at the mirror, large block letters written in red lipstick proclaimed. "I killed Jimmy."

"Oh, God." I put my hands to my face and backed up. Destiny's skin had lost its color. The cat stood with its front paws against the tub and meowed at the nude lifeless form. Rather than throw up again, I ran out of the apartment. It took three deep breaths to get air into my lungs and a rational thought into my head.

I willed myself to be calm and made a plan. Call the police. Call Jack. I repeated the plan like a mantra as I dug through my purse for my cell phone. My fingers fumbled over the keypad and I reported the body in the bathtub. I identified the victim and myself but my mind went blank when the operator asked for the address. It took a moment to page back through my memory simply to get to Costa Mesa, but I finally recalled the apartment complex and street.

The operator remained calm. "We'll have an officer there in a minute. Stay on the line, please."

Stay on the line? I needed Jack. Once the police got here, I might not get a chance to make another call immediately. "I'll try but the battery's low on my cell phone. Tell the police to hurry. We might get disconnected any—"

I pressed End. Jack answered on the second ring with a sleepy grunt.

"Jack. I need you. Destiny's dead. I'm at her apartment. Can you come?"

He woke instantly. "Are you okay? What happened? What's the address?"

I gave him the information and one final instruction to hurry. When he hung up, I put the cell phone back in my purse, and wrapped my arms around my waist. Finding Jimmy O'Reilly's body hadn't been half as bad, but then, I'd never known him alive and there hadn't been so much blood.

The cat ran out and I caught it. "No, Kitty. Things are bad enough tonight. You don't need to get lost."

I held the cat and stroked its fur. Its purring helped calm me. A flashlight bobbed down the path, alternately illuminating the sidewalk or shining on the buildings. I tried to make out the silhouette. The man had a cop bearing, noiseless soft-soled shoes, and a heavily laden belt. I gathered up my voice. "Are you the police? Over here."

The officer flashed the light in my face. I squinted and hugged the cat as he approached and asked my name. We hurried through the identification formalities and a brief description of where I found the body. He cautioned me to stay put while he went inside. A few minutes later, he came out and started asking questions.

He eyed me suspiciously when I told him about finding the door unlocked and walking in when I heard the cat meow. He examined the lock and the windows and I began to doubt the wisdom of telling the truth. Two more officers joined the first and stepped inside to talk while I leaned against the cold stucco wall and waited. The cat had less patience than I had. It squirmed in my arms and I persuaded the officers to let me put it in the apartment.

I hugged myself. What was wrong? Why did I feel so bad? Destiny's confession printed on the bathroom mirror would certainly clear Willow. That was what I wanted, so why didn't I feel relieved? Probably because I knew it wasn't suicide.

An occasional inhabitant of the apartment complex wandered by on their way home and rubbernecked a little, but no one volunteered to talk to the police. About twenty minutes after I found the body, an Asian man in a suit came up the walk and took charge. He pulled the officers aside and they spoke in low voices. The first officer motioned toward the apartment and then pointed at me.

The Asian man left one officer by the door and sent the other two to canvass the neighbors. He introduced himself to me as Detective Lau. I tried to tell him Destiny had been murdered, but he stopped me before I could get two words out and asked me to wait.

So much for being a good citizen. I zipped up my jacket. Another male silhouette appeared on the path, but I recognized his shoulders and his gait and I ran to meet him.

Jack wore tight jeans, a sweater, and his old leather bomber jacket, the most elegant clothes he had at my place. He had his badge on his belt and his ID in his hand. When I jumped into his arms, I felt his weapon. I held him with all my might and made sure he was wearing his vest.

"Excuse me." Detective Lau interrupted our reunion. We forced ourselves apart. I stood by Jack's side while Jack showed Lau his ID and his badge. Lau shook his head. "I don't recall asking Newport Beach for support on this."

"She's my girl. She called me."

"Ahhh. I see." Lau raised his eyebrows and scrutinized me. "So why did you feel you needed your boyfriend here?"

"Because it's the third body I've come across in a week." I held up my hands. "Fourth, if you want to count a rape victim. And I'm feeling a little stressed."

My voice must have sounded like a ten on the maniac scale and Lau visually measured me for a straitjacket. He raised four fingers in disbelief. "Four bodies?"

Jack put his arm around my shoulders and explained about Nicola, Jimmy O'Reilly, and Jimmy O'Reilly's lawyer.

Lau snapped his fingers and pointed at Jack. "You're the cop who got shot Monday night." He smiled and held out his hand. "Good to see you up. How are you feeling?"

I slipped my arm around Jack. "Well, he just got out of the hospital today. He shouldn't be on his feet too long."

Jack clenched his teeth. "Liz, please, I'm fine." He gave Lau a manly shrug and drawled. "She saw me get hit and she's still a little skittish. You know how it goes. You don't mind if I sit in while you talk to her? I'm sort of interested in what's happening here myself."

"It's okay." Lau shrugged. "I don't like interviewing people in the dark. Why don't we go to the clubhouse?"

He escorted us to the clubhouse. The bulletin board in the entry was covered with brightly colored papers advertising social events, but we had the place to ourselves. Lau chose to work at a simulated wood-grain table suitable for playing cards or conducting interrogations. The cushioned chairs had casters and I rolled mine next to Jack's. Lau sat across from us with his back to the glass wall overlooking the pool.

Jack wasn't going to like what I had to say, but the best solution was to tell Lau why I knew Destiny had been murdered as soon as possible and get him on the right track. I knitted my fingers together. "I think I can clear this up quickly."

Lau took out his notepad. "Ms. Matthews, I prefer to ask the questions. Could you tell me how you found the body?"

A control freak. Fine. Instead of arguing, I hurriedly explained about the cat and unlocked door, finding the body in the bathtub of bloody water and throwing up in the sink. "I'm really sorry about throwing up but, I mean, I've never seen so much blood before. I don't think I touched anything."

Lau put his pen down. "Let's go back a little. You just walked into the apartment?" I nodded. "Are you a friend of the deceased? Was she expecting you?"

"No, not really. We met at her ex's funeral yesterday. I just dropped by to talk."

"What about?"

Why do cops have to question everything? "I wanted to ask her some questions about her ex-husband's murder."

"Why would you do that?"

I sighed and looked at Jack as I explained about Willow.

Lau stood and walked across the room to a floor lamp. He twisted the switch three times. With each click, the light grew brighter. He pointed to a spot on the carpet. "Ms. Matthews, I want you to come over here."

Whatever Lau wanted, it couldn't be good. I looked at Jack, hoping he'd protest, but he waved me away. I stopped about four feet from where Lau pointed. "If you'd just listen to me for a minute."

He held out his palms. "Let me see your hands."

He examined my hands and sleeves under the light. He was looking for bloodstains. Even though I knew he wouldn't find any, watching him work made me sweat. Why didn't Jack make him stop?

Lau dropped my hands. "Take off your jacket."

I did. Lau pointed at my chest. "What's that?"

My gasp could've been heard in Riverside. Blood was smeared on my sweatshirt. "I was holding her cat. It tried to run away. See, there's cat hair, too. It must have gotten into some of her blood. You can ask the officer."

Jack joined us. "May I?" Lau motioned toward me and Jack tilted the lampshade to shine more light on my breast. He bent over and stared at the streaks, his nose just inches from the fabric. Lau bent beside him. My boobs had never had so much attention in my life. They could see my heart pound. Jack pointed. "Those are definitely paw prints." Lau nodded and Jack glanced over the rest of my shirt. "No spatters."

"No, no spatters."

Both men straightened and assumed the negotiating posture with their arms folded. Lau began. "It may be weeks before I know if I've got a homicide or a suicide. I have to collect all the evidence. I want her clothes."

Jack rubbed his chin. "I'll admit Liz is too damn snoopy and that she had no business being here, but she's not a murderer. I don't think you should rush to any conclusions without hearing more about the O'Reilly case."

The men stepped away and I tapped my foot to calm my nerves. When the men finished, they shook hands and came back to me. Jack spoke calmly. "Detective Lau is going to hold your clothes until he sorts out things. He won't test them unless it's absolutely necessary."

I crossed my hands over my breasts. "I'm not going home naked."

Lau spoke up. "I'll have an officer follow you."

I made a face. "If you insist, but would you please listen to me. I'm sure Destiny didn't kill herself." I looked at Jack and took a deep breath. "I'm really sorry. I should have told you, but I was here earlier this afternoon."

His mouth opened. "You lied to me."

"In a way. I knew if I told you, you'd get mad and we'd have another fight. I didn't want that. Things were finally right between us. I was going to tell you later."

Jack turned away, his jaw welded shut. If anything had been left in my stomach, it would've come up. Lau took over. "Tell me what happened."

I told him the entire story, including Destiny's wrist-slitting comment. "But then Andre Lefebvre called. He owns a recording company in Newport Beach. He offered her a contract. She was ecstatic. She went down there to sign it."

"Maybe things didn't work out."

"Maybe." I nodded. "For the life of me, I can't figure out why Andre called her in the first place, let alone offered her a recording contract. He really doesn't think much of her, but she seemed positive it was a done deal. She said Andre told her he'd wanted to do it for years but her ex-husband wouldn't let him."

I glanced at Jack. At least he appeared to be listening, even if his jaw remained stiff. "The real point is, when I was there earlier, her place was a pigsty. There were clothes and shoes and cigarette butts and trash all over. She was in such a hurry to get to the recording studio, she didn't stop to clean the place. And if I were going to commit suicide, I sure as hell wouldn't bother to pick up my apartment."

Lau reminded me of Destiny's cat as he narrowed his eyes. "Suicides often try to put their lives in order first."

"Maybe, but, I think she was entertaining someone. Someone who likes expensive French wine."

"Well, I will look into it. If you'll wait here, I'll send an officer to escort you home. First thing in the morning, I want you to come to the station. We'll need your prints and I want you to make a statement."

Jack squared his shoulders as if nothing had happened and I'd disappeared. "If you all don't mind, I'd appreciate seeing the crime scene when you're finished."

Lau agreed and they started to leave. I caught Jack's sleeve. "Please. May I talk to you?"

Lau went on ahead and I tried to apologize. "I'm really sorry." Jack's face remained an angry mask. "Please, Jack, don't be mad."

"I can't talk now."

"Then listen. It wasn't so much a lie as just not telling you the whole story. I told you, I didn't want to start another fight. See what's happening now?"

His voice shook. "I trusted you."

I bowed my head and put my hands to my face. God, I'd blown it. I felt Jack walk away and I glanced up. My voice squeaked. "Are you coming home?"

He kept his back to me. "Don't wait up."

29

403809798274981798409197

Under normal circumstances, having a cop follow my car would make me nervous, but I felt dazed. I knew Jack would be angry, but I'd expected him to yell, not to walk off.

I'd carry the memory of Jack's face and Destiny's nude body in a tub of bloody water for the rest of my life. My relationship with Jack was beyond repair, but it wasn't going to be for nothing. While I waited for a red traffic light on Bristol, I called Andre.

I rattled off the words like a machine gun. "Andre, Liz. We need to talk about Destiny."

His melodious voice had a smile. "Yes, we should. It keeps bringing us together."

"Fuck you. I was with her when you offered her a contract this afternoon. Why did you do that?"

The line went silent. "My goodness. I never know where you're going to turn up. I simply invited Destiny to audition. It was a friendly gesture that, unfortunately, didn't work."

"Bull shit." I carefully enunciated each word. The light turned green and I tucked the phone on my shoulder. I shifted into first and waited for the car in front of me to move. "From the end of the conversation I heard, it sounded like a done deal. Her feet weren't touching the ground."

"Perhaps Destiny simply heard what she wanted to hear. It's not my fault. But you're right about her feet not touching the ground. She was high when she got to my office. The audition was a disaster. I couldn't possibly sign her to a contract. You can listen to the tape, if you like."

"Maybe later." I hung up and, pushing the car into second gear, slipped through the intersection as the traffic signal turned yellow. The cop stayed on my tail. I managed to get home with textbook driving, but every movement took a conscious effort. I couldn't let that bastard get away with murder again.

Even if I had to give up my favorite sweatshirt for forensic tests, I didn't have to let a cop in my apartment without a search warrant. I made the officer wait on the landing outside of my door while I changed. At least Useless and Puddles were happy to see me, although I suspected part of their frenzy came from their need to go outside. I pushed past them into the bedroom and stopped at the sight of the unmade bed. Just a few hours ago we'd made love on it and I could still see the impression of Jack's body. I yanked up the sheets and punched the pillows to obliterate the memories.

What I needed was a walk. A quick trip in the salt air would help clear my mind, and I could take Useless back to Jack's place along with his things so we could avoid any awkward moments while we dismantled our relationship. Then I could call Mom and apologize for being so late. I put on running gear and strapped on my fanny pack with my survival kit.

When I opened the door, Mom was standing beside the officer wringing the strap of her purse. "Is this a bad time?" Her eyes played ping-pong between the cop and me.

I handed the cop my clothes and invited her in. Useless and Puddles gave her a good sniffing.

"What nice dogs." She stooped to pet them. "What was that police officer doing here? I've been waiting in my car for an hour. Did something happen?"

I explained about finding Destiny's body and getting her blood on my clothes. Her eyes widened. "Oh, Sweetheart. That's awful. I hope you're not in trouble."

"Oh, they're just covering their you-know-what's." I shrugged as if nothing could possibly go wrong. "How was your meeting with Detective Peters?"

"We didn't have it. He was called away." She glanced around and sniffed. "Is something burning?"

I ran to the kitchen and opened the oven. In another ten minutes the roast would have become charcoal. Mom surveyed the disaster. "I bet the bottom half is fine."

"Yeah, it's a good thing Jack likes blackened pork."

I dropped the pan on the counter and buried my face in the hot potholders. Mom put her hand on my back. "What's wrong? Is it Jack?"

I nodded. "He's, he's…." She stroked my hair as I choked out the story. "He's never going to forgive me."

"Of course, he will. He adores you. You'll see."

"But you don't understand, he's just like Dad. He sees everything in black and white. It's ruined. He'll never trust me again."

I felt so empty inside. Why had I let myself fall in love? Why hadn't I predicted this? Mom wrapped her arms around me and I bent over to let her hold me while I fought to maintain control.

"I'm sorry. Don't know why I was getting all upset like that over some stupid man. I don't need him. I just want to take his stuff back to his place and then I'll be okay." I straightened up. "Want some wine?"

I opened a bottle of Merlot. Before it could take a breath, I poured it into glasses and saluted Mom. "To our first meal together, even if it is burnt."

She held up the glass. "I don't mean to pry, but who is this poor woman and why did she get murdered tonight?"

We moved to the dining room table and I explained about Destiny, Jimmy O'Reilly, Tara Tourville and her baby, the payments to Destiny, and the man who shot Jack at the wake.

"You see, I thought Jimmy killed Tara because he was the baby's father and he paid Destiny to keep her mouth shut and that she killed Jimmy to keep her son out of trouble. But when I found her body, I realized she hadn't killed herself and I knew it had to be Andre."

"Andre Lefebvre?" Mom's mouth almost hit the cherry table. "But why would he do that?"

"Because he killed Tara Tourville. He was the baby's father. Jimmy and Destiny must have been blackmailing him."

"Then why did he wait so long to kill them?"

"Well, I guess because...Oh, my God. Ryan." If my rapist logic applied to Destiny and her son, it also applied to Andre and Ryan. Except that I'd seen Ryan at the wake and he was with Willow when two of the rapes occurred.

Unless he sneaked out while I was upstairs with Andre, we were up there long enough. But Willow—damn, was she in on it?

I put my hands over my face. Mom tapped my arm. "Is something wrong?"

"Yeah, Mom, a lot. You said you don't take the newspaper."

She nodded.

"And you haven't watched the local news this week?"

"It's too depressing."

I took her into my study and pointed to the sketch of the rapist's mask taped to the wall. She regarded me curiously. "What are you doing with that picture of Ryan's mask?"

My heart dropped. "Ryan's mask? You've seen him with it?"

"Well, not exactly." She ducked her head as if she'd been caught cheating in class. "Willow made it. She works on all her art projects in her bedroom, and I'm not supposed to go in there. You see, we went to this therapist who said Willow needed her own space. They decided I should never go in Willow's bedroom. But sometimes when Willow's out and she forgets to lock the door I go in." She flushed. "I just like to look at what she's making. I'm not spying, really—"

Before we went on a long excursion down Mom's stream of consciousness, I interrupted. "It's okay. Dad still goes through my things. That's why I live here. Just get to the point. You saw the mask. Why did she make it?"

"Oh. Ryan and Willow are supposed to go to a Mardi Gras party Saturday night at his father's office. I gave her money for a dress but she wanted their costumes to be a surprise."

I sank in the swivel chair. It fit. Ryan had grown tired of beating on high school girls and needed bigger thrills. The answer had been this close all along.

"You're not going to tell Willow I went in her bedroom, are you? She'd kill me."

"No, Ryan would." Mom stared at me, totally clueless, and I explained. "Have you heard about the man who wears a mask while he's been raping women down at the beach?"

"Yes." Her expression turned to open-mouthed horror. "Oh, no. You don't mean. How could he do such a thing?"

"I don't know, but the picture was in the paper Saturday morning. It's plastered all over the beach now. Ryan knows Willow can identify the mask."

My fingers wanted to press Jack's extension at the police station, but I called Hal instead and left a message. As I drove up to the hospital,

I hoped Hal wouldn't treat me like the boy who cried wolf. Part of me wanted to rush in and confront Willow, but the police needed to see her reaction, so I paced. When Hal arrived, I told him about the mask. "Ryan knows Willow can identify the mask. I think he tried to kill her."

"It's damned hard to make a person swallow pills."

"I know, but let me handle it. I think I know how to get the truth from her."

"Liz, no." He shook his head firmly. "I can't do that. What if she's in this with him?"

"Then she's all yours. Do you agree, Mom?"

"Mrs. Forrester, you might want to call your attorney."

For the first time since I'd met her, Ann stuck up her chin. "I trust both my daughters."

Hal laid down the ground rules. We waited in a room decorated in early cozy. Willow came in wearing the same jeans and T-shirt she'd worn earlier. She plopped on a chair and twisted her arms and legs into a pretzel.

"They said I had to come here but I'm not going to talk."

Willow stared at the ceiling while she hummed tunelessly. I wanted to slap her silly but I shrugged. "Fine, if that's the way you want it. I was going to try to get you out of here, but oh, well. Catch you when you get out of jail."

She kept her nose up and avoided looking in my direction. "Ryan's going to get me out. He promised we'd be together."

"Why would he do that? The word's out that he's available. The girls are lining up and if I were you, I'd get my butt out of here ASAP."

She glared at me. "Ryan would never look at another girl."

"Listen to Big Sister. I saw him at Uncle Jimmy's last night with some cute little chick with maroon hair named Magenta."

Willow's baby blues became murderous slits and she hissed. "That slut. How were you going to get me out of here?"

"You have to talk first." I showed her the sketch of the mask. "Have you seen this before?"

Her eyes widened then narrowed again. "It sort of looks like the mask I made for Ryan, but how'd you get it?"

"A friend of mine saw some guy wearing it. It made a real impression. We were wondering, what was your inspiration?"

She made a critical face at the sketch. "Ryan gave me this old photo of his dad and Uncle Jimmy when they were in a Mardi Gras parade back in college. It was so gross. They were on this float wearing loin cloths." She wrinkled her nose. "Ryan wanted me to make him a mask like theirs to wear to this party. He thought it would be funny."

"Did Uncle Jimmy see it?"

Willow nodded. "I gave it to Ryan on Valentine's Day when we were at Uncle Jimmy's."

I sat back and let Hal take over. "When was the last time you read a newspaper?"

She looked at him as if he were hallucinating. "Why would I read a newspaper?"

"Have you seen the news since you've been here?"

"Duh? In this place? Are we through yet?"

I raised my hand. "Almost. We know Ryan called you Saturday morning."

She lowered her eyes and stared at the floor.

"He woke you up so you could let him in, didn't he?"

"I told you he wasn't there Saturday."

I whispered. "He's probably with Magenta right now."

Her voice squeaked. "He called. I let him in."

"Did he know the security code?"

"Sure. We let ourselves out all the time."

"So, what did he want?"

She sighed and went limp in the chair from the exertion of speaking to adults. "He said my mom and his dad planned to keep us apart and the only way we could be together was to show them how serious we were. He gave me some sleeping pills. He said if I took them, Mom would know that we belonged together."

My father's favorite expression came out of my mouth. My voice even sounded like his. "And nothing inside your head said this was stupid?"

"He said he'd come back and find me and I'd be okay and we'd be just like Romeo and Juliet except that we'd get married as long as I didn't tell anyone he'd been there."

Hal shook his head. "But when you woke up and you found out Jimmy O'Reilly was dead, why didn't you tell us about Ryan?"

"I told you. He promised to marry me if I didn't say anything and I didn't want to get him in trouble. Like he wouldn't kill Uncle Jimmy."

"Was anyone else there?"

She bit her bottom lip. "I'm not sure. He was alone when I let him in. But I thought I heard the front door open when I was almost asleep and it sounded like his dad calling him."

I nodded. Of course, Andre was behind it, the bastard. "Willow,

Ryan's raped four women in the last week. He wore that mask each time."

Blood came up in her cheeks. "He wouldn't do that."

"I'm really sorry, but it's the truth. He gave you those sleeping pills to kill you so you wouldn't identify him."

She stood and shrieked. "You bitch! You're making it up!"

"But he did. And I think he killed Jimmy O'Reilly because he could identify the mask, too. Then Ryan left the gun in the bed beside you with your fingerprints on it to make it look like you'd shot Jimmy."

"Stop it! Stop it!" Willow sobbed as she flailed at me.

Hal pulled Willow out of the room. My heart pounded from the attack and I slumped forward on the couch with my forehead nearly touching my knees. Proving I was right wasn't supposed to feel this bad.

Mom sat beside me and I recognized her perfume and her touch. She leaned her head against mine. "Thank you."

"You'd better get out there with Willow before she does something else incredibly stupid."

"I want to sit with you." She rubbed my back. "She didn't mean those things. She needs a sister like you. I need you."

I nodded. "You need to get your attorney down here."

My mother tried to talk me into staying, but since the psychiatric unit wasn't passing out Prozac samples, I needed to be alone. My autopilot got me home. As I pulled in the alley behind my apartment, I punched the remote on my visor. The garage door rumbled open and I parked. As I switched off the engine, Andre darted in and aimed a gun at me. He pressed the button on the wall and the garage door opener motor grumbled as the door started back down. It clunked when it hit the concrete and silence echoed through the small space.

"Put your hands up and get out slowly."

My heart boomed as I edged out of the car. "Who are you going to pin this one on? The cops aren't buying suicides today." Losing Jack made me feel reckless and I bragged. "I found Destiny's body and told the police about the audition. They're looking for you."

Andre walked toward me. "You are, without a doubt, the most annoying woman I've met. You can't leave anything alone."

I backed up and nearly got tangled in my mountain bike parked against the wall. "And I've never met a man who's left such a trail of bodies. Let's see." I counted on my fingers. "Tara Tourville, Jimmy O'Reilly, Destiny, and Jimmy's attorney, no, wait. That was Ryan."

"Aren't you smart? What else do you know?"

I scooted around the rear end of my car. "Well, Tara's a no-brainer. Destiny said you slept with her. It must have been your baby. Tara wanted to get married but you were engaged to the boss's daughter."

"I didn't mean to hurt Tara but she was stubborn and naïve. I would have made her a star if she'd had an abortion."

"Big surprise. She can't be the only Catholic school girl you dated." I inched back between the passenger side of my car and a stack of boxes. If I could get to the door, I could get out. "Jimmy and Destiny knew you killed Tara."

"Jimmy was in the control room at the church. He taped our argument. He's used it against me ever since."

"But Jimmy recognized Ryan's mask in the newspaper. He knew Ryan was the rapist."

His voice dropped. "You know about the rapes?"

"Yeah." I basked in my brilliance. "Willow identified the mask and told the police you were at Jimmy O'Reilly's the day of the murder. They probably have Ryan in custody by now."

"You bitch." He put his gun on the hood of my car and pushed up his sleeves. "I'm going to enjoy killing you."

I yanked a stack of boxes and ran for the door. My college math books thudded on the floor between us. Andre scrambled over the books and my Corvette. He grabbed my wrist, spun me around, and caught me with a right. I tasted blood. He hit me again and I saw the Milky Way galaxy. I doubled over. My hand touched my fanny pack.

His fingers dug into my hair as he twisted my head around while my fingers wrapped around my pepper spray.

30

03809798274981798409197

Pepper spray burns like hell. At least the residual mist that floated in my eyes stung like crazy. Andre bent over with his hands to his face and cursed, then swung blindly at where I'd been. I grabbed my hockey stick. All the hours I spent playing with the boys back in Detroit paid off.

I hammered him until he crumbled then I grabbed his gun from the hood of my car. My hands shook as I held the gun and fumbled in my fanny pack for my cell phone. I barely managed to punch 9-1-1. Thank goodness Officer Eric responded first up and recognized me, making the explanation easier. My trembling gave way to shivering as I stood watch over the Armani-clad lump on the garage floor and listened as the sirens reached a crescendo and faded to silence in my driveway.

All I wanted to do was crawl to my apartment and grab some ice and some food, but the paramedics insisted the cut near my mouth needed stitches. They hauled me to the hospital. Hal caught up with me at the emergency room as the doctor finished. Hal examined Andre's handiwork and whistled.

"You look like you just went fifteen rounds with Tyson."

"Yeah, well, you ought to be on this side of it," I lisped. My eyes hurt. The entire left side of my face ached and my lip felt as if the doctor had injected a quart of collagen in it. And I really didn't want to see my nose. When I tried to sit up, the room went fuzzy like static on a television screen. I flopped back on the pillow with a moan and closed my eyes.

"Oops, none of that." The nurse gave me a whiff of ammonia. My head cleared and she checked my blood pressure twice to make sure I was alive. "Are you a fainter?"

"Only when I have stitches on an empty stomach."

She handed me a cold compress and I held it against my face while she went for orange juice. Now I could add embarrassment to my list of injuries. I'd never been good with needles.

Hal wheeled over a stool and sat beside the bed. "Can you tell me how this happened?"

It hurt to move my lips and with a broken nose, I sounded like a ventriloquist with a cold.

When I finished, Hal nodded. "Good work, champ. But next time, leave the rough stuff to us. We've got Ryan Lefebvre down at the station. He's a real piece of work, but we'll break his story." He checked his watch. "I'd better get going. Where's Jack? He should be here. Want me to call him?"

"No, don't." I explained about our fight, or rather our complete lack of a fight. "I don't want him to come back because I got hurt."

"I think you're blowing this way out of proportion."

"No, Jack did. Please, don't say anything to him."

"It's your life." He shrugged. "Want a ride home?"

I shook my head. The nurse returned with the orange juice. The first swallow bounced around my stomach but I kept it down. As soon as my blood pressure returned and I could sit up without falling over, I signed the release forms and called Nicola.

I slumped in a chair and watched the ER entrance, praying Jack would rush in, yet hoping he wouldn't. Nicola flew through the doors, her cheeks flushed and her red hair wild with worry. When she saw me, she put her hand to her mouth. "Oh, God, Liz. Not you, too."

I gave her the *Reader's Digest* version about Andre and Ryan and she threw her arms around me. "Oh, Liz, if there's anything I can do for you, just say it."

"Can I crash at your place?"

"Of course, but I thought Jack was staying with you."

I held the compress against my cheek and repeated the story.

She shook her head. "Liz, you need to talk to him."

"He's the one who doesn't want to talk."

During the trip to her place, I made some calls. Once we were safely inside her apartment, she handed me a fresh Harvard T-shirt to replace my bloodstained sweatshirt and I slipped into the bathroom. The first glimpse in the mirror made me dizzy. The last time I broke my nose, Dad said it gave my profile character. Now it had enough character for three people.

After I finished cleaning up, Nicola installed me on the sofa in her living room with a bag of ice wrapped in a soft terry towel, a forest green afghan, a carton of Ben & Jerry's, and a glass of brandy with a straw. The dark chocolate ice cream soothed my lips and filled the inner void with enough sugar and caffeine to keep me vertical while the brandy numbed my mind. I checked Mickey and wondered how long it would take the news to reach Jack.

Viper arrived first. The silver studs of his black leather jacket and matching collar coordinated nicely with his multiple body piercings. Nicola wrinkled her nose and held my house key at arm's length, ordering him to fetch my dogs. He grumbled, but after a quick glance at me, he agreed.

She darted about straightening the room, shelving law books and jamming the articles on rape in the end table drawer. Travis came in his chef's whites as Viper returned with the dogs. Puddles jumped on my lap and sniffed, but Useless had a strange affinity for Viper. Maybe it was their matching studded leather collars, but Useless sat by Viper and let Viper stroke his head.

Travis twittered above me like a swarm of anxious flies around a jar of jam, but Nicola wouldn't let me talk until my mother arrived. She ran in and gasped. Her fierce hugs almost made my nose bleed again. Travis poured her a brandy while I assured her everything would heal.

Once Mom calmed, Travis cleared his throat. "Now can Liz tell me who killed Tara?"

"And what about Dad?" Viper added.

I sucked down some brandy. "Andre killed Tara." I lowered my voice to a whisper. "He got her pregnant."

"The fucking bastard." Travis clenched his fists.

I put my hand on his and explained what happened. Travis stood and circled the room. "God, I want to kill him." His hands were poised to strangle; all he lacked was Andre's neck. "But how could he do it? How could he murder my sister and look me in the eye."

"Andre doesn't have a conscience. He was engaged to the boss's daughter and Tara got in his way."

Nicola handed Travis a brandy. Viper took Travis's place. "What about Dad?"

I tried to phrase my answer delicately. "Your father was in the control booth the night Tara was killed. He videotaped the whole thing and used it against Andre to get a singing contract and the job."

Viper shook his head. "But Dad was good. He knew more about the recording industry than that asshole Andre."

"I'm sure he did, but Andre's not a generous man. Your father needed leverage with Andre and Andre resented him."

Viper sank back into the cushions, his knuckles pressed to his lips in thought. "Andre hated Dad's guts. Some of it's starting to make sense to me now. But why did he kill Dad after all these years?"

"When your father realized Ryan was the rapist, he couldn't stomach it. He knew Ryan needed help and he was going to the police."

Nicola handed Viper a brandy. She sat on the other corner of the couch with a glass in her hand.

Travis pulled up a chair. "If they were both involved in Tara's death, why did they invest in my restaurant?"

"Jimmy thought you had talent and I think he felt a little remorse. He wanted to do something for Tara's family." My enunciation was off a little, but my meaning was clear.

Travis gulped some brandy. "But, if Jimmy was blackmailing Andre for twenty years, why didn't Andre kill him before now?"

"Jimmy warned Andre that if he died mysteriously, his lawyer would turn the videotape over to the police at his wake."

"Oh!" Nicola's face glowed in a Eureka moment. "I see now. That's why he killed the attorney Monday night, to get the tape."

"Yeah. It was a risk, but he had to do it. Jimmy planned to reveal everything at his wake, that's why he invited Travis, Reverend Anderson, and Jack. Andre brought Ryan to the wake, made certain enough people saw him, then Ryan slipped out and waited. When the attorney came, he grabbed her briefcase and shot her. He stashed the things in Andre's Mercedes around the block. In all the confusion, when everyone went outside to see what happened, it was easy enough for Ryan to get back into the house."

"So, how did you find out that Ryan Lefebvre—," Nicola stopped in mid-sentence and swallowed. "How did you find out that he was the man who raped me?"

I explained about Willow and the mask. "Andre and Jimmy didn't know what Ryan was doing until they saw the sketch of the mask in the newspaper Saturday. They recognized it from their college days. Jimmy called Andre and told him he was going to the police. Andre had to get rid of Willow and Jimmy fast and he took advantage of Willow being at Jimmy's house. He decided to make it look like a murder/suicide. Except Willow didn't die."

Viper sneered, "I told you Ryan was fucking twisted."

Nicola frowned. "But why didn't your sister just tell the truth? Didn't she realize she was in trouble?"

"No. She has more hormones than brains. Ryan promised to marry her if she kept her mouth shut."

Mom held my hand. "But why did Ryan's father attack you?"

"I ruined everything. He was afraid Willow would crack, but she was out of his reach. So, he killed Destiny and made it look like suicide, complete with a confession to Jimmy O'Reilly's murder. As soon as Willow got out of the hospital, she was going to overdose again." I traced quotation marks in the air. "But I figured it out and I told him and the police."

Nicola sighed. "I'll never forget what Ryan did to me, but it helps to know he's in jail. I owe you so much, Liz."

"I do, too." Travis raised his glass to me. "It's been hard all these years, not knowing who killed Tara. Anytime you're hungry, you just come by the restaurant and you'll eat on me for as long as I live."

Mom squeezed me and beamed. Viper realized it was his turn to say something gracious. He raised his hands. "Hey, I helped." Travis and Nicola stared him down and Viper colored. He dropped his hands. The silver stud was back in his tongue and he clicked it on his teeth as he searched for the words. "Okay. I appreciate what you did, Liz. I thought you were a real bitch at first, but you're cool. And you trusted me." He lowered his eyes and scratched Useless's ears. "I'm glad you found out who killed Dad. If you ever want to hang out or anything, I'd like it."

A knock at the door interrupted us. Jack had finally found me. The painkillers wore off and I felt every stitch, even the ones that hadn't been taken yet in my heart. Puddles fell on the floor when I stood. "Tell him to take Useless and go home."

I hurried into Nicola's room and closed the door. I curled up on the bed on with the icepack on my cheek and a pillow over my head to muffle the sound of voices.

The door opened and the light came on. I opened my good eye a crack. Nicola, Travis, Viper, my mother formed a semi-circle around me.

Nicola stepped forward. "I've spoken to the defendant. He pleads guilty to the charge of being an asshole and throws himself on your mercy."

I closed my eye. "Tell him to go home."

She sat on the bed. "Liz, he's only a man and if we could jail men for being childish, there wouldn't be any on the street. You wouldn't let me hide, I don't think you should."

"He'll never trust me again."

"Does he have you on a leash?"

"No."

"Then what you were doing was none of his business and you should've told him that. This is simply a matter of poor communication. You shouldn't let that ruin your relationship." Nicola sounded like a lawyer. I tried to grin at the thought, but my face wouldn't co-operate.

I opened my eye and considered what she said. My mother knelt in front of the bed and pushed my hair back from my face. "Sweetheart, don't make the same mistake I did. Your father and I never talked. If I'd tried harder, I wouldn't have lost you."

Travis took the floor. "I've known Jack a long time. He's like an old hound dog. He may growl, but he's loyal and he doesn't give up. He's worried crazy. He won't leave until he talks to you. Please?"

Before I could answer, Jack slid to his knees by the bed; Useless sat by his side. Jack tried to lift the ice bag from my face, but I swatted him away. Everyone tiptoed out.

Viper paused at the door and frowned. "I'd tell him to fuck off." He shut the door behind him. Viper, the relationship expert.

"Oh, Lizzie." Jack's soft drawl was filled with worry. "I came as soon as I heard. Are you okay?"

He inhaled sharply when I sat up and he saw my face. He buried his head in my lap, his chest heaving, and I panicked. I touched his shoulder. "Jack? I'm fine, really. Just a little tired. Please, would you leave? I need some sleep."

He peered up at me, his eyes sad and damp. "Why wouldn't you let anyone call me?"

"You walked out on me."

"I'm sorry. I made a mistake. I was pissed and I needed to cool off. As soon as Hal told me, I came running, but I had a hell of a time finding you." He buried his face in my lap again.

My resolve defrosted but I steeled myself. "And if he hadn't told you, when were you going to talk to me? Tomorrow? Next week?"

"I was going back to your place tonight as soon as we finished the crime scene."

"Yeah, right. You don't trust me anymore."

He popped up. "What the hell are you talking about?"

"I lied to you about where I was this afternoon, that's why you walked out on me. You'll never trust me again."

Jack groaned as he pushed himself from the floor. I helped him settle beside me and he rubbed his ribs. "Lizzie, now you're overreacting. I love you. I trust you. I'm mad that you lied but I know why you did it. It came out of your heart. It was just really stupid."

I folded my arms. "It wasn't stupid. I caught a murderer."

"Yes, Ma'am, but badgering the suspects until one of them gets pissed enough to beat the crap out of you is damn' dumb. You could've been killed."

My face ached from talking and I put the ice bag to my cheek. "Well, at least I got Andre real good."

He grinned. "Tell me about it."

I described the battle in my garage, complete with graphic details. "He's going to need plastic surgery."

"I know. I saw him at the hospital. I wanted to take him apart but there wasn't enough left." He took my hand and laced his fingers in mine. "Lizzie, we had a fight. That's all it was. Couples have them. Will you forgive me for being an asshole and let me take you home?"

My face throbbed and my head felt as if it was stuffed with cotton. Maybe Nicola and Mom were right.

I squeezed my eyes shut.

I took the leap.

THE END

Timberwolf Entertainment

TIMBERWOLF MISSION

To acquire the rights to exciting entertainment titles, release them in text (book and electronic) and audio (illustrated streaming episodes, MP3's, Tapes, etc.) and leverage the resulting brick-and-mortar and online sales, publicity and fan-base to promote back-end movie, television and other rights optioning, production contracts and sales.

Timberwolf Press/Timberwolf Entertainment: A holistic approach to content incubation, distribution, sales and rights marketing.

Timberwolf Press founder Patrick Seaman was the first person hired by the founders of broadcast.com (now Yahoo! Broadcast). Patrick helped develop technology and negotiate major media deals as Director of Technology and later Vice President of International Development & Special Projects. After four years, Patrick aided in the transition during Yahoo!'s $5.4 billion acquisition of the company. At that point, Patrick decided to use the technology he pioneered to pursue his true passions: writing and publishing.

MERGING ENTERTAINMENT AND TECHNOLOGY

Timberwolf Press publishes fiction titles in book form, but goes a step further by using *real actors* to perform dramatic, unabridged weekly episodes in performances broadcast at **http://www.TimberwolfPress.com**. Not the dull, dry droning of so many of today's old-style "audio-books" but fresh, dynamic, unabridged performances by professional actors in an exciting weekly episodic format. The performances will also be available on cassette tape, CD, and via popular downloadable formats such as MP3.

CULT FOLLOWING

Timberwolf's prototype book and series, **A Small Percentage** (ISBN: 0-9653210-0-2), was the world's first Internet audio-book. It quickly developed a loyal following and global fan-base. One listener from Australia commented that the weekly series "kept him on the edge of his computer." Consistently in the top 5 audio-books on Yahoo! Broadcast, the title remains one of the all-time most-listened-to Internet audio books in history.

ALL THE TEA

by Ken Carodine

The U.S. and China have emerged in the new millennium as the pre-eminent superpowers. Japan and the U.S. have secretly perfected a viable nuclear fusion reactor at a disused nuclear safety research center on a remote island in the South China Sea. Suddenly, just as the project is on the verge of breakthrough, the black veil of secrecy is shredded and the Chinese want the prize for themselves.

Desert Storm combat-veteran Commander Ben McGuire, a small SEAL team, and an isolated group of scientists struggle with sabotage, typhoons, a rapidly approaching and extremely well-equipped Chinese fleet and a radical new reactor that some of the scientists are terrified of shutting down.

Ken Carodine is a Naval Academy graduate, Desert Storm Veteran, (Currently Commander, USN Reserve), and winner of the 1997 Rose Trilogy Award for Best New Work. Since leaving active duty in 1989, he has worked as an Information Systems professional. Carodine serves as the Commanding Officer of a fifty-member reserve unit. He is now a Managing Consultant for a software company.

Book: ISBN 1-58752-000-1, $14.95, trade paper, 4-color cover, 220 pages

E-BOOK: Rocket Edition, ISBN 1-58752-036-2, $14.95
Microsoft Reader, ISBN 1-58752-032-X, $14.95

Eight-hour Unabridged Dramatic Audio:

Cassette Tapes (5), ISBN 1-58752-001-X, $29.95
Audio CD's (6), ISBN 1-58752-002-8, $34.95
CD-ROM (1), ISBN 1-58752-003-6, $14.95
MP3 Download, $15.00

Free Weekly Episodes at http://www.TimberwolfPress.com

Timberwolf Press / Timberwolf Entertainment
http://www.TimberwolfPress.com
Distribution: Hervey's Booklink (800)-413-3300

CALCULATED RISK

by Denise Tiller

Newport Beach, California actuary Liz Matthews discovers counting dead people for a living can be murder when the bodies start multiplying.

Liz builds her life around things she can count on: numbers, her father, and her cop boyfriend Jack. Order is disrupted when she literally stumbles upon the latest victim in a string of brutal rapes.

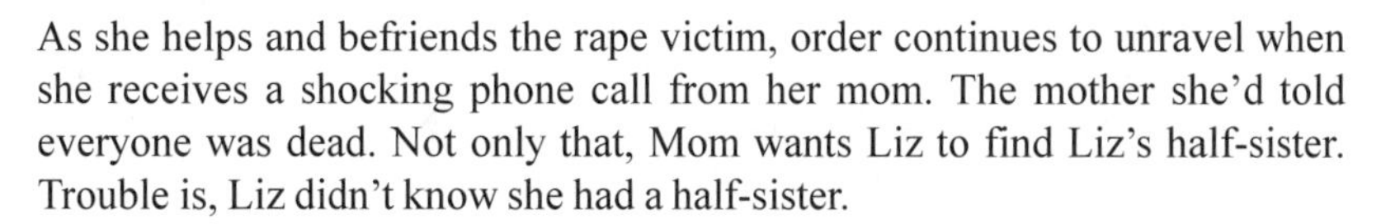

As she helps and befriends the rape victim, order continues to unravel when she receives a shocking phone call from her mom. The mother she'd told everyone was dead. Not only that, Mom wants Liz to find Liz's half-sister. Trouble is, Liz didn't know she had a half-sister.

But first, Liz finds a freshly dead body, then uncovers a twenty-year-old murder. A Mardi Gras mask connects the serial rapist, her missing sister and the murders. Armed with a black belt in mathematics, she uses intuitive and analytic skills to unearth a trail of blackmail and betrayal. Meanwhile her relationship with Jack splinters and even more bodies turn up that need counting.

Denise Tiller is a Fellow of the Society of Actuaries and worked in Newport Beach for several years. Her textbook, *Life, Health, and Annuity Reinsurance,* is the industry standard textbook.

Book: ISBN 1-58752-015-X, $14.95, trade paper, 4-color cover, 249 pages

E-BOOK: Rocket Edition, ISBN 1-58752-035-4, $14.95
Microsoft Reader, ISBN 1-58752-031-1, $14.95

Eight-hour Unabridged Dramatic Audio:

Cassette Tapes (5), ISBN 1-58752-016-8, $29.95
Audio CD's (6), ISBN 1-58752-017-6, $34.95
CD-ROM (1), ISBN 1-58752-018-4, $14.95
MP3 Download, $15.00

Free Weekly Episodes at http://www.TimberwolfPress.com

Timberwolf Press / Timberwolf Entertainment
http://www.TimberwolfPress.com
Distribution: Hervey's Booklink (800)-413-3300

“Science fiction has gained a bold new voice in Jim Cline.”

— **Ben Bova**, Author, editor, futurist,

A SMALL PERCENTAGE

by Jim Cline

Alien battle fleets converge on earth at the beginning of the twenty-first century. Technology and intrigue blend to form a graphic study of politics, morality and the brutality of total war. A bitter, hard-fought war that ranges from the depths of interstellar space, to a nuclear Battle of the Atlantic, to savage assassinations and Machiavellian usurptions of power and control.

Timberwolf's first fiction project, ***A Small Percentage***, was the first audiobook on the Internet and is now available in forty-two dramatic episodes at timberwolfpress.com! It remains one of the all-time most-listened-to audio books on the Internet.

Jim Cline is an electrical engineer with over 17 years as a design engineer, systems engineer and engineering manager in the defense industry, and holds five US patents. He co-authored the ground-breaking book *WebSite Sound.*

Book: ISBN 0-9653210-0-2, $21.95, hard back, 4-color cover, 544 pages

E-BOOK: Rocket Edition, ISBN 1-58752-038-9, $14.95
Microsoft Reader, ISBN 1-58752-034-6, $14.95

Eight-hour Unabridged Dramatic Audio:

Cassette Tapes (5), ISBN 1-58752-004-4, $39.95
Audio CD's (6), ISBN 1-58752-005-2, $44.95
CD-ROM (1), ISBN 1-58752-006-0, $14.95
MP3 Download, $15.00

Free Weekly Episodes at http://www.TimberwolfPress.com

Timberwolf Press / Timberwolf Entertainment
http://www.TimberwolfPress.com
Distribution: Hervey's Booklink (800)-413-3300

★(— @dotrs.gov.au) Canberra, Australia - The longer I listen, the more I want. A great story that just keeps me on the edge of my computer, the weeks in between go so slow!

★Jesse (here2do@wans.net) Tampa, FL - I started listening to a Small Percentage about 5 months ago. I've been hooked ever since. I'm amazed that this book hasn't been made into a movie yet. If you're a Sci-Fi fan as I am you'll be HOOKED soon too!

★(dgr@cjnetworks.com) Topeka, KS - Imagine "Independence Day" written by Tom Clancy, with the character development of the "Star Trek" sagas and a dash of the action of a Schwarzenegger film, and you'll start to get a feel for this electrifying novel. Would make an excellent blockbuster film or TV miniseries. Mr. Spielberg or Mr. Lucas, please take note. Stop reading this, clear the rest of your daily schedule. Take your phone off the hook, and begin the adventure NOW!

★Frank Price (— @hotmail.com) Sherwood, Arkansas - A spell-binding story that will keep you on the edge of your seat. The waiting for the next episode is the only bad part of this story. Full of plot twists and surprises, you will find your self listening again and again to past episodes in order to keep up.

★Jeff Bates (— @aol.com) Hot Springs, Arkansas - What a great book... keep them coming. Me and my son look forward to every episode -- we have made it part of our life... can hardly wait from week to week to here what will happen next. Like I say, you're doing a great job. Thank you for the book.

★grendal (— @yahoo.com) sareeooh planet earth - It's worth listening to BACKWARDS. This book is my second read through.

★Mary Ann (— @erie.net) Corry, PA, USA, Earth :] - The hardest thing about reading this series is waiting for the next installment!!!!...A truly entertaining novel with twists and turns the reader rarely anticipates. I have been thoroughly entertained and highly recommend this wonderful book to anyone who enjoys Science Fiction reading or media mind-blowers like Jeff Rense "Sightings" or Art Bell...The audio production is chilling at times! Thank you Jim Cline, Timberwolf Press and broadcast.com!!!!!!!!!!!

"Ron is unfairly talented! I expect he'll get fed up with being called the new J.B. Cabell."

— Sir Arthur C. Clarke

BRADAMANT
THE IRON TEMPEST

by Ron Miller

Before Xena™, before Wonder Woman™ was fantasy fiction's first warrior-woman, Ludovico Ariosto's Bradamant. In this modern retalling of her story, Bradamant, a knight in the service of Charlemagne, remains steadfast in her love as she searches for Roggero, the Saracen champion. She fights on the side of right, vanquishing evil knights and rescuing the unfortunate while pursuing her quest. Roggero himself must defeat magicians, mythical beasts, giants and no small number of mere mortal knights in his struggle to find Bradamant, his enemy in battle, who in an act of unthinking chivalry had nearly died in order to save him from an unfair blow. Bradamant's story is richly illustrated by the author and Gustave Doré.

Ron Miller is the author and illustrator of nearly 20 top-selling books, including *The Grand Tour, Cycles of Fire, A History of Rockets* and *The Dream Machines*. He was the production illustrator for *Dune* and a consultant for *Contact*, A&E *Biography* and Disney Imagineering.

ISBN 1-58752-027-3, $16.95, illustrated, trade paper, 4-color cover, 331pages
E-BOOK: Rocket Edition, ISBN 1-58752-037-0, $16.95
Microsoft Reader, ISBN 1-58752-033-8, $16.95

Sixteen-hour Unabridged Dramatic Audio:

Cassette Tapes (11), ISBN 1-58752-028-1, $34.95
Audio CD's (13), ISBN 1-58752-029-X, $39.95
CD-ROM (1), ISBN 1-58752-030-3, $16.95
MP3 Download, $15.00

Free Weekly Episodes at http://www.TimberwolfPress.com

Timberwolf Press / Timberwolf Entertainment
http://www.TimberwolfPress.com
Distribution: Hervey's Booklink (800)-413-3300